Tales From Alternate Earths Volume III

An Inklings Press publication

Copyright ©2021 by Inklings Press

Follow Inklings Press on Twitter @**InklingsPress**

Find us on Facebook at
www.facebook.com/inklingspress

Website
www.inklingspress.com

Tales From Alternate Earths Vol III includes the following stories:

story of magic and technology set in the Roman-Helenic Empire? ose yourself in the cleverly woven tale of **Steel Serpents** by Ricardo ictoria. And if you're wondering how war has changed our world, nd out through the perspectives of the larger-than-life marines of Jeff Provine's engaging story **Going Over the Top**.

Need a good detective mystery with humorous elements set in a richly built alternate ancient Rome? **Dying to Alter History** by E.M. Swift-Hook and Jane Jago is just the remarkably crafted world for you. And finally, if you're wondering what it would be like to go on a mysterious journey with two former KGB spies, the fast-paced brilliance of **A Short Story by Somerset Maugham** by D.J. Butler has what you need.

No matter your question or wish, no matter what worlds you seek to escape to, the stories in this anthology can transport you there. Sit back and buckle up...for you're about to take a wild ride!

Minoti Vaishnav

Table of Contents

Foreword
By Minoti Vaishnav

Every question has a million possible answers. In Tales fro
nate Earths Vol. III, these answers come in the form of stories.
are powerful, for they not only open up whole new worlds to u:
also show us possibilities within the world we already know. W(
have to ask ourselves what we desire.

Would you like a take on what would have happened if the 16
Gunpowder plot was never thwarted? **Gunpowder Treason**, brilliantly written by Alan Smale has an answer. Do you wonder what
would have happened if Alfred Hitchcock had directed Titanic first
Hitchcock's Titanic, Matthew Kresal masterfully breaks down how
this might have worked out. Do you seek a saga set a few years after
the Peninsular War with an action-oriented female protagonist and a
spooky, ghost story-esque feel? Then **Ops and Ostentation** by the
ingenious Rob Edwards is the story for you. Or perhaps you're a fan c
dinosaurs and the power of storytelling in flashbacks. If so, the superbly crafted **Dust of the Earth** by Brent A. Harris will keep you hooked.

Do you crave a story featuring a woman of color on a quest to take
down a notorious killer? **To Catch a Ripper** by yours truly might just
scratch that itch. Or perhaps you're curious about what would happen
if neanderthals were the dominant species and had the technology to
wipe out all sapiens. If so, the engrossing world built by Aaron Emmel in **Second Chances** will reel you in. Would you transport yourself
to 19th century Bulgaria in a fast-paced adventure if you could? Then
check out the skillfully woven tale of **Levski's Boots** by Daniel M.
Bensen. Do you wish to ask a Zulu witch doctor how the world would
have been different if Napoleon IV had lived? If so, the artfully structured **Woza Moya** by Christopher Edwards might have the answers
you're searching for.

Are you looking for a noir detective story with a surprising protagonist and a science fiction-esque twist? Read **Not My Monkey**, a
brilliantly innovative narrative by J.L. Royce. Or what if the aftermath
of the Challenger shuttle disaster created a new plan for space exploration? **Heaven Above, Hell Below** by Leo McBride takes you on a
gripping journey through what that might look like. Are you craving

Table of Contents

Foreword
By Minoti Vaishnav

Every question has a million possible answers. In Tales from Alternate Earths Vol. III, these answers come in the form of stories. Stories are powerful, for they not only open up whole new worlds to us, but also show us possibilities within the world we already know. We only have to ask ourselves what we desire.

Would you like a take on what would have happened if the 1605 Gunpowder plot was never thwarted? **Gunpowder Treason**, brilliantly written by Alan Smale has an answer. Do you wonder what would have happened if Alfred Hitchcock had directed Titanic first? In **Hitchcock's Titanic**, Matthew Kresal masterfully breaks down how this might have worked out. Do you seek a saga set a few years after the Peninsular War with an action-oriented female protagonist and a spooky, ghost story-esque feel? Then **Ops and Ostentation** by the ingenious Rob Edwards is the story for you. Or perhaps you're a fan of dinosaurs and the power of storytelling in flashbacks. If so, the superbly crafted **Dust of the Earth** by Brent A. Harris will keep you hooked.

Do you crave a story featuring a woman of color on a quest to take down a notorious killer? **To Catch a Ripper** by yours truly might just scratch that itch. Or perhaps you're curious about what would happen if neanderthals were the dominant species and had the technology to wipe out all sapiens. If so, the engrossing world built by Aaron Emmel in **Second Chances** will reel you in. Would you transport yourself to 19th century Bulgaria in a fast-paced adventure if you could? Then check out the skillfully woven tale of **Levski's Boots** by Daniel M. Bensen. Do you wish to ask a Zulu witch doctor how the world would have been different if Napoleon IV had lived? If so, the artfully structured **Woza Moya** by Christopher Edwards might have the answers you're searching for.

Are you looking for a noir detective story with a surprising protagonist and a science fiction-esque twist? Read **Not My Monkey**, a brilliantly innovative narrative by J.L. Royce. Or what if the aftermath of the Challenger shuttle disaster created a new plan for space exploration? **Heaven Above, Hell Below** by Leo McBride takes you on a gripping journey through what that might look like. Are you craving a story of magic and technology set in the Roman-Helenic Empire? Lose yourself in the cleverly woven tale of **Steel Serpents** by Ricardo Victoria. And if you're wondering how war has changed our world, find out through the perspectives of the larger-than-life marines of Jeff Provine's engaging story **Going Over the Top**.

Need a good detective mystery with humorous elements set in a richly built alternate ancient Rome? **Dying to Alter History** by E.M. Swift-Hook and Jane Jago is just the remarkably crafted world for you. And finally, if you're wondering what it would be like to go on a mysterious journey with two former KGB spies, the fast-paced brilliance of **A Short Story by Somerset Maugham** by D.J. Butler has what you need.

No matter your question or wish, no matter what worlds you seek to escape to, the stories in this anthology can transport you there. Sit back and buckle up...for you're about to take a wild ride!

Minoti Vaishnav

Gunpowder Treason
By Alan Smale

See Moll Frith, nineteen years young and dressed like a boy, cap squared and head lowered, doing the cutpurse dance along the cobbles behind the half-cheering crowd and pulling in coins every minute. Lining her pockets while emptying others.

Still only noon, but Moll had been out and about for two hours. Worth the early morning, given the crowds for the State Opening of Parliament. Rich, poor, everyone crammed in along Whitehall to watch the fancy carriages go by. Many a man wouldn't miss his purse till he reached for it later in an alehouse and found all his money gone, gone, gone.

Some in the crowd were dark and quiet. Those, Moll avoided. Cockney sparrows not so chirpy today, not sure of this King with two numbers, James VI of Scotland and now also James I of England. King here for just two years, though King of Scotland since he was a wee bairn of thirteen months.

Many in London had loved Gloriana, the Virgin Queen, James's predecessor. Elizabeth had been solid. James, though? Son of Mary Queen of Scots, warmaker, murderess, and beheaded Papist, now warming her toes in Hell?

So James earned suspicion from both sides. No Papist, at least by vow, raised by Scots Calvinists and sworn to the Anglican faith, but many a Protestant doubted where his heart truly lay. After all, his Queen was Catholic. As for the Catholics themselves, they'd been persecuted since the latter years of Elizabeth, their Mass illegal, Anglican church-going compulsory. Recusants underground, just-in-time deathbed 'conversions' to Catholicism rife.

And even setting aside religion, who could trust a Scot? James had a thick Edinburgh accent, and favored his own Lowlands lords with money, houses, land, jewels. For the English, warming to their new Scottish king would take time.

The grand carriages passed soon enough. Streets reopened, crowds dissipated, and Moll walked all the way back to her lodgings off Fleet Street to change out of boy-clothes, get herself girled up for the afternoon and evening trade. Soon enough she'd be back in Whitehall hunting a different sort of money. Moll spoke well and looked clean, so toffs regularly opened their wallets and their breeches to her. She made good coin outside theaters and gentlemen's clubs, too.

She was early. James VI and I would still be addressing his English Parliament, so she dawdled, looking out over the greasy Thames with its colliers' barges and eel-boats, ships carrying grain and lumber, the watermen ferrying passengers and goods.

But here came a man striding fast, eyes darting and disturbed. Nice jerkin and hose, but a shabby cloak and his hat had seen better days. Tall, powerfully built. Reddish hair, moustache, and beard. No toff: his demeanor, boots, and spurs called 'soldier' loud and clear.

Moll smiled, her gaze lingering overlong for an honest woman, then looked back at the Thames and the mudlarks that waded its filth hunting for driftwood.

The man passed her, then looked back. "Come away."

"Not likely." Hadn't asked nicely, hadn't made an offer, had he? That wasn't the game played right.

He chewed his lip. "Your name?"

"Mary." Her born name, why not? Respectable, that.

He shivered, a whole-body shudder. Because of her name? Tiredness lurked behind his eyes. "And yours, sir?"

"John."

Moll grinned. "Ha." He'd wanted to say another name, but settled. Men often did, as if telling Moll their real names would give her power over them.

Sometimes, it did.

He looked out across the river. "There was supposed to be a boat." Apropos of nothing.

"Was there, now?"

"Just come away. I ask no more. Grant me that boon."

Either way, odd John wasn't waiting. He strode on and something in his agitation, well: Moll just turned to follow, and chased in his wake for a quarter-mile, giving the occasional hop-and-skip to keep up.

A rattling crack. A world-shaking thunderclap. A sudden storm that slammed her in the back and effortlessly tossed her head over heels. Moll landed with a thump that knocked the wind from her and skidded painfully along the road, shredding skin. Opened her mouth in a scream she couldn't hear over the din that surrounded her. Banged her head, came to a merciful halt. Lay on her back panting, staring at a black-hot fug of smoke that roiled across the sky, heading east.

She smelled burning, harsh and acrid. Blinked red. Spat red, too; she'd bitten her tongue.

Panic, fast and furious. She pushed herself onto her elbows, sat up. John lay prone, head raised and nose bleeding, eyes staring. Moll followed his gaze.

Hell had come to London.

Houses of Parliament gone, replaced by what looked like a volcano, its fire blasting the Heavens. The entire Palace of Westminster, the Abbey next to it, and the many buildings that surrounded them were already razed, the buildings further distant wrecked and ablaze. Burning rubble fell from the sky behind her, ahead, and across the Thames. Day turning to night with all the sudden smoke, and the ground still shook.

A fierce wail that Moll felt in her throat, while still unable to hear it with her ears. "John!"

Unsteadily, he rose to his feet. Looked around in a daze. Reached out to pull her up. His lips moved as he grabbed her hand. Then they were running together, away from the inferno.

• • •

See London burn.

The vast explosion and the blazing Parliament had set alight all the buildings around them. The rain of burning wood from the sky had scattered more fire throughout the city. It was November, but summer had been dry and autumn mild; fire begat fire, and houses went up like tinder. Soon whole streets were ablaze while others sat untouched, at least for now. The flames kept spreading.

Aside from the Palace and Abbey, Westminster wasn't so grand. Within a quarter-mile radius of the House of Lords lay the usual collection of houses, inns, shops, and stews. The ordinary had rubbed shoulders with the dignitaries, and today had perished with them. Anyone within that radius who'd avoided death in the blast had likely been burned alive in the sweeping firestorm that followed, searing all in its path. Everything from St. James's Park to the Thames on an east-west line, and north into Whitehall, a rabbit-warren of Government offices mostly built in wood. The westerly wind carried debris into the heart of the city, where the multiple fires linked arms and created ever-fiercer conflagrations. The old Gothic cathedral of St. Paul's was visibly aflame, and parts of Cheapside beyond. Across the river, Southwark blazed.

By now she and John had slowed to a brisk walk, both grunting for breath. Looking around in dread they passed through Charing, the Eleanor Cross in the road's center now undermined and leaning drunkenly.

The slums and rookeries of St. Giles were aflame. People running every which way, trying to put out fires in their own houses or their neighbors'. Gangs of other men pulling down perfectly good houses downwind of the blaze with firehooks, thirty-foot-long poles with strong iron pegs to yank a house down by its roof tree. In this way they made firebreaks, gaps in the combustibles that perhaps a flame might not leap over.

Fistfights here, knife-fights there. People not so happy to have their homes and livelihoods destroyed, just to save others further distant.

Horrors all around, and in her mind. This man, still clutching Moll's hand, dragging her along: had he known what was about to happen? But the shock and terror on his face, his sheer disbelief at the scale of the destruction, belied that. An enigma.

Right now, Moll hardly cared. Their bond had been literally forged in fire, the mutual bond of almost being blown up. Leaving skin and blood on the cobbles in similar measure. John's urging had likely saved her life. In those minutes she'd hurried a good way further from the Palace of Westminster, rather than sauntering a hundred yards closer.

An inn called the Duck and Drake, almost to Holborn. They were beyond the worst of the blazes now, and Moll could see John's relief. She could hear again too, after a fashion: ears ringing, they had to shout to hear each other.

"You'll come in?" he asked, eager. Pumped up, somehow. From surviving, making it out beyond flame and smoke.

"Your lodgings? Nay, sir; honest girl like I? My reputation..." Their eyes met. Ridiculous, this, a seduction at full volume. No one paying attention, though. Streets full, but everyone rushing around so.

Something in John's hand, a glint of gold. Drawn like a magpie, Moll claimed it without a moment's thought.

Upstairs, a room, sparsely furnished, a bed and an empty wardrobe. A small bag on the floor. John traveled light.

He locked the door, turned to clasp her as if they were long-separated. He reeked of smoke, but Moll's nose was blunted to that now and besides, it went with his fiery beard.

"Mary. My woman of flame. My blessing," he said in endearment, though still too loud of voice. And then he took her with a passion she had hardly expected, as if they were truly lovers and not merely a Moll and her John, and to her surprise Mary found she needed this too, needed it beyond all else on this explosive, disastrous day.

At the end, he called out her name. And once they were done, Mary Frith knew she was truly alive.

• • •

Thousands weren't, though.

King James dead, both the Sixth and First of him. His son and heir, Henry Prince of Wales. And all the members of the Privy Council, and the Lords and men of the Commons who were present. Many other Londoners, when large swaths of the city were razed, destroyed, undermined, burned.

Only gunpowder could have done that. A *lot* of gunpowder, likely right under the Queen's Chamber, where the House of Lords met. A deep conspiracy, then.

Papists. Who else?

In an odd, detached way, Moll wondered how many men she'd pleasured over the past years had died in the blast. A slippery thought. Hardly seemed real.

• • •

"You knew it would happen," Moll said later, entwined in the sheets. "What's the trick of that?"

He nodded soberly. "I received warning from a man I trusted. One... deep within a certain group. I fear I can tell you no more."

"You're a spy, then?" she said, half in jest.

"Of a sort."

"And your real name? For it most surely ain't John Johnson. A *good* spy might have chosen better."

He grinned, but said: "I think I shall not tell you."

Moll gave him that hooded-eyed stare that worked so well on men, and reached out her fingers for him again. "Your name, sir, or I shall surely cease."

"Mary, Mary." He lifted her hand away with ease, and now she felt foolish and a little hurt.

"Your secrets would be safe with me," she said.

"But it is for *your* safety that I do not tell them." He paused. "Forgive me. Your faith?"

"Anglican, by family. For myself?" She stroked his thigh. "Not so big on praying, truth be spoken."

Good enough, his expression said. "All right. I work for Cecil."

"Course you do," Moll said, none the wiser.

A wry cloud passed before his eyes. "'Worked', I should say. Sir Robert Cecil, no? Lord Privy Seal and Secretary of State? Last spymaster to the Virgin Queen, and first to James after her. Which, now he has perished, there can be no fault in revealing."

"So, you *are* a spy?"

"Everywhere, plots. Two against the King in just his first year donning the English crown."

"Had you pegged for a soldier."

"And a soldier I was, in the Dutch War. But I'd rather leave wars behind me. Enough blood, and much I cannot reveal. Do not ask me more of that either, I beg."

Moll didn't desire to. Soldier-men, prompted, talked at fine length about campaigns and slaughter. With London still burning, Moll welcomed that kind of talk even less.

"Then, perhaps... some dinner?"

If they could find food anywhere. But Moll had a feeling John's guineas might do the trick.

• • •

Londoners started dragging out Catholics that very night and hanging them. Known Catholics and recusants, suspected Catholics, and more than likely several non-Catholics whom some in the mobs held a grudge against. They hanged Ben Jonson, a popular playwright of masques and a known Papist, and Will Shakespeare, a writer of historical plays and comedies and also fancied to be a Catholic, and that saddened Moll; she'd roared with laughter at his *Twelfth Night* while fleecing his audience.

November 5th, 1605, was a Tuesday. The fires kept spreading on Wednesday, but by Thursday the city was getting a grip on it. By that time, they'd moved to Moll's room off Fleet Street, a good mile and a half from Parliament. Fleet was as wooden and overcrowded as much of the rest of London, but it was close to a water conduit, and by Thursday the wood of every building along the Street had been soaked.

No rookery, stew, or coney-burrow this, but a timber-framed tenement with lodgings for respectable working folk, all set above a needle-maker's shop with a weaver's next door. Moll had never brought a mark home before, but by now she was by no means sure that John was merely a mark.

She'd watched his face as he'd walked in, alert to any wrinkling of the nose. And to be true, Moll could have afforded a finer billet than this on her wages of sin, but she chose to keep her life unremarkable. Who knew when she might get beaten by a toff or injured in an accident, or get sick, and need to live off the savings she'd squirreled away under the floorboards?

But John showed no judgment. Just smiled and thanked her kindly, and set about preparing the meager victuals he'd paid ridiculous, gouging prices for at the Covent Garden market along the way.

He seemed like a good man. For once.

• • •

"There'll be an uprising," he said. "Mark me. A bloody conspiracy of this nature? And now no one in power?"

He wasn't wrong.

News arrived of a popular revolt erupting in the Midlands. Elizabeth, James's oldest daughter, captured from Coome Abbey near Coventry. A man called Robert Catesby behind it all, a name that brought a grimace to John's face.

Many of the great magnates in Britain were still Catholic, practicing their faith quietly, and tactfully disregarded. All Jesuits and Catholic priests were supposed to have left the country, but no: they'd gone underground. Along with many more covert Catholics laying low, greater in numbers than anyone had expected, common folk whose hearts belonged to Rome first.

Most of them as shocked and horrified as anyone at the carnage, hating and reviling the treachery, the slaughter, the destruction. Many, nonetheless, willing to heed the call, step into the breach, have their day.

Several of the Catholic Lords had stayed away from the Opening of Parliament. Pure luck and ill health the tale, though Moll gave that short shrift. The Earls of Arundel, Worcester, and Northampton, the Lords Monteagle and Vaux: these men bravely put their grief behind them and marched smart-like into the power void the murders of their colleagues left. They secured the city, arranged for tents and other facilities for the suddenly and catastrophically homeless. Sent in the Navy to blow more firebreaks across the map of London and bring the remains of the fire to heel.

And quietly took control.

The King was dead, long live the Queen! Within a week of the fire's quelling came the coronation of Queen Elizabeth II. Moll went to see it, even though it was in Windsor. Ever one for a procession, despite the long cart ride. Pageantry, plus all those purses dangling unguarded during the cheering.

The newly-minted Queen owned unusual poise for a nine-year-old. Despite the recent deaths of her father and brother, her sole expression was a numbed frown.

Henry Percy, Earl of Northumberland, would serve as her regent and bring her up properly in the Catholic faith. For Elizabeth II would be their puppet Catholic Queen, long may she reign!

And across England stone altars were restored, and the communion rails and surplices returned. And here came the cardinals again.

No. London was having none of that. The Great Fire may have been quenched, but the city still simmered. A pot on the boil. That bubbling spilled over into riots. Steps were taken, and the streets ran with blood as well as ashen water.

The conspirators had wanted Charles as well, James's sickly four-year-old son, but they hadn't got him. Charles had been spirited North with haste, hurried to Scotland to be pronounced King there. And so once again Britain had two monarchs: Elizabeth II down here, and Charles I up there, over the border in the hands of Calvinists.

This likely wouldn't go well.

• • •

John Johnson showed no signs of leaving, and Moll none of evicting him. He left early each morning and was out most of the day. Doing his spywork, whatever that was, "for the good of the Realm." He'd sometimes come home with a frown, bone weary, and she'd need to try and cheer him. But he was paying more to her in board than the rent she owed, and was little trouble, so she stowed his money away and was grateful.

She, too, went out as before. John showed no inclination to trim her activities in the name of fidelity, no interest in whatever she might do when he wasn't around. They'd relaxed into an understanding without ever discussing it.

But the streets of London during the clearing and rebuilding were dangerous enough that she sometimes welcomed a dashing protector by her side. Desperate men, with no homes. Mobs still hunting for suspected Papists to string up.

Sometimes, Moll even yearned for more. John's guineas seemed inexhaustible. Perhaps he had a house somewhere? Perhaps he might even be her route to a real life? A thing she'd never thought within reach, until now.

Best not to rush, though, and risk scaring him away. Better to just work at making herself indispensable.

"If ever you need help?"

John looked at her sideways. They were in bed, of course, where most of their conversations took place.

"You've already helped me to quite a degree, I'd say." He scratched himself comfortably.

"In terms of business, I'm meaning. Yours. Whatever it is you do. If you happen to need a female touch. Or myself on your arm in a nice dress to give you," she swallowed, "respectability, or the thing next best. Even a man-and-wife cover. For your work."

John raised his eyebrows, grinned. "Might come a time. All eyes on you, rather than me. And doors might open. Aye, I'll think on it."

The very next week he brought her quite the dress: bodice tight, skirt wide over a whalebone farthingale, and very fine. To a soiree they went, Moll's heart in her mouth. Him talking to groups of gents – even some still-extant Lords – in a very serious way while the elegant Mary engaged in light conversation with polished-up vowels, distracting the other "wives", decrying the slow state of the rebuilding and other such issues. John brought her the popular pamphlets and broadsides to read, so she might appear well-informed.

Fun enough, to be a spy's Moll. Hard to keep her hands off the purses, of course. But for John's sake, she controlled her itchy fingers.

• • •

Lively rebuilding under way, all across the city. Can't keep old London down. Mostly in wood, like before. Ideally they'd have rebuilt in stone but few had the time, and even fewer the money.

A wall around the new Parliament, and the building itself looked like a fortress. Villains wouldn't be renting space in the undercrofts of this one. That innocence was gone forever.

Insurance brigades, formed by property companies and insurance offices, sprang up even as London rebuilt. Well-heeled buildings new and old soon wore the badge of whatever company would swoop in and save them from a future blaze with fire-wagon, pump and leather hose. At the soirees men debated the merits of brass nozzles versus copper, and proclaimed on the topic of gooseneck valves. No one expected another Parliament-bombing, but London had had its fill of fire. Likely, after the Great Fire of 1605, London would never again face a conflagration as great. Unless...

Civil war. A counterstrike against the Catholic usurpers of power. Scotland-led, sweeping down through the English shires like a dose of salts, and heigh-ho, before anyone could quite fathom what was going on it was all-change, Elizabeth II gone as if she'd never been, disappeared, and who's this?

Charles I, Charles the First and First (of Scotland and now England), a weakly child ascending the throne at the tender age of almost six. At her coronation his sister had looked calm and confident. Judging from Charles's face he'd already peed his hose and would do it again ere long.

The joke throughout London: monarchs are getting younger every day.

"Are we all Papists, Protestants, or Presbyterians now? It's making me dizzy."

That was the one and only time Moll thought that John might strike her, his expression was that dark, but he swallowed it down. "Protestants," he said, shortly. "Or pirates, perhaps. Knaves, at any rate."

A brooding anger consumed him most of the day. As wary of angry men as any woman, Moll kept her distance, kept quiet, avoided his touch; who knew when he might erupt? Seeing this, John softened his tone. Reassured her. Yes, he was shaken. Yes, he was worried sick about the rule of law, in London and the rest of the country. But he'd not take it out on her.

And that seemed to be true. But still, it made Moll think, and once she started thinking, she couldn't stop.

• • •

She had to walk back and forth along Whitehall for a day and a half before she glimpsed one of the four or five men who'd do for her purpose. She crossed the street and fell in beside him, not too close. "Sir, a moment, if you would."

He glanced at her in her boys' clothes, and did a doubletake so perfect it was almost theatrical. "*Moll*?"

"I've a need to tell you something."

"Great Gods, woman, not here!"

The horror in his eyes wounded her. "Rest easy, I need just a word. 'Tis for the sake of your calling, not mine."

"A word with a noted whore, dressed as a man? If someone were to see—"

"If you'll keep a civil tongue," Moll said sharply, "and try to look natural, we'll draw fewer eyes. And this is a thing you'll want to hear."

• • •

John came home in triumph that night, mood lifted, clutching a brace of quail. Moll's heart sank – that would be a mighty feast – but this couldn't wait.

"I bid you," she said carefully, after greeting him. "Tell me about the boat that wasn't there."

His face blanked. "Boat?"

"Almost the first words you spoke to me, on the embankment before Parliament blew. You'd expected a boat. To take you away? Maybe even all the way out of England?"

He shook his head, said nothing.

"To Spain, even?"

Now it was the brace of quail he shook. "Mary, are you hungry, or are you not?"

"Soon enough. Please, John. It's been on my mind. I swear I don't care tuppence what faith you follow. But I care if you lie to me."

He exhaled, such a long sigh that Moll half expected him to crumple to the floor at its end.

"I know you haven't liked it. The lying. I've seen that in your eyes. Rare enough in a man."

A long, thick pause. "All right, then. When I fought as a soldier, aye: it was for Spain. Not for the Netherlands."

"For the Pope," she said bluntly.

"Yes."

"And you knew about the blast because the plotters warned you. Not because you were on the verge of stamping out their wickedness."

"Yes."

"And since, you've worked on the quiet for the new Popish Lords, while never quite trusting their grabbing of the throne would hold fast—"

"Take the damned birds," he said.

"Right you are." She accepted the quail from him at last. Stepped back toward her pots. Watched carefully, to see if he'd pounce on her.

He did not. In fact, he was looking at the door. "Even as I tell truth, you now lie to me?"

"'Twas no lie. John, I truly don't care how you pray. But I do care that you murdered thousands, with a giant and cowardly blast."

"I told you, I was merely warned—"

"John. You lit the fuse."

"And how could you know that?"

"By your hurry, back then. And your stillness, now."

Again, he eyed the door. "They're out there, aren't they? Star Chamber?"

Moll nodded. In the hallway, and in the next room. Listening through the walls, but she didn't say so. He'd likely guess, anyway.

He shook his head. "Why?"

"Because maybe you'll do it again one day. Maybe even soon. Light another fuse. Try to burn out the new lot as well. I couldn't have that on my soul, John, not now I *know*."

His gaze turned slowly back to her.

Moll leaned on the table. Inches away, behind the flour tin, was the cosh she carried when she was out at night. Lead shot in it, heavy. She'd blooded and stunned many a man with it when they'd presumed, raised a fist, turned wild. Just in case John lunged across the room to wreak his revenge on her while he still could.

He merely shook his head. "You can't possibly think that of me. Not after... all that. And everything since." A fierce shudder racked his body, like the one he'd suffered when first they'd met, and he sat suddenly. "Once was enough, by God."

"Once was too many. You really did it, then?"

"I did. I was born in England, yet I consider myself no Englishman, not now. Not till the day when all England again accepts the true God, and the supreme power and holiness of Paul the Fifth in Rome, and purges this Anglican heresy from its heart. Though I suppose now I'll not live to see it."

Tears in his eyes. "I'm a good man, Mary. A Godly man. Please remember that, always."

Unexpectedly, his sadness pricked tears in her own. "And now you hate me."

"Never."

"Tell me your name? Your real name?"

"Fawkes," he said.

"*Forks?*" An unexpected note of wry levity.

He grinned, tiredly. He likely got that a lot. "For the love of God, Mary. It contains a W."

"What sort of name is that?"

"Mine. And for what it's worth, that bastard Robert Cecil perished in flame in Westminster without ever knowing it." He paused. "I love you, my Mary. I'll love you unto death, and beyond. And I forgive you."

And with that John stood again, turned to the door, and raised his chin and his voice. "Gentlemen! Let us end this charade. My name is Guy Fawkes, and I bid you enter—"

But before the five burly officers of Star Chamber burst in to drag him away to the rack, Moll ran to throw her arms around him.

One last time.

· · ·

Fawkes was hung, drawn, and quartered, the penalty for high treason. Another procession, men and women cheering along the way. Moll Frith quiet and alone in the crowd in her boys' clothes, taking no purses, just looking on in silence.

Tied to a hurdle and dragged by horses. Hanged by the neck until he was almost dead and then cut down, his beautiful body dismembered, his guts out and head hacked off, corpse chopped into four more pieces. That was Guy Fawkes's punishment for his vile and callous murder of thousands. His atrocity, in the name of God.

Forcing herself to watch it all: that was Moll's, for harboring him so long. Her hand on her belly, fighting back the nausea.

Eventually, and much later, she wept.

· · ·

The years spun by. War with France, then Spain, much noise and bluster but little by way of conclusion. Irony there, for as Charles I reached his majority and consolidated his power, he was ever more the absolute monarch in the French and Spanish style, albeit Anglican rather than Catholic. And after a graceful death of old age he passed his crown to the even more rigid Charles II. But a peaceful transition for once, no one this time needing to be slaughtered in the streets to make it so.

· · ·

See Edward Frith, son of Mary, otherwise known as Meg Markham and – long ago – Moll Cutpurse, standing by his mother's grave.

Edward, close to sixty years old as far as he can guess, red hair greying, is not too proud to share a tear. His mother, hardly virtuous – a doxy when young, burnt on the hand as a thief, later a brief sensation on the stage and a scandal for aping men's attire and smoking tobacco. Gross sins, that repelled him. Yet those had been excesses of her youth. For all of Edward's remembered life his mother had been a woman of good heart, who'd repented long since and died having confessed her sins to Almighty God. A woman who had loved Edward, and done right by him.

Edward's father? A mystery. Certainly not Luke Markham, who married Mary a decade after Edward's birth. She'd never told. But Edward has his suspicions. And why?

Because, Edward's whole life, his mother would never approach the new Parliament closer than a half-mile, but would stare on it from afar with complicated eyes.

So: his father likely a political man. Edward might even be a Lord's by-blow. A virtuous man, surely, else why would his mother dwell on his memory so?

Probably a man who'd perished ablaze in the Gunpowder Treason and the Great Fire that had followed. The timing of Edward's birth was hazy, but that might be about right.

And so Edward Frith, pious Puritan, agent of the Crown and scourge of Papists, has always sought to be a good man. One to make his mother proud, and – Edward prays long and hard on his knees each night before his frowning, relentless God – to be worthy of his long-martyred father.

Meet Alan Smale

For his Tale, Alan takes us to an alternate England where the Gunpowder Plot succeeded in all its horror and devastation. Recent analysis has shown that if the 2500kg of gunpowder placed beneath the Houses of Parliament had really gone up, the cataclysm might have been even more devastating than Alan describes. Had Guy Fawkes witnessed what he'd wrought, he might have had a few mixed feelings.

Mary Frith (aka Moll Cutpurse) was a real woman of her times, though her life proceeds rather differently in this newly transformed London.

Alan's novella of a Roman invasion of ancient America, "A Clash of Eagles", won the Sidewise Award, and his associated novels Clash of Eagles, Eagle in Exile, and Eagle and Empire are available from Del Rey (and received a second Sidewise nomination as a trilogy). His Roman baseball collaboration with Rick Wilber, The Wandering Warriors, appeared recently from WordFire Press, and Hot Moon, his alternate-Apollo thriller set entirely on and around the Moon, will be released by CAEZIK SF & Fantasy in 2022. Find him at www.alansmale.com, Facebook/AlanSmale, and Twitter/@AlanSmale.

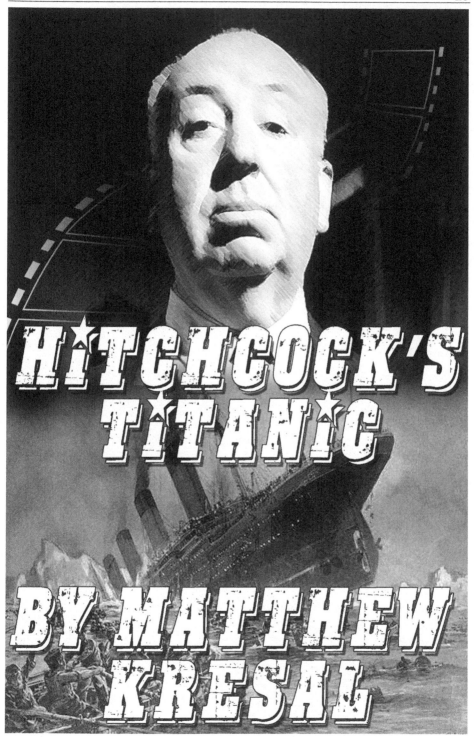

HITCHCOCK'S TITANIC

BY MATTHEW KRESAL

Hitchcock's Titanic
By Matthew Kresal

We all know the opening scene. The opening credits play out over a tight close-up of a rivet used to hold together the hull of a mighty vessel. Franz Waxman's beautifully haunting music plays over the titles, offering not a hint of anything wrong. At least not until the camera pulls out to reveal the rivet is next to a letter, painted white against the black hull. As it pulls back, the music takes on dark tones until it strikes a chord as we see the full name.

Titanic.

Such is the opening of the 1940 film *Titanic*, a film which seems to be undergoing something of a revival at present. The restoration of the film led to a successful art house release which has been followed up by a superb home video release via the Criterion Collection. Given the film's place in the history of the medium, it seems appropriate that it is, perhaps belatedly, receiving the attention it deserves. It is, after all, the only American film that noted British director Alfred Hitchcock ever made.

The Director & The Producer

The story of Hitchcock's *Titanic* begins in the late 1930s just as the director was reaching his zenith with films such as *The 39 Steps* and *The Lady Vanishes*. It was those films, successful both in England and in the United States, that brought the 40-year-old filmmaker to the attention of

American producer David O. Selznick.

Though younger than Hitchcock by three years, Selznick was already a towering figure in American film. Moving to Hollywood in his mid-20s, Selznick's career took him from MGM to Paramount and then to RKO. Having risen from an assistant story editor to Head of Production in less than a decade, the still ambitious young man went one step further. Leasing RKO's Culver City and striking a distribution deal with United Artists, Selznick attached his name to Selznick International Pictures in 1935. Selznick's streak of success continued with films ranging from 1937's *The Prisoner of Zenda* to *Gone With The Wind* in 1939.

Perhaps it was no surprise that the director and the producer, both on the rise, fell into each other's orbit. It was through Selznick's brother Myron in London that, first, the notion of Hitchcock coming to Hollywood and then later the negotiations of his contract took place with Selznick sending telegrams from America to London. In the summer of 1938, Hitchcock and his wife made their way to America aboard the Queen Mary which docked in New York on the sixth of June. Met by Selznick representative Kay Brown, they traveled across the country via train, arriving in Los Angeles on June 14th.

The following day, the two men at last met face to face. As well as Selznick being younger than Hitchcock, he was also taller and thinner. On the surface at least, the two men could not have been more different both in physical stature and in temperament. Selznick could be loud and talkative, Hitchcock quiet and observant. Selznick, thanks to the still unreleased Gone With The Wind, had already acquired a reputation as a prodigious memo writer who seemed to meddle in all aspects of his productions before, during, and after filming. Hitchcock was a great planner, planning things to the smallest detail while also allowing for small amounts of improvisation. They should have been worlds apart.

And yet, it turned out the two men had something in common. Two things, to be more precise, with one of those things being an interest in filming Daphne du Maurier's Gothic romance *Rebecca*, that was riding high on bestseller lists on both sides of the Atlantic even then and which Selznick had the film rights. It seemed a natural fit for Hitchcock and Selznick was keen to make a film of the book.

At least, until the moment the second topic was broached. Exactly where in the conversation the subject of the *Titanic* came up is unclear with accounts differing as to the timing and even who mentioned the ship first. Whatever the case might be, it soon became clear that both men had put at least some thought into the idea. A surviving memo from the Selznick archive reveals that Hitchcock had already conceived one of the film's signature sequences set in the first class smoking room involving a game of cards and fluid shifting inside a glass. Given the report in London's *Daily Telegraph* about the trunk full of research material Hitchcock had, perhaps this shouldn't come as a surprise with hindsight. At the time, it was a convergence that accomplished the director's goal of landing him a deal in Hollywood, one he would take up after returning to England to film *Jamaica Inn*. It would be some months before the director, with his wife and daughter, returned to America for good.

It was on arrival in the New World that Selznick surprised him. For no sooner had the Englishman stepped off the *Queen Mary*, then he was ushered onto another boat. A boat that was, as Hitchcock's daughter recounted years later, far smaller than the one they had crossed the Atlantic on. The Englishman reportedly wasn't surprised by the turn of events for Selznick's reputation, which was being secured by the filming of *Gone With The Wind*, had already become widely known even in British film circles.

And yet, it seems doubtful that even Hitchcock could have foreseen the twist that was coming as they traveled out into New York Harbor that day. Selznick had himself made the cross-country not just to greet Hitchcock but first to inspect and then introduce the director to his new film set: the SS *Leviathan*.

The *Leviathan*, which had sailed a little more than two years after the *Titanic* sank, was on the brink of being scrapped. Originally named the *Vaterland*, it was, in fact, a German vessel that had been seized by the American government upon entry to World War I. Having served as a troop carrier, it became a passenger line once more in the 1920s under its eventual name. Though popular with passengers, by the 1930s both rising costs to maintain her and the Great Depression had grounded her. Unlike the *Titanic*'s sister ship the *Olympic*, it had managed to avoid the scrapyard until Selznick had found her and decided it was to be the stand-in for *Titanic*.

Hitchcock, however, was not as impressed with the vessel as his American producer. As well as being younger than the *Titanic*, the *Leviathan* bore little resemblance to the famed British liner. It had only three funnels instead of the *Titanic*'s four (though one of its smokestacks too had been a dummy) in addition to the fact that its art deco interiors, remodeled when the vessel had entered American passenger service, bore no match to the White Star liner's Edwardian splendor. Could Selznick not see the problems that would create?

As it happened, he had. Indeed, he offered a solution to the director right there in New York Harbor that day. The *Leviathan* would stand in for the *Titanic*'s exteriors and perhaps some interior scenes. The majority of the ship's interiors, including its famed Grand Staircase, would be built on the stages in Culver City. Besides, Selznick insisted, shooting on a real ship would give the film an extra layer of authenticity and suspense.

In the end, Hitchcock found himself agreeing with the producer. Over the next few months, the *Leviathan* would set sail once more, ironically under the command of the *Olympic*'s former master Captain John Binks, on a voyage that would see her traverse the Panama Canal on its way to the West Coast. There she spent some months in a dry dock undergoing a series of alterations to both her interior and exterior to make her look more like the *Titanic*.

Even with the alterations, which were both time-consuming and expensive, the *Leviathan* was not a perfect match for the sunken vessel. *Titanic* researcher Paul Lee has noted the inaccuracies in the relevant article on his website as well as how the model built for long shots had changes made to it to fit certain aspects of the stand-in ship. And yet watching the film it's clear that Hitchcock made the most out of the vessel, shooting sequences with an authenticity that would have been difficult to match on a soundstage with rear projection.

The time needed to refit the *Leviathan* had another consequence for the film. It gave Hitchcock and Selznick, along with a team of screenwriters, the chance to hammer out a script. It was here that the two men began to butt heads and the first storm clouds appeared.

The Script

When Hitchcock arrived in California, it still wasn't clear what shape the *Titanic* film would take. Outside of the specific shots that he had discussed with Selznick during their earlier Hollywood meeting, there wasn't much of a storyline laid out. Such a thing was not unheard of for Hitchcock and, after all, Selznick had bought the rights to at least one

Titanic-related work already in the form of the article *R.M.S. Titanic* by Hanson W. Baldwin. In theory, then, Hitchcock had something of a starting point.

Looking through the surviving treatments, it's clear that Hitchcock wasn't particularly keen on getting the exact historical details of the sinking correct, at least not at first. In looking at his British films such as *The 39 Steps*, it's clear that Hitchcock had little respect for source material. The style he used on those adaptations was to use them as the foundation for his film, and *Titanic* was to be no exception to that rule.

Evidence suggests that the director was already working on a story-line for *Titanic* even while filming on *Jamaica Inn* was underway. So much so that he presented one to Selznick shortly after they finished their inspection of the *Leviathan*. That version no longer exists except for notes in a Selznick memo which makes mention of the producer being "very unhappy with the ending. The audience wants to see *Titanic* sink." Another note mentions "Too much like your earlier pictures," which suggests that Hitchcock might have been planning a return to the espionage genre he had mined so well during his British career.

Sadly for film scholars, Hitchcock's reply has been lost while so many of Selznick's memos have survived. What is clear is that a back and forth took place between the two men on the topic of precisely what the film would include. If Hitchcock had indeed planned to end the plot before the sinking, it seems odd that he would have done much research into it only to dismiss it. Or perhaps that would have been in keeping with his earlier style of adaptation or, conceivably, even in diffusing audience expectations of what the film would contain.

There's another possibility as well. Even at this early stage, there were storm clouds on the horizon regarding its release. British film censors, as well as the British Board of Trade and the Cunard White Star Line (which had once owned and operated *Titanic*), had voiced their displeasure over the film's announcement. Indeed, less than a decade earlier, they had forced more overt references to the liner to be removed from the film *Atlantic* (which, coincidentally, had starred *39 Steps* actress Madeleine Carroll). Before leaving England, Hitchcock had met with officials from all parties and assured them the film would present the *Titanic*'s crew in the best possible light. Could this explain why Hitchcock seemed less than keen on showcasing the sinking?

Whatever the case, Selznick wanted the sinking. Indeed, the man who set fire to the RKO backlot to stage the 1864 torching of Atlanta had initially planned on sinking the *Leviathan* to add further authenticity to planned scenes. Reportedly, it was only the expense that went into refitting the vessel that convinced him not to take that course of action. While the sinking would be filmed using both canted camera angles and specially built sets, those original plans perhaps show how keen Selznick was to feature it in the film.

From surviving memos, we can ascertain that it took a struggle but, eventually, Hitchcock agreed to the producer's demands. Instead, he chose to go down a route of recreating events on the ship with an eye for authenticity. So much so that he convinced Selznick, who perhaps saw a chance for publicity, to bring two of the *Titanic*'s officers over from England. Charles Lightoller and Joseph Boxhall, who had served as Second Officer and Fourth Officer, respectively, were brought on in the role recognized today as "technical consultants," with Lightoller's memoir, *Titanic and Other Ships*, serving as the credited source for the film.

Despite the involvement of those *Titanic* officers, or perhaps because of it, Hitchcock and his writers (his British collaborators Charles Bennett and Joan Harrison) focused on a fictional officer. Originally named Lawrence and later Stanley, using a fictional officer based on Lightoller and Boxhall allowed them to cover various aspects of the ship at different moments. That and to include something Selznick described as "feminine appeal": romance. Specifically, a blossoming one between Stanley and a First Class passenger originally named Mrs. Fisher and Mrs. Bellamy before becoming Mrs. Katherine Mead. The story of the officer and the widow would become the basis for the script's narrative, something which met with the approval of Selznick though Hitchcock remained resistant to putting too much emphasis on it.

Students of the auteur school of film-making have noted that, in their way, both Selznick and Hitchcock fit the description of what makes an auteur. In England, Hitchcock had increasingly had control over his films from script to screen. With *Gone With The Wind*, Selznick had been the vision behind the film as it transitioned between numerous writers and directors. Perhaps it should come as no surprise that, with *Titanic*, the two men had a clash even as early as the script phase. It was, like the ice warnings sent to the *Titanic*, also a harbinger of things to come.

Casting

The next point of clashes between the two came in casting the lead couple. Oddly enough, the two started at points of agreement that due to the film's subject matter, at least the leading man would need to be British. Doing so meant finding a star established in both America and Britain (it doesn't appear that making Stanley American was considered, unlike with the 1943 Nazi propaganda film *Titanic* which saw a fictional German First Officer inserted into proceedings).

It was there that the point of agreement between the two men ended. Hitchcock's first instinct was to try and lure his *39 Steps* star Robert Donat into bringing the role to life. Donat, however, was suffering one of his periodic bouts of ill health and had to turn down the role. Selznick favored Ronald Coleman or Leslie Howard, whom he had just used in *Gone With The Wind*, but Hitchcock disagreed vehemently. "[Howard] looks like a schoolmaster," he informed Selznick in a memo which has survived. Coleman was busy on another project which led to Orson Welles being considered, the feeling being that his accent might allow him to play British without much issue. Welles, however, was soon to be busy filming *Citizen Kane* as part of his RKO contract.

Ironically, it was in casting the role of Mrs. Mead that they found their leading man. Though Margaret Sullavan, Anne Baxter, and Loretta Young both auditioned, Selznick hit upon the notion of casting Vivan Leigh in the role. Leigh was a hot star on the back of *Gone With The Wind* and was, perhaps just as important, under contract to him. Hitchcock was initially unconvinced and requested she screen-test for the role. Needing someone to play the role of Stanley, Leigh asked for Laurence Olivier (with whom she was in a relationship with) to play the part for the test.

That screen test with Leigh and Olivier was the moment the film's casting clicked. Those who have seen the scene (included as a supplemental feature on the Criterion Collection release) immediately noted the chemistry between the pair, a case of art imitating life. From it, Hitchcock found himself casting Olivier and Leigh in the lead roles with Selznick's approval.

On the rest of the cast, there was much broader agreement. Much of it was made up of the contingent known as the "Hollywood English," whom Selznick has used to grand effect in 1937's *The Prisoner of Ze-*

nda. Zenda veterans appearing in *Titanic* included C. Aubrey Smith as Captain Smith and Douglas Fairbanks Jr. in the role of White Star Line managing director J. Bruce Ismay. Fairbanks' casting raised eyebrows at the time since Ismay was a supporting role and the actor was nearly a dozen years younger than the real Ismay had been at the time of the sinking. That Ismay had also only passed away in the autumn of 1937 further raised eyebrows, particularly upon *Titanic*'s British release, but as the film neared production, that issue had yet to surface.

Filming

As filming commenced, Hitchcock found himself temporarily outside of Selznick's clutches. The producer was focusing on the post-production and premiere of *Gone With The Wind*, the filming of which had contributed to the delays on *Titanic*'s production. Selznick, usually hands-on as we have seen, was thus forced to temporarily hand over control to Hitchcock.

It was something that the director relished in. Filming began on the converted *Leviathan* off of Long Beach in a flurry of publicity orchestrated not by Selznick but by Hitchcock himself. After a series of photo calls, filming began with a week dedicated to shooting the limited number of daytime scenes. These scenes included the *Titanic* leaving Southampton, various encounters between Stanley and Mrs. Mead, and a scene involving Captain Smith and Ismay discussing ice warnings delivered to the ship by wireless.

The completion of these scenes gave way to weeks of night shoots required to film the sinking sequences. The initial plan had been to film as much of the sinking as possible here, using the boat deck of the *Leviathan* and the sea around it to stage the lowering and rowing away of the lifeboats in addition to some scenes of panic set towards the ship's final moments. At first, all seemed to be going well with Hitchcock's pre-planning allowing him to shoot a large amount of material in comparatively little time.

However, all was not plain sailing. The night the *Titanic* sank was both moonless and still, the lack of waves contributing to the ship's demise. Unfortunately, neither the Moon nor Long Beach harbor cooperated with moonlight over illuminating scenes while swells around the moored *Leviathan* spoiled the illusion of a calm North Atlantic.

Hitchcock became aware of both problems and attempted to compensate for them with the aid of cinematographer George Barnes. While their combined effort minimized reshoots of the scenes filmed on board the *Leviathan*, Hitchcock abandoned the lifeboat scenes for the moment.

It was the abandonment that raised the first alarm with Selznick. A flurry of memos went back and forth between producer and director until Selznick watched the rushes from the night shoots and discovered the problem. "How did we not consider this?" he asked Hitchcock in one memo. The pair agreed to postpone scenes with Selznick agreeing to look into using the same tank the *Titanic* miniature was to be filmed in for the lifeboat scenes. When that proved to be impractical due to the tank's size, Hitchcock and his effects men struck upon the solution of using model lifeboats in long shots with camera angles inside the boats restricted largely to close-ups and limited rear projection.

Selznick's watching of rushes as he continued to focus on *Gone With The Wind* did lead the producer to a realization. Hitchcock was doing in-camera editing with sequences leading in and out of one another. Coverage, the shooting of scenes with multiple angles and line-readings to allow for additional choices in the editing room, was not on Hitchcock's menu. Selznick was annoyed with the decision, realizing that the British director was leaving little room for him to re-edit the picture potentially. Whether this was part of Hitchcock's meticulous planning or his having learned the lessons others had learned the hard way with Selznick isn't clear. What is clear is that Selznick attempted to have the director shoot coverage, only to be turned down.

As the film moved onto elaborate sets built from blueprints loaned to the production, Selznick was trying to exert more influence on the film. And yet, Hitchcock still worked to get around that by having a closed set that would shut down once Selznick appeared. Officially, filming would stop due to "technical issues" but, according to Oliver's memoir *Confessions of an Actor*, it was clear to everyone on set that a game of cat and mouse was in progress between the two men. Selznick would talk with Hitchcock mainly, occasionally with his lead actors, and leave. Once he did so, the "technical issues" would be resolved and filming would continue.

Such occurrences were not uncommon on the *Titanic* set. Despite that, Hitchcock kept the production on schedule, even when filming was extended to reshoot scenes abandoned during the *Leviathan* shoot. In that regard, Selznick had nothing to complain about since the production had managed to come in at just under its original budget. Indeed, Selznick was so pleased that he confirmed to the press that once *Titanic* was "put to bed," Hitchcock would be starting working on adapting *Rebecca* for cinemas.

A Question Of Music

Before the men could set about working on *Rebecca*, they had to finish the film they had already shot. While Hitchcock may have been able to close his set to Selznick and ignore his memos during production, when it came to post-production Selznick was in charge. Indeed, it was here that the producer made himself most felt.

The first place was in the editing. Hitchcock and editor W. Donn Hayes prepared a rough cut for Selznick which the producer viewed in early 1940. In watching it, Selznick noted that the film "shows great promise," while also saying that it was "slow" in places and questioned, "how accurately are we portraying events?"

Specifically, Selznick pointed to the *Titanic*'s band. Those familiar with the *Titanic* story will know the famous story of the ship's First Class band playing until nearly the last moment, their final selection remaining a hotly debated topic among *Titanic* historians. Back in 1940, it was to be the source of disagreement between Selznick and Hitchcock for, as originally shot, Hitchcock went with *Songe d'Automne*, which the director decided was both most likely to have been played and a dramatic piece.

Selznick disagreed and insisted that the hymn *Nearer, My God, to Thee* be used as it was better known to the public in regards to *Titanic*. Hitchcock was to resist until the final cut when Selznick, overseeing the dub, had it put into the film. The decision to do so led to one of the best-known goofs in film history as the band on-screen plays their instruments to one song while another plays. It was a decision that infuriated Hitchcock who, when asked in interviews after the film's release, was happy to blame the producer for the mistake.

Selznick oversaw much of the post-production of the film alongside Hitchcock in the winter and early spring. This time, the director could not keep the producer off-set when it was decided to reshoot certain scenes on the still-moored *Leviathan* to add to the montage of panicked passengers as the ship takes its final plunge. Despite their earlier animosity, the two men did not clash much and the rest of post-production went comparatively smoothly including a small amount of looping (which likely cost the film an Academy Award nomination for Best Sound Mixing) and the recording of Franz Waxman's score.

For the moment, at least, all looked up for Hitchcock's *Titanic*.

A *Titanic* Release

Titanic had its premiere in Miami on the 14th of March, 1940. The choice of date, just one month before the 28th anniversary of the sinking, was a deliberate move by Selznick. The film would have limited engagement in cities across the country before going into a wider release on the anniversary of the sinking. It was an interesting strategy and one that seemed to be paying off.

Reviews from critics were mostly positive. Frank S. Nugent of *The New York Times* gave it a glowing review where he referred to it as "an altogether brilliant film, haunting, suspenseful, handsome and handsomely played." The reviewer for *Variety* described the film as "an artistic success" noting Hitchcock's pacing as "the impending disaster begins to take a firm grip on the imagination and builds a compelling expectancy."

Not all reviews were entirely positive. One particular sour note came from Hearst newspaper columnist Hedda Hopper who declared that "the actual sinking looks like a nautical tragedy on the pond in Central Park." Also, in *Variety*'s otherwise glowing review, its critic did issue a warning that they felt that the film was "too tragic to hit the fancy of wide audience appeal."

Variety's critic was proven wrong. *Titanic* earned a for the time impressive $3.5 million at the American box office on its initial release, showing that even after the passage of nearly three decades the story could still hold sway over an audience. All looked up for an early summer release in the UK.

From the beginning, Selznick and Hitchcock had concerns over releasing the film in Europe, and Britain in particular. Both the British Board of Trade and Cunard White Star expressed strong reservations about the project, expressing fears that Hitchcock summed up as "They seem to think that if I recapture all the horror and violence of the situation, it will stop people from going on cruises."

The atmosphere had changed little when the film arrived for the British Board of Film Censors to certify for release. The film also had, due to the outbreak of war in Europe in September 1939, to be signed off on by the Ministry of Information. Both agencies announced to Selznick and distributor United Artists that edits would be needed. Specifically in the scenes of panic towards the end of the sinking sequence. For a nation at war that would soon face the Blitz at the hand of the German Luftwaffe, perhaps the scenes would be seen as too much or likely to inspire real panic.

A flurry of memos went back and forth between Selznick and Hitchcock. Both were reluctant to make the edits and yet Selznick, who had bankrolled the film, was aware that the war had squeezed the European film market as it was. Reluctantly, he forced Hitchcock to make the edits which led to stories about multiple versions of the film which continue to do the rounds in film circles.

There was another issue facing the film's British release. J. Bruce Ismay, the managing director of the White Star Line in 1912 who had survived the sinking to great scandal, was portrayed in the film by Douglas Fairbanks Jr, and the film implied that Ismay was a party to the circumstances which caused the disaster. Though Ismay himself had passed away in the autumn of 1937, his widow was very much alive. When she and her children received word of the portrayal via letters from friends in America, there began to be rumblings of legal action. Controversy raged in the British press which led to calls for Hitchcock to return to England to account for his "uncharacteristically anti-British sentiments" and for the film to be banned.

Circumstances favored the film. Selznick and Hitchcock, through sympathetic members of the British press, were able to release stories that pointed to testimony given both the American and British inquiries into the sinking, statements they felt back the portrayal of events in the film. An additional aid came from surviving *Titanic* officers Lightoller and Boxhall who, while not agreeing with the depiction of their former boss Ismay, stated that they felt that they and British seamen, in general, were well represented by the film. Though the Ismay family refused to attend the film's London premiere, as well as their public announcement they had no wishes to see it, the controversy subsided in time for the film's release in May 1940.

The timing too proved to be in the film's favor. *Titanic*'s British release date coincided with the beginning of Operation Dynamo, the evacuation of Allied troops from Dunkirk. The removal of 336,000 British and French soldiers under siege by the Nazi military was aided by more than 800 small craft from England, among them Charles Lightoller's yacht the *Sundowner*. Perhaps because of the film, Lightoller's role was highlighted by members of the British press among the soon to be named "Little Ships of Dunkirk."

Critics were quick to make a connection between the seamen of the *Titanic* and those who had participated in Dynamo. Despite having been accused of being anti-British just weeks before, Hitchcock's *Titanic* was now finding itself praised for its presentation of "supreme British seamanship under pressure," as one British reviewer noted. Audiences began to flock into cinemas to see the film, allowing it to become the most successful film at the British box-office that year with earnings of $1 million by year's end.

The End Of An Era

The film's British success had an unlikely side-effect, one that neither Hitchcock nor Selznick could have foreseen. Critics and audiences had made the unintended connection between the film and the events at Dunkirk. Among those doing so was the British government of Prime Minister Winston Churchill who suggested that Hitchcock next tackle Dunkirk.

While Churchill was known to make similar suggestions to filmmakers still based in Britain (a similar suggestion led to Alexander Korda filming *That Hamilton Woman* which coincidentally starred Olivier and Leigh), this was the first time he'd done so to Hitchcock. Being based in Hollywood away from the war and under contract to Selznick, there are some indications that while Hitchcock wanted to make a pro-British picture regarding the war, doing one about Dunkirk wasn't what he had in mind.

Neither did Selznick. Aware that America was deeply isolationist, the producer was worried not just about whether such a British-based topic would be viable but also about violating American neutrality laws. As odd as the latter may sound, it may be worth remembering that the Senate Foreign Relations Committee investigated a number of films in

1941 for pro-British propaganda, including *That Hamilton Woman*. The Hitchcock/Selznick Dunkirk could well have fallen into that category.

The matter seemed to be settled when word reached Hitchcock that there were rumors of him being, in effect, drafted into the British military to make the film. The director had also become aware of criticism from the home front that he was "sitting out the war" safe in Hollywood. Selznick too was aware of the pressure and, through Korda's American company Alexander Korda Films Inc., struck a deal to let Hitchcock return home. The director left his wife and daughter behind with the intention of having them follow later, aware that he would have to re-establish a home in Britain in the midst of wartime conditions.

Neither would ever follow him. Twelve days after leaving Hollywood, the ship carrying Hitchcock back to England was at the bottom of the Atlantic. It had been the victim of a German torpedo, fired from a U-Boat in mid-ocean. He died just short of his 41st birthday.

His death had a marked effect upon Selznick. The producer shelved plans for a film based on the novel *Rebecca*, only briefly returning to the idea in 1950 but passing on the idea once more. *Titanic* also marked the end of Selznick's most productive period as a producer though he loaned out contracted players and produced films such as 1949's *The Third Man* (once again with Korda). His health deteriorated in the 1950s, leading to his death at the age of 53 from a heart attack.

What Ifs?

As spectacular as Hitchcock's *Titanic* is, there still lingers questions around it and the films that Hitchcock might have made if he had not drowned in the North Atlantic. The "what if's" pile up around it as they do they the factual ship. What if producer and director hadn't made *Titanic*? What if they had made *Rebecca* instead? What Hitchcock's *Rebecca* might have been like remains one of the greatest what-if moments in film history. Would it have the launch of a successful American career for the director or would he have run into similar issues? Would Hitchcock have found another film to make about the war, one that wouldn't have put in the path of a Nazi torpedo?

We'll never know, of course. Like the *Titanic* itself on that night in April 1912, what Hitchcock might have done next had sunk into the dark depths of history. There have been other films of *Titanic*, of course, including 1958's *A Night To Remember* (made by Hitchcock protegee Roy Ward Baker) and James Cameron's career-ending flop twenty years ago. None of them match Hitchcock's ability to recreate the wonder of the ship and the nightmare of the disaster quite the same way.

And, I suspect, none ever shall.

Meet Matthew Kresal

Matthew Kresal is a writer, critic, and podcaster with many and vary-ing interests. He's written about and discussed topics as wide-ranging as the BBC's Doctor Who, Cold War fact and fiction, and the UFO phe-nomenon. He has appeared on podcasts including Spybrary, Dead Hand Radio, The 20mb Doctor Who Podcast, and The Saucer Life. His prose includes the non-fiction The Silver Archive: Dark Skies from Obverse Press and short fiction including The Aurora Affair in Belanger Books' A Tribute to H.G. Wells and The Light of a Thousand Suns in in D&T Publishing's After the Kool-Aid is Gone. He was born, raised, and lives in North Alabama where he never developed a southern accent.

Matthew's story so very nearly came true in real life. He was indeed hired by David O. Selznick, having agreed to work on a film about the *Titanic* disaster, but there our worlds part. Instead, he made *Rebecca*, and from there went on to make a catalogue of films so famous you know them already.

You can find Matthew on Twitter, as @KresalWrites. He also has a novel, Our Man On The Hill, available through Sea Lion Press.

OPS AND OSTENTATION

BY ROB EDWARDS

a candle holder. Enough candles had been lit that the rooms were almost too bright. The risk of fire seemed ever present, but the threat of the dark too much to bear. The scent of wax and candle wick cloyed the air, making it hard to breathe amongst the throng.

And throng it was. It seemed the whole town had craved some respite and chose to attend whether they had been invited or not.

"So pleased you could make it, my dear Mrs Briggs!" called Mrs Drake from across the room.

Constance smiled tightly, nodded, and let the flow of the crowd sweep her away.

"A marvellous turn out, don't you think, Mrs Briggs?"

She didn't even turn to see who had spoken, instead Constance ducked through a doorway, pretending not to have heard. She let her steps take her further from the furore, until at last she came to a dark corridor beneath the main hall. The sound of life from above echoed around the walls, the stomping of feet rattled the ceiling as the dance began in earnest.

Constance leaned against the wall, hugging herself. "You are being ridiculous," she told herself crossly. "If all you are going to do is hide, why attend at all?" Yet she did not move.

One voice cut through her regret. A man's voice, warm and rich, speaking too low for Constance to determine his words, but his tone of authority was unmistakable. It was closer than the rest of the clamour, here on her level. Curious, Constance stepped away from the wall, followed the voice.

Three men she did not immediately recognise huddled deep in conversation. Two were obviously gentlemen, in their forties, the third was a younger man, perhaps a tradesman by his attire. One of the gentlemen was tall, dark-haired with a beak of a nose, the other was a shorter man, his face dominated by a vast beard, clearly intended to distract from his bald pate. After a moment's thought, Constance decided that these must surely be the brothers Fenton that Mrs Charles had described. Who the third man was, or what the three of them were doing here in the dark, she could not imagine.

As she watched, she met the gaze of the bearded Mr Fenton. His eyes burned with fierce intelligence and she recoiled in shock. She must have made a sound, as the other two men turned their attention towards her.

The taller Mr Fenton took a step forward, then bowed to her. "My apologies if we startled you, dear lady. My brother and I were taking a moment away from the most enthusiastic welcome we received upstairs. Are you in need of aid that we may render?"

"No, thank you, Mr Fenton. I, too, was seeking a moment's solitude. I apologise for intruding upon yours."

He inclined his head in a bow again. "Then perhaps we may isolate together? I, as it seems you may know, am Arthur Fenton; this hirsute fellow is my brother John. May I beg the honour of learning your name?"

"Mrs Constance Briggs."

"Sir William's wife? My dear Mrs Briggs, my sincere condolences on your loss. He was a good man."

"You knew William? I do not recall him ever mentioning you."

Mr Fenton put a hand to his heart. "The acquaintance was brief, but your husband left an impression. He earned great honours at Badajoz, I understand."

"Thank you, Mr Fenton. May I extend my condolences, also. Your wife I understand was…?"

He stiffened, straightened, looked away. "In London, yes. It seems this new age breeds condolences aplenty, but they never do seem to dull the bite of the loss, do they?"

John put a hand on his brother's shoulder. Arthur nodded.

"Let us return upstairs," Mr Fenton suggested. "John must, from there, return home. Would you, Mrs Briggs, consent to reinforcing me against the assault of Hetherton society, perhaps allowing me to do the same for you?"

At the top of the stairs, John Fenton and third man left without a word. Constance thought it rude, but to comment such would only compound the rudeness. Instead, she followed Arthur as he weaved through the crowd, nodding greetings to those they passed.

They took the field, Arthur claiming a spot near the dance floor, but making no move to join it. They had a good view of the action without obligation to participate. To Constance's delight, the strategy seemed sound. They were both curiosities to the assemblage, each in their own way, but by standing together in conversation, they each deterred those interested in the other.

Mr Fenton offered humorous remarks upon proceedings, never mean or mocking, but witty and insightful. More than one remark prompted Constance to laugh. A tightness in her chest she had never noticed eased, voice. "It had no interest in us. We are quite safe here within these stout walls. Take heart, Anna."

"Yes, ma'am."

Constance clutched at her robe to stop her hand from shaking. "Now, I think after a little adventure like that, we have both earned a nip of sherry. Would you be so kind as to fetch glasses for us both?"

A task to focus on, however simple, was just what her girl needed, it seemed. Anna stood, smoothed down her skirts and bobbed a passable curtsey. "Yes, ma'am, thank you ma'am." She really was a steady sort. Not for the first time, Constance was glad of her company.

Still, Constance could think of no task, however simple, with which to distract herself. She knew the vision of the thing in the moonlight would stay with her. Sleep would not come quickly that night.

• • •

The household was roused early the next morning by an urgent rapping at the front door. Cook, who had slept through the entire night-time incident was good enough to answer the door. Constance heard her ask the visitor to wait, then slowly mount the stairs, presumably come to alert her mistress.

Constance was in no shape to receive guests. "Send them away, Cook," she said through her closed bedroom door.

"Begging your pardon, ma'am, Mr Fenton seemed quite insistent upon seeing you."

"Mr Fenton?"

"Yes ma'am."

"Tell him I shall be down directly."

"Yes, ma'am." Was that a chuckle in Cook's voice? Surely not.

Constance readied herself as quickly as she was able, then bustled down the stairs to meet her visitor.

"Constance!" Mr Fenton declared, then caught himself. "Mrs Briggs. It is good to see you well."

She assayed a smile. "Did you have reason to think I would not be?"

"I received word of the presence of certain beings near town last night. I have men… friends, visitors, out checking the locale to see what damage they wrought, if any, but I found myself compelled to call upon you directly to ascertain your condition."

"I thank you for the consideration, Mr Fenton. We remain well, as you see, though our night was indeed a troubled one."

"They were here?" Mr Fenton's eyes darted about, as though seeking signs of the creature under the chairs.

"I saw… something. Out on the road, just beyond the gate. It left us unmolested, but I confess we found the encounter somewhat dismaying."

He took a step towards her and for a moment it seemed that he might throw all propriety to the wind and embrace her. Instead, he drew back at the last moment. "I am pleased that you are well, but troubled that you would be disturbed here. I shall examine the lane and determine if any trace of the creature remains. If so, I shall see that it is cleared away, you may rely upon it."

"Thank you for your concern, Mr Fenton. It is most gratifying."

He nodded a bow. "Then, reassured that all is well, I shall take my leave. I very much hope we can expect to see you at the Hall next week?"

"It would take more than last night's adventure to prevent it, Mr Fenton. Arthur."

• • •

If all of Hetherton had turned out for the dance at the Guild Hall, Constance mused, then surely the celebration at Brandon Hall had summoned up luminaries from across the county. Carriages snaked up the long path to the Hall through its expansive and picturesque grounds, delivering a veritable flood of the worthy and the curious to the Fentons' door.

Any other establishment would be overwhelmed by this sudden influx of guests, yet it seemed Mr Fenton was prepared. An army of staff stood ready to guide and assist the guests, to make sure they found their way to the entertainments and provisions, simultaneously keeping certain areas of the Hall politely off-limits.

Constance laughed to see one curious stranger deftly collected and diverted away from the door to the Fentons' private quarters. "Oh, splendidly done," she said.

For her part she drifted from room to room, admiring the tasteful restraint of the decorations here. The Hall had a celebratory air, for certain, but it was neither extravagant nor indulgent.

assured, I shall keep this confidence. For I intend never to speak of you again to anyone of my acquaintance."

She marched from the stable and back to her carriage, ignoring Arthur calling after her.

• • •

Constance permitted no outward sign of her broken heart to display. Indeed, she threw herself back into society as she had not even when William had lived. There were obligations Constance had neglected, duties to which she returned. She visited with the sick and elderly. Helped arrange the business of the parish. Allowed her home to be again a place of bustling welcome.

Cook and Anna, at least, seemed to realise it was all charade. Cook outdid herself, filling tables with Constance's favourites, whether she asked for it or not. Anna was attentive and, within the bounds of propriety made herself available to her mistress so she need not feel alone.

Both discouraged word of the doings at Brandon Hall in their mistress's hearing, but their seal of secrecy was not infallible. Word reached Constance of a stream of visitors that attended the Brothers 'Fenton'. Men of military age flocked to the Hall, though the explanations for it ran wild. Most popular was that Mr John Fenton had some grand new invention that necessitated a growing workforce to prepare to bring to market. Hopes of some new prosperity in the area ran high. Others remembered word that Arthur Fenton was rumoured to be some kind of scholar, and suggested he was creating a place of learning and study at the Hall. Those who favoured this theory spoke of the honour and reputation such an establishment could bring to their small town.

Constance saw it for what it was, and slept only fitfully, visions of that strange undulating being returning to terrorise their village and put a stop to Arthur's machinations.

While she no longer sought the company of Arthur Fenton, Constance's renewed participation in the affairs of Hetherton did, on occasion, cause their paths to intersect. At such times, Constance held her tongue and Arthur's secret, relying instead upon the rules of civilisation to carry them through any awkwardness.

"The weather has been most pleasant for the time of year," she told him, when circumstance and etiquette obliged them to communicate.

"All of the indicators point to a warm summer," Arthur replied in similar empty formality, his eyes dark.

"Indeed," she agreed, heart aching.

"Indeed," he concluded, before taking his leave.

• • •

And so it went. Weeks became months, and the promised warm summer arrived. Until, on the morning of Saturday June 17th, everything changed.

Mrs Charles fair flew through Constance's door with news that the Hall was suddenly deserted. "I really do not understand what can have happened," she wailed. "I had rarely seen so many fine young gentlemen in town. The girls were to have their pick, I'm sure, but now? All hope is lost. All that remain at the Hall are a few of the elderly attendants and the more reclusive Mr Fenton."

"Arthur Fenton has quit the house?" Constance asked, despite herself.

"I really do not know what to tell you," said Mrs Charles, all evidence to the contrary. "Only that he and many of his students are no longer in residence today, and none can say when they left or to where they went."

Constance looked out of the drawing room window, and once again her imagination painted that formless thing glistening beyond the garden hedge. She shivered. "Well, I suppose it is no business of ours," she said, fearing the lie rang in her voice.

"Oh, but I quite forgot the other news, about my dear Mary," Mrs Charles said.

Constance felt secure in letting the triviality flow past her, and instead let her mind turn over the meaning of Arthur's departure.

• • •

Sunday morning was marked by thunder in a cloudless sky, a sound which recalled the similar cacophony that had marked the fall of London. People stayed within their homes and prayed. If this was the precursor to further attacks, perhaps a harbinger of Armageddon itself, people wanted to be with their families.

Constance dismissed Anna and Cook to go be with theirs. For her

DUST OF THE EARTH

BY BRENT A. HARRIS

and scoured the sun-scorched cliffs of Montana's Hell Creek, searching the strata.

Fossils from *Triceratops* and *Tyrannosaurus* and, of course, *Dakatoraptor* had been discovered here. But the dig site at this part of Hell Creek, due to lack of funding, had all but dried up. Jess was convinced that she could bring life back to this place. *I need to find a fossil to prove the link between dinosaurs and birds...*

The scorching summer sun stretched shadows across stony outcrops of spiraling gargoyles. Cretaceous era rock beckoned her through whispers of wind which tugged long, black hair. She scanned her immediate surroundings of flat plateau, swirling dust, and clumps of cordgrass to the edge of a drop-off through darkened lenses of Aviators.

Nothing.

Jess removed a scrunchy from over a wrist tattoo and used it to tie her hair back. She was well tanned, lithe, and athletic from bouldering as a hobby and bone-digging for a living.

Tattoos covered each leg; the cliff notes of her life ingrained in ink symbols, each one telling a story. A skull there. A Rebel symbol there. A rose with a sharp thorn stretched across her calf.

But none were so important as the ink-black semi-colon on her wrist above a long, thin scar. No amount of ink could confuse the story there.

She continued her trek, drawing closer to steep cliffs that led to a gorge below. There had been a windstorm last night, bringing a perfect opportunity to reveal what the earth had secreted away.

Yet, half a day in, an hour's hike away from her Jeep, and being somewhat foolish to investigate alone, she'd come up empty.

Again.

Jess should have been out digging in China. The real spot for significant finds. She shook her head, the argument she had with Dr. Maxwell in their museum back home still fresh in her mind and hot in her heart.

People had tired of the same fossil finds. He wanted her to find something bigger, scarier. More teeth. Perhaps it might re-ignite interest, sell more tickets, and bring dinosaurs into the limelight she knew they deserved.

She shook her head. She wasn't interested in Rex. Professionally, to find a *Dakotaraptor* specimen, complete with the impressions of feathers —- cotton-candy-like fuzz — pressed into the rock? Solid proof that dromaeosaurs were evolutionarily linked to modern-day birds? *Jackpot.*

Her colleagues had found such evidence in Liaoning, half a world away. No such find had been discovered in North America. Not yet. And unlikely.

Even if she could discover feather impressions on a species out here, she'd still face an uphill battle with public perception. The Chinese population, not just scientists, embraced the idea of a dinosaur, perched and poised — as if to fly. Americans, skeptical of science and tuned to their TVs, still pictured dinosaurs as slow, lumbering, lizards, dismissing the Chinese image. She sought to change that.

I just have to find my fossil.

She stepped closer to the cliff's edge, and carefully peered out over the deeply cut gully. Dangerous, yes, but she was desperate. Below, about twenty feet she guesstimated, she eyed some nice boulders to "cushion" her, should she fall. A snake-like path of Juniper and sagebrush demarcated a dry stream bed.

Climb down? See what might have been exposed by the wind and winter rains within the crags? Unfortunately, her harness, helmet, and rope were back in her Jeep. All she had was a chalk bag, better suited for bouldering up rather than scrambling down. She mulled her problems while fiddling with her rock hammer, leaning over the windswept precipice.

How do I spur people's interest into dinosaurs? How do I change their perception? And where the hell are my fossils?

John Ostrom had long since argued that dinosaurs were warm-blooded, agile creatures, more akin to birds, facts generally accepted by paleontologists the world over. The problem wasn't with the research, but the awareness. Westerners largely ignored advanced theories of paleontology in favor of pop-culture candy.

Archeology.

Most notably, everyone had fixated onto one figure: the Hollywood hero with a fedora, bullwhip, and a penchant for punching Nazis while in search of artifacts he sought to put into museums.

It was hard to beat that kind of popularity. Paleontology was just old rocks. Boring for anyone but five-year-olds who could pronounce *Stegosaurus* before they could perform basic math. Once that childhood curiosity was lost, people became empty vessels, ready to devour anything dished out by Disney.

Defeated, Jess gave up for the day when the cracked, dry earth beneath her collapsed—

She slipped off the dirt and fell with a scream.

A low thrumming sound stirred her attention away from her computer screen toward a transparent plastic cup of water beside it. Rings rippled outward from the center. Each ripple different from the last, each one impossible to predict, as she studied them, struggling to place the sound of the thrumming.

The noise stopped and so did the vibration. Jess picked up and gulped down the contents of the cup. *That'll stop the ripples altogether.*

The reverberations began anew. *That's right*, she finally recalled: *construction had started on the expansion to the museum's Egyptology wing.*

The money funneled into that project was going to make her case for funding even harder to present today. Jess put her computer to sleep. On the screen had been a novel she'd been toying with but had struggled to write. It seemed she had everything in her mind but the pesky parts, like the actual story.

I'll pick it up later. It's Death by PowerPoint time. She picked up a set of file folders, printouts of budgets, and shoved her raptor claw between them for good luck.

She headed out of her closet-sized office, excavated out of a corner in the paleontology exhibit. In the museum, she wore heels, which echoed along the long tile hallways. Being on a dig meant she could ditch them for shoes more her style.

She passed a mural reprinting by Zallinger called *The Age of Reptiles*. It annoyed her for its outdated depiction of reptilian dinosaurs which had somehow stuck in the public mind, like a piece of popcorn kernel caught in the gums. Every time she walked by, she frowned, yet a look toward the main hall gave her a sudden and unexpected smile.

In the center of the room was a *Nodosaur* mummy on loan from the Canadians. Well, it wasn't a mummy. But since mummies sold tickets and dinosaurs didn't, the moniker of *mummy* stuck.

This *Nodosaurus* was one of the best-preserved fossil specimens ever, showing an ankylosaurid in amazing detail of armored plates from head-to-tail. A remarkable find, considering she was over 110 million years old. Most mummies were, at best, 6,000.

Take that, Anubis.

But it wasn't the *Nodosaur* that had made her smile. It was a little girl poring over the glass display.

She approached the girl, cautiously. She was about nine or ten, with blond hair and a phone in her hand. She wore jeans and a t-shirt with a pyramid on it that said, "Boys dig me."

So much about that isn't right.

After a few moments, the girl lost interest with the creature.

Jess sprang into action. "Isn't it cool?" she asked the girl, introducing herself. "I'm Dr. Yang." She made sure to emphasize the doctor. There weren't many women portrayed in the media, especially as scientists. No harm in impressing on the girl that she could be a scientist too.

She continued, "This is as close as we may ever get to knowing just what a real dinosaur would look like. Can't you imagine him bounding over hills and wagging his tail like a puppy?" Unlike other ankylosaurids, *Nodosaur* didn't have a bony club. Just a stubby, unadorned tail. "What do you think?"

"Looks more like a ten-foot turtle to me." The girl turned to leave the room unimpressed.

"You could become a paleontologist yourself—"

"I want to see a real mummy," the girl said as she dashed to the Egyptology exhibits.

"But—"

It was no use.

The girl had passed a life-size cardboard stand-up of Indiana Jones advertising the museum's archeological offerings. This stand-up was more recent than the last. Under Harrison Ford's fedora stood the unlikely Chris Pratt (life is stranger than art, she admitted) who'd traded out the bullwhip for a Tommy gun to keep up with the times.

How many spin-offs and sequels were there? Jess let the girl go from her mind, conscious of a losing battle as she braced herself for yet another, as if she were falling, spiraling out of control...

Jess instinctively reached out for something, anything to grab onto.

She flailed. Deliberately. Letting her arms and legs hit and kick anything that might break her fall as the ground rose to slam against her.

She missed the boulders by inches as she fell against earth, stumbled,

Jess recalled the former paleontologist. He'd had a few famous finds and been on a few documentaries. With more funding or public support, he could have been the face of paleontology. Or that eccentric Bakker guy, the one with the big book. Neither had acclimated themselves well to obscurity and failure. And she sure as hell didn't want to end up like them. *Hell Creek it is, then.*

She slunk her head in surrender, wondering what her brother would think of all this, the one who'd helped save her and set her on this path.

The prairie rattler grew bored. The sun had dipped from its noontime high, and the wind whipped through the ravine. As the snake slithered away, it gave Jess one last disapproving glare, then went off in search of a meal or burrow for the night.

"What, where you goin' little guy?" Jess propped herself back up on her elbows and watched as the snake left her company. "I was just starting to like you."

She doubted the snake had envenomated her much, it was a precious commodity to them, after all. And she was clearly not a meal.

It could have been worse. If she had stumbled off a cliff and fallen through a mysterious gateway to the Mesozoic. With dinosaurs chirping and rumbling about. A snake was nothing compared to being *Dilophosaurus* dinner.

Alright, humor in check. That's step one. Maintain a positive attitude. It's not too bad, right?

Her leg throbbed and her head spun, but she could manage if she focused. And she had to focus. Otherwise, she wasn't leaving Hell Creek.

Ever.

She dug her phone out of a leg pocket. The screen was cracked. No, the fall hadn't broken her phone, she'd done that a long time ago on the tile floor in the bathroom. Still, she frowned, no signal.

I need a plan. She thought her actions out, as calmly as she could, addressing each problem at a time.

First, she took off her black tank top to reveal a black sports bra underneath. She tied the shirt around her leg just above the snakebite. Slow the venom, if any.

She took her chalk bag belt and cinched it around her leg, letting slip a yelp, thankful it hadn't been a compound fracture. *Or I'd be dead.*

She wasn't sure if she had gotten the order right, and with the chemicals rushing through her system, from adrenaline to toxins, it was possible she'd made a mistake. But it was the best she could do under the circumstances.

Looking around, she saw nothing she could improvise as a splint. Which would mean hell for her leg for the long journey back.

But first, she needed water. Desperately. Her glasses and her canteen hadn't bothered to make the journey with her downhill. She looked around for her rock hammer, cursing that it too had been separated from her by the fall.

She remembered from looking over the edge that there was a dry stream bed below. Now, she was on top of it. She inched over the tough prairie earth and in between two juniper bushes among a long, thin line of shrubs.

Dry.

But, not underneath, she was sure.

She examined the hard earth and then her hands, sighing. Tiny, dull fingertips wouldn't be enough. There were rocks scattered about but none nearby and she needed that water now.

I need my hammer. It was dull on one side, pointed like a pickax on the other. A paleontologist's primary tool. But she had something else that might work.

With a spark of an idea in mind, she removed her raptor claw from the chalk bag, and dug the sharp end into the dirt. She imagined a *Dakatorapter* giving her a disapproving look. Still, it worked. Within minutes, she had dug down deep enough for water to pool. She drank at it, greedily.

Thanks, Big Bro. Sam had given her the claw as a gift when she had decided to pursue paleontology, shortly after her incident. This was the second time he had saved her life.

Her thirst slaked, it was as good a time as any to stand. She used her good knee and hands to hoist herself upright. To her own surprise, it didn't hurt nearly as much—

She cried out as her leg resettled into its new position.

Never mind. Oh, this is gonna be fun.

Still, she stood. And she could ambulate, as evidenced by a slow, steady hobble toward the crags.

On any given day, she could scramble up it, minimal effort required.

Meet Brent A. Harris

Brent A Harris is a two-time Sidewise Award finalist of alternate history. He writes about dinosaurs, fantasy, the fears of our future and the mistakes of our past. While he considers Southern California home, he currently resides in Naples, Italy. You can learn more by visiting www. BrentAHarris.com.

Other books by Brent include: A Time of Need: A Dark Eagle Novel (an alternate history of the American Revolution); Alyx: An AI's Guide to Love and Murder; and Dickens Meets Steampunk in: A Twist in Time and A Christmas Twist: A Twist in Time Book II.

You can find Brent on Twitter at @brentaharris1.

"You're not him," I said. "You're just a common thief."

The man, who I suspected was the Bill Street Mugger, a thief the police had been seeking for a fortnight now, gave me a venomous look from the ground. "And yer justa dirty curry coon," he spat at me.

It was a slur I'd heard so many times, it had ceased to bother me. I'd come to expect the vitriol spewed my way most days. Thus in this moment, I was not interested in what the man I'd just kicked to the ground had to say. Instead, I moved my gaze down, from his face to his trousers. Confused, the man followed my stare, wondering perhaps if he'd wet himself in all the excitement. But he hadn't. I was in fact looking at his belt.

In my native homeland of India, I had trained in combat with the Bengali army. Over the last eight months, I'd called upon that training to aid me in my quest for Mary Ann's killer. Unchecked by the police, The Ripper had taken the lives of ten women, and it seemed to me that the only way to halt these killings was to apprehend the culprit myself. Along the way, I stumbled upon many a crook, just like this rogue, and I now knew well enough how to bring reprobates like him to justice.

Tying the man up with his own belt, I escorted him through the maze of back alleys that I'd now memorized. Though he struggled at first, he could not get me to loosen my grip, nor get near enough to kick me, for my training had served me well. The mugger had no choice but to let me guide him to the back of a building, one that criminals of London found both familiar and formidable – the London Metropolitan Police Station.

I wouldn't go inside, of course. There'd be too many questions, and if the police caught on to the fact that I, a maid, moonlighted as a vigilante, well they'd tell the Wentworths what I was up to, and it would become a gargantuan scandal. This world has certain expectations of people like me, one being that I am to always remain invisible and do the job that is appropriate for my station and race. If Londoners at large were to ever find out that I am capable of far more than they could ever conceive, well, they'd punish me simply for being bold.

There is only one person above my own station who understands this. We are childhood friends. His parents were stationed in Calcutta when I was a child, and he and I would play cricket together, even though his father had forbidden him to play with "the rabble", as many British officers called us Indians. But my dear Iain never saw me as rabble, and wrote me frequent letters even after he and his family had moved back to England. Six years later, when I moved to London as the Wentworths' maid, Iain was the first person I sought out. We'd picked up our friendship right where we'd left off, except this time, we had a more quiet, hidden friendship. We weren't children anymore, and as I've already said, London society can be cruel.

Our long history means that Iain often voices his concerns about my new nighttime obsession. But he never stops me. Sometimes I think he wishes I would step out of the shadows and become an official police woman, but this is purely fantasy for they would never let a woman, let alone one with my skin tone, work in the force. Thus for now, every time I catch a villainous varlet trying to steal or stab some poor unsuspecting soul in an alleyway, I come to Iain (or Detective Campbell as the police call him), and hand him the criminal in question so that he can take them in.

That night, I approached the window to Iain's ground floor office, holding the mugger as tight as I could by his belt, my handkerchief tied around his mouth so he could not squeal. I had done this enough times to know Iain would likely be at his desk this night, and sure enough, as I drew closer to the building, I saw a dim light on in his office. I pressed my face to the window. Inside, Iain sat at his desk, scrutinizing photographs of what was likely a grisly crime scene, deep in thought.

Thap. Thap. I knocked softly on his window. Iain looked up, alarmed at first, and then relieved when he saw it was me. Approaching quickly, he opened the window and stuck his head out. I grinned at him, still holding the mugger tightly by his belt.

"Samira," said Iain. "What the—"

"I have a present for you," I explained with a grin. "I'm going to push him through the big, main station doors and then scarper."

"No," said Iain. "Commissioner Warren will ask too many questions. I—"

"Well, then climb out here and bring him into the station yourself, as if you caught him," I said, somewhat irritated. We had played this game perhaps a million times before. Why was this instance any different?

Iain looked at me as if he'd read my mind.

"I have a strange feeling in my gut," he said, his eyes locking with mine, trying to convey something that he couldn't fully comprehend himself. "I cannot explain what it is, but I do not think you should be out alone tonight."

I looked at Edith as if I were seeing her for the first time. The remorse she projected didn't reach her eyes. It suddenly dawned on me that butchers never delivered meat to customers, and if they did it was certainly never this late at night. Then, for the first time, I noticed Edith's choice of attire for the night – she was dressed like a man, with a long heavy coat wrapped around her person. Even her long hair was tied up in a bun and hidden underneath a hat.

I forced myself to look at the body on the ground once again, fixating on the woman's throat. The cuts were surgical, as if someone with a skill for cutting had made these incisions.

Someone...like the Butcher's wife.

Slowly, I looked up at Edith's face. I wondered if I should feign ignorance and perhaps escort Edith home without letting her know what I suspected. But it was too late. The expression on my face had betrayed me, and Edith could see that I had deduced the truth.

Slowly, she opened her coat to reveal a sharp and still bloody knife. I took a few steps back, my hands held out in front of me, attempting to stop the woman I thought was my dear friend from coming any closer.

"Edith," I said. "There is no need for this."

"I'm afraid you've seen what I've been doing, Samira," said Edith. To my alarm, I noticed her accent had vanished. In a flash I realized I'd never truly known the woman standing before me, for she had been putting up a facade. I was meeting the real Edith for the first time...and I was terrified. "I cannot let you tell your policeman friend that I am this Ripper he's been looking for," she continued as she approached me slowly.

I stepped back once more. I was aware that the more I backed away, the more I'd come up against the back wall of the wash house. But I had no means of escape yet. "Why did you do this, Edith?" I asked, trying to keep her talking. "You killed Mary Ann."

"She was a sinner, as were they all," said Edith. "Perhaps God would have forgiven them. Perhaps he still will. But their sins were corrupting our men."

As Edith advanced closer, I continued to back away, my eyes darting along the alley for some kind of weapon I could use, but I couldn't spy anything useful.

"Corrupting our men?" I asked. "You mean...your husband?"

"He was tempted!" screamed Edith, and I knew I'd guessed correctly.

Jacob the Butcher had clearly been seeking pleasures of the flesh outside his marital bed.

"Mary Ann was his first," said Edith. "Then he was tempted again by nine others. But he was not at fault. These women were quite like the snake that corrupted Eve in the Sacred Garden, manipulating my poor husband. I could not abide their sinful actions."

As she drew closer, I was saddened by how much Edith had perverted the meaning of her own religion. She did not seem to comprehend that a true woman of God would never take another's life. Besides, the indiscretions that ruined her marriage with Jacob the Butcher were entirely his fault, and if Edith simply *had* to take a life, the simpler thing would have been to murder her husband instead of these poor lasses. But I held my tongue and kept this to myself. Speaking this out loud would only give Edith more ideas.

"Tis not your place to take matters into your own hands like this, Edith." I said instead.

"Murder is a sin too. And you will hang for it."

"I believe not," said Edith as she continued to approach me. I realized I'd finally been backed into a corner. I looked at Edith, calculating the best way to attack her so I could make my escape. Had she been any other vagrant, I'd have had her winded on the ground by now. But she was my friend, and attacking her came with a hesitation I did not know I possessed.

"The police shall only find out if you tell them," Edith continued, the knife she held glinting sinisterly in the moonlight. "But you will not get the chance, Samira. I am sorry to do this to you, for you are a kind soul. But perhaps you too will end up on heaven's gate as well."

As Edith raised her knife, ready to strike, I aimed a kick at her gut. But the shock of her true nature must have uncentered me, for I missed. This gave Edith the advantage, and she managed to kick me to the ground. I was now at her mercy. As Edith's razor-edged knife came down upon me, I closed my eyes. A last thought floated through my head – Iain was right. I should have let him escort me back to the Wentworths. Alas, now I'd never see him again.

Boom. A shot rang out in the quiet night. Startled, Edith dropped her weapon with a loud clang. I opened my eyes and looked past her to see Iain, holding his pistol high, staring in shock at the scene in front of him. He hadn't struck her, but his arrival had served as a distraction, allowing me to rush at Edith and pin her to the floor.

Edith, however, was fueled by adrenaline, and she would not surrender so easily. Throwing me off her person, she quickly righted herself... then went straight for Iain. Before he could comprehend what was transpiring, Edith had punched him in the gut and wrestled his pistol away.

Fortunately, my reflexes were quicker than his, and by the time Edith turned towards me, pistol in hand, I had her butcher knife ready.

I saw the pain on her face before she felt it. Wide-eyed, she dropped the pistol as the knife slid into her gut like butter. In horror, I looked down at what I'd done, expecting Edith to fall to the floor in agony, for our battle to finally be done.

But it was not. Edith still had some strength left in her. Retracting the knife from her belly, she pushed me aside, and fled down the alleyway with surprising speed for someone who had just been stabbed. Iain reached for his pistol. *Boom* it went again, but Edith was running with increased haste, and Iain missed once more. I watched as Edith slipped out of the alleyway and into the street beyond.

Quickly recovering from my shock, I ran after her. I intended to catch her if it was the last thing I did. I sprinted down the alley. But alas, when I reached the corner of Bill Street I could see no trace of her. I looked on the ground for a trail of blood, but there was none. I recalled Edith's heavy coat. Perhaps the fabric had shielded her from being too grievously wounded.

"She'll be long gone by now, Samira," a voice behind me said. I turned back to the alleyway to see Iain approaching me.

"She murdered Mary Ann!" I said, in tears. "She killed all those poor women. We have searched for this mysterious Ripper for nearly a year, and by God's grace we have found her. If we do not apprehend her now, she will surely kill again."

"We *will* apprehend her, Samira," said Iain, trying his best to comfort me by patting me in an awkward manner on my shoulder. "We will look for her together, you and I, until we bring her to justice. You must give your testimony to Commissioner Warren, and–"

"You know I cannot do this," I said, disappointed. "The Wentworths will be utterly mortified if I'm involved in any sort of investigation."

"Samira," said Iain, his blue eyes looking at me in exasperation. "Without your testimony, the police will never believe the butcher's wife is the notorious killer they've been searching for. They will continue to look for a man."

"They will not believe me," I said. "In fact, they will arrest me for stabbing her. Why don't you tell them what you saw?" I asked. "Perhaps you can say you witnessed an unidentified woman in a scuffle with the Butcher's wife."

"I will do so," said Iain. "But as you well know, Commissioner Warren is prejudiced against Scotsmen like myself. He does not trust me, and will not accept my testimony unless I bring in a witness from the scene."

And sure enough, though I hated to admit it, Iain was right once again. Not only did Commissioner Warren not believe him, the police went to the Butcher shop the next day and arrested Jacob the Butcher instead. The wounds on all the corpses had already made them suspect a butcher's expertise, but then they learned Jacob's wife was missing, and this gave them cause to question Jacob and deduce that he had solicited the services of all the dead prostitutes. They instantly concluded that Jacob was not only the Ripper, but that he'd probably killed his wife too. They simply could not fathom a world where God fearing, wide-eyed, docile, and now missing Edith, was the infamous Ripper they'd been after all along.

For a while, Jacob the Butcher became the perfect scapegoat for the crime. But since the murder weapon was never found, the police lacked the evidence to convict, and eventually they had to let Jacob go and resume their search for the real Ripper. Iain and I continued to search for the woman we knew to be the correct culprit, but she never resurfaced.

It has been six months now. The killing of prostitutes has stopped, or rather, the few that have been found dead haven't been cut up in a way that suggests Edith is behind their murders. Little Johnny the urchin has fewer tips for me than he once used to, for the ladies of the night have moved on from Whitechapel to other London neighborhoods.

Iain and I have concluded that Edith is either dead, or that she has stopped killing because she knows her identity has been compromised. As for the police, they continue to look for the "man" that has evaded their capture for over a year. The Wentworths say that Jack the Ripper will go down in history as one of London's most notorious killers, but nobody except Iain and I know the Ripper's true identity, and that it is not a man who took the lives of nearly a dozen prostitutes, but a quiet, unhinged woman named Edith, who, if she is still alive, could very well kill again.

The possibility of her return is the reason I continue to walk these streets at night, still apprehending the occasional thief or mugger along the way. Every night I think of the women who lost their lives to Jack the Ripper, whose manufactured name will be remembered for all time, while their names, the names of *her* victims, will rarely be uttered. I will never forget these women. If Edith ever dares to come back, I will find and confront her, and this time, I will best her. Mary Ann and her comrades will be avenged.

This is my promise.

Meet Minoti Vaishnav

Minoti Vaishnav is a short fiction author who has had five short stories published in print anthologies this year alone. She is also a television writer most recently staffed on The Equalizer on CBS, a former pop star with three albums under her belt, and a documentary television producer who has created shows for Netflix, NatGeo, Travel Channel, and Discovery Channel among other networks. Minoti also has a Masters degree in Creative Writing from Oxford University and is an alumna of the ViacomCBS Writers Mentoring Program.

Woza Moya
By Christopher Edwards

In 1879 Louis Bonaparte, son of the deposed Napoleon III of France and great-nephew of the first Napoleon Bonaparte, was an ambitious 23-year-old. He had lived in exile in England since before his 15th birthday. He studied artillery with the British Army and made himself conversant with law and economics. He was in fact an emperor-in-waiting.

Although his supporters in France urged him to return, he was very aware that he was a young man who had done nothing of note.

Then an opportunity arose...

"Human history of the last five thousand years was written on the plains of East Africa half a million years ago."

We had found early on in our travels Alan was in the habit of making statements like this. It was, this time, accompanied by a gesture with a liver-spotted hand at the African landscape passing by the windows of the minibus. What he wanted was someone to ask for an explanation so that he could talk, for half an hour or more, on the subject.

I was enjoying our tour of the battlefields of South Africa too much to endure one of his long lectures. Alan's wife, Sandra, was wisely keeping silent; she usually did. Moses, our Zulu guide and translator, flashed a brief smile of white teeth in his ebony face but likewise said nothing. Mswazi, the driver, didn't speak much English. And I wasn't going to play Alan's game this time.

exchanged words; neither of them looked happy.

There was a conversation between Moses and the old woman that seemed to attract the attention of all the Zulu, even the children and especially the handicraft seller. All the villagers turned to regard us expectantly.

He turned to us. "It is possible for you to see something Europeans don't often see. The old woman there is a..." For once Moses' fluent English failed. He tried a Zulu word "*sangoma*" and saw our uncomprehending looks. He took a moment. "I think you would say a 'witch doctor'," he finished uncertainly.

The four of us looked at the woman. If we were expecting a necklace of skulls we were disappointed. She looked the same as virtually all the other women wrapped in their standard red blankets.

Moses continued. "She, and men and women like her, are part healers and part priests. She was asked to come to this village because that young woman, is worried about her husband. The healer is asking for too much money to call the spirits and won't lower her price.

"Would you pay? I do not think she will ask so much."

Alan, Sandy, Susan and I put our heads together. Alan, probably still sulking from earlier, was against the idea. I thought I would quite like to see a real Zulu summoning of spirits. Susan agreed but it was the usually taciturn Sandy who was the most enthusiastic. She began to rummage in her purse.

"Wait on," I said. "Let's find out how much it is first."

Moses was asked to negotiate with the witch doctor-ess. The discussion seemed to take a long time but I did notice that all the Zulu seemed to relax as soon as the bartering began. It was as if it was all decided but the formalities had to be observed. At last, the old woman gave a sort of nod of agreement. I'd noticed the older Zulu tend to lift their head up and down rather than the European nod of down and up.

Moses came up with a price. It wasn't that much for us but probably expensive for the locals. Moses said that we four could all ask one question of the spirits. Sandy seemed delighted. Alan just snorted but didn't prevent his wife handing over their share of the money. The villagers and ourselves walked back to the monument to take advantage of the shade afforded by the trees. The villagers sat on the ground while we elderly tourists sat gingerly on the dry stone wall.

"This is all nonsense!" complained Alan in an aside to me.

It possibly was to a European but Zulu belief was that even a single Zulu wasn't alone; the spirits of their ancestors always went with them. The Zulu greeting of "*Sawubona*" translated as "We see you"; the accompanying spirits were included in the "hello".

"Maybe," I told Alan, "But the old Zulu witch doctors knew a few things. They were quite skilled healers, at least of battle wounds, and the warriors that they 'doctored' for war often talked of a 'red mist' before their eyes as they closed for battle. Whatever concoction they were given made them more aggressive and fearless."

The spirit summoner sat opposite the villagers, the woman with the missing husband sitting closest to her. I got the impression there was a well-understood formula being followed by all the Zulus here. The woman with the question spoke at some length with lots of gestures. The villagers began murmuring. I assumed at first they were confirming what was being said but the murmuring continued throughout the proceedings; sometimes louder and sometimes quieter but it never disappeared completely. Occasionally, I thought I could make out words but I had no idea what they were saying.

Moses had taken up station behind us. He spoke softly and since I was furthest from him I didn't hear everything he said. The young woman's husband had gone to work in one of the South African cities and he had not returned when he had said he would and was now long overdue.

The old medicine woman stared at the ground until the murmur had almost began to falter. Then she opened a pouch that had been suspended around her neck with a strip of leather. She took a pinch of powder between her thumb and forefinger and threw it in the air, letting it fall back to the ground.

She said loudly "Woza Moya! Woza Moya!"

"Come spirits! Come spirits!" Moses translated.

This was repeated two or three times. Then she stared around as if watching the spirits assemble. The old lady knew how to put on a show.

She spoke to the air in front of her. Moses explained she was telling the assembled spirits what the problem was. She spoke in short phrases which Moses duly translated. I noticed the background murmur was louder or quieter depending on what she had stated to the spirits.

"This woman's husband went away to work." (Murmur.)

"He needed money for his family." (Murmur.)

"He said he would be back before winter." (Loud murmur.)

This part went on for some time as the old lady recounted all the characteristics of the missing husband. I guessed that the volume of the murmur related directly to how accurate it was. A couple of them were interesting.

"He doesn't get drunk too often." (A slight drop in the volume for this one I fancied.)

"He doesn't beat his wife unnecessarily." (Quite a loud murmur for this one but it was accompanied by an outraged "Unnecessarily!?" from both Susan and Sandra. Moses pleaded with them to keep quiet.)

"He hasn't phoned." This must have surprised Alan as he echoed the last word, "Phoned?"

I don't know why this was surprising; the whole world is connected now. No wonder the wife had gone old school with the healer woman. She hadn't been able to contact her husband and had no way to get in touch with him. Once he had gone over his expected return, she must have been frantic.

By the end I'm sure the healer had a good idea of what the village thought of the missing husband; that is, he was a poor man who had accepted separation from his family to earn some money for them.

The villager's murmur stopped. It was time for the "Spirits" to reveal what they knew. The old woman's voice changed. From its shaky warble, it became strong and measured. *She really is a showman or rather show woman.*

"The husband is on his way home. The journey is long and difficult. Phones do not work everywhere. He expects to be with you before you next harvest the corn."

The wife gave a cry of joy and the village gathered around her sharing her joy.

I don't know if the husband ever did arrive. If he did, the witch doctor's prediction would enhance her reputation. If he didn't, well, something must have happened to him after the reading.

The wife of the missing man came to us and pressed bead necklaces into the hands of Sandy and Susan and refused to take any payment. She was obviously grateful. She and the rest of the villagers moved off.

The old spirit summoner looked at Moses expectantly. He in turn asked us what we would like to ask her.

I wondered how she would perform without the background murmur. Even if we had wanted to aid her, each couple had only met for the first time just over a week ago. Sandy didn't talk much about anything. We and the rest of the tour had quickly learned Alan only wanted to talk about what interested Alan.

I think Sandy was going to ask something but Alan suddenly blurted out, "Ask her how the world would have been different if the Prince Imperial had lived."

The normally silent Sandy gave a cry of exasperation. "Alan!"

He was unrepentant. "I'm serious. It's what I want to know. Did history carry on unchanged or did one person change it?"

Moses was reluctant to translate the question but Alan now had the proverbial bit between his teeth.

I don't know how Moses phrased the question but the old woman listened dispassionately. She said something in Zulu with a glance at Alan.

I think Moses was regretting the whole business. He seemed uncomfortable but said that the old woman would ask the spirits. "She has a warning. The spirit of the foreign lord was released in this place. His spirit will be strong here." *I suppose foreign lord meant the Prince imperial.*

"I don't care about a gypsy's warning," said Alan. "Ask away."

We were all still sat on the wall. The old witch doctor sat down in front of us and repeated her call to the spirits. She threw more dust into the air again. Maybe it was a mark of how difficult a question it was but there was a lot more dust and she threw it with some force. Some of the dust landed on Alan and me. I imagined that if any of the cloud of dust landed on Sue and Sandy they weren't going to be pleased.

"Woza Moya. Woza Moya!"

The old woman began speaking to the empty air in front of her. Moses didn't translate word for word. "She's asking the spirits now."

• • •

I was thinking of my medication, trying to decide if I could eke out the pills by splitting them in half or if it would be better to take them less frequently; every other day instead of daily. Maybe I could still find a pharmacy somewhere, although we had been told rioters and looters had targeted such places.

Alan started talking. "They say the human race started here in East Africa."

protestant princess marrying the very devout catholic Louis but neither did they want to be seen to be capitulating to German demands.

"An international conference was called. It was decided that Louis would not marry Princess Beatrice and France would not form an alliance against Germany. The Kaiser agreed to return the provinces to France that had been annexed after the Franco-Prussian War. Most of Europe thought the new emperor had done well out of the treaty. The return of Alsace-Lorraine went down well with even the Republicans in France.

"European borders have remained, more or less, unchanged since then."

"I wonder which one it was." pondered Alan. "Do you think it was the Tzar or the Kaiser?"

I realised he was talking of more recent history. "Does it matter which one attacked first?' I answered bitterly. "Anyway, it could just have easily been one of the half dozen emperors, caliphs or shahs. They all had nuclear weapons. Everyone scrambled to develop them after the Japan America war. It could have been that upstart American emperor. He seems crazy enough to do anything."

Alan shook his head. "I thought no one was going to use nuclear weapons; it guaranteed... What did they call it? Mutually assured destruction?" I thought he was going to cry. I felt like bursting into tears myself.

I nodded towards the memorial. The French tricolour emblazoned with the golden letter 'N' was hanging from the flagstaff before it. "We could have done with Napoleon the Peacemaker again, couldn't we? Susan says he prevented the fall of Christendom in 1914."

"Christendom?" queried Alan.

"A bit of an old-fashioned word, nowadays," I explained. "I guess it means Europe in this case. All of the crowned heads of Europe claim to be anointed by God, or at least the local priesthood."

Susan had come up beside me. "I was just telling Alan about how we avoided war thanks to this guy," I told her pointing at the memorial.

"Perhaps it's a pity he succeeded. A war fought with rifles and artillery would at least have left survivors," she said. "He wanted to build a France to overtake the economic success of Britain and Germany. A war would have interfered with his plans. It's why he was so cautious when he made treaties with other powers. His reform and build-up of the

French army was done gradually, so as not to alarm the Kaiser."

"In any case France was the model the rest of the world wanted to emulate for most of the 20th century," I said.

"Yes," said Sue. "The royal houses found that economic prosperity was the way to keep their people from revolution. As Louis said, 'A war will unite a nation but only so long as it is winning'."

Alan snorted. "It's human nature to want war. Everyone knew that, sooner or later, some nuclear power was going to attack another." Alan had espoused this before. It was if he was able to take comfort from being proved right. He added angrily, "You know, he didn't make peace, he just postponed war."

It was a measure of how distracted we all were that Sue didn't argue with him.

A red-eyed Sandy joined us too. "How long do we have?"

Alan deliberately misunderstood. "We can go back to the hotel when you like."

"No Alan, how long before the nuclear winter affects South Africa?"

Alan embraced Sandy. "It already is," he said gently. "You can't see the sun and won't be able to for months, maybe years."

I put my arm around Susan. I didn't say anything. I didn't know what to say.

I heard the old woman speaking in Zulu.

Someone said, "She says that you have your answer."

It was Moses.

• • •

My mind must have wandered. I was sitting on the wall surrounding the memorial watching the old Zulu healer walking away. I looked around. The four of us looked a bit shell-shocked. I looked back at the memorial. I had an odd memory of a large marble construction dominating the landscape but there was only the modest Victorian tribute to a dead young man.

I looked back at my fellow tourists. Sue and Sandy seemed perplexed by their surroundings. Alan was slowly shaking his head.

Moses asked. "Are you ready to go back to the bus?" There was concern in his voice.

Nobody answered but we all stood up and started moving towards the

SECOND CHANCES BY AARON EMMEL

Second Chances
By Aaron Emmel

Neven closed his hand around the programmable microchip in his pocket and tried to lose himself in the line of departing shoppers. The Protectors were coming closer, but they didn't seem to be watching him in particular. If they found the chip, the size of his thumbnail and sheathed in plastic, they'd send him to the worklands.

"Too bad we can't get in the express queue, huh?" the woman in front of Neven said. Neven nodded in the affirmative. He didn't want to say anything that might draw the Protectors' attention.

The woman didn't get the hint. "You work in Mohom?" She was his age, mid-twentyish, with dark hair and a confident smile. On any other day, he would have been happy to talk to her.

"Yeah."

"I'm just visiting. Must be a good job. Yeah?"

Neven nodded again. Even if he escaped the Protectors, if Kathu caught him with the chip his job would be over. On the other hand, getting fired would be the least of his worries.

The pair of Protectors glanced his way. Did they notice how quickly he turned his head? They moved purposefully in his direction.

Up until a few weeks ago — when he had helped Kathu demonstrate that his impossible machine worked, and he'd started to think about what that actually meant — he would have been the last person to risk getting caught with restricted tech. He would have focused on how much he had to lose.

He would have looked back at the free section of the market behind him, where stalls sagged beneath the weight of produce from across Fihoma that was available to anyone who needed it, one basket per household. He might have glanced at the main market behind it, arranged in a great arc, where he had met his contact and traded for the chip. His eyes would have skipped quickly over the walled section where he wasn't allowed.

He would have been grateful for the rail service that could connect him to anywhere in Fihoma, no trade or payment necessary, as long as there was space. He would have pushed away any resentment about the express queue, the one just beside the line he stood in, that he couldn't join. He wouldn't have complained about the shuttles that he couldn't board, the ones that leapt the great waters in a matter of hours. And most of all, he would have been grateful for Kathu and his job, as he'd been grateful ever since Kathu hired him, instead of planning to betray him with what he carried in his pocket.

But now, those things — the walled market, the shuttles, the express queue — they were all he could see, and he tried not to stare, tried not to let his hand slip protectively back into his pocket as the Protectors closed in.

"It looks like they're coming this way," the woman whispered. "Just be cool. They'll walk right past us."

The Protectors stopped in front of Neven. A male and a female. "Are you a resident?" the female asked.

"Yes, Gowan." For the first time, the title of respect galled him. It was an honorific that would never be used for him.

"What is your name, resident?"

"Neven the Swift of Ilhom, Gowan."

"Neven the Swift, please show me what is in your pockets."

They had seen him. No matter how careful he had been, they had seen him. He pressed his hands against his sides. "There's nothing there, Gowan."

"Raise your arms."

Neven raised his arms, and everyone could see that his hands were trembling. The male Protector, who had not yet spoken, tapped Neven's body and clothing, from his ankles to his shoulders. Then he reached into Neven's pocket, first left and then right. His hand emerged with the microchip between his thumb and forefinger.

There were gasps. Everyone around them backed away.

"I don't know him, Gowans, I swear," the woman with the dark hair said.

The male Protector inserted the chip into a bag and sealed it. "Your contact had a change of heart," his companion said. "He came to us and confessed to trading a microchip to a Sapiens. He will be sent to the worklands for a rotation. But you, you will be there for the rest of your life. Come with us."

For an instant, he thought of running. But there were gates around the market. There was nowhere to go. And his ingrained fear, his life-long training in submission, stopped him from bolting. He followed the Protectors across the flagstone tiles, beneath the shade of mighty maple trees, away from the line.

The female Protector stopped and lifted a rope-bind. "Hold out your hands, Neven the Swift."

The swiftness Neven had been known for wasn't physical speed. "I work for Kathu the Inventor."

The Protectors looked at each other. "Kathu Gowan the Inventor is much respected," the female said. "That is a great honor, for a Sapiens no less. That makes it even more disappointing that we are forced to detain you and send you to the worklands."

Neven said the first lie that came to his mind, one that might save him now but would certainly make things worse down the line. "The chip isn't for me. It's for Kathu."

"Use his full name or call him Gowan, Sapiens," the male said, the first time he had spoken. His voice was low and deep.

"Kathu the Inventor is busy. He's finalizing a new type of machine for the Parliament of Sciences. You must have read about it in the gazettes. That's why he sent me."

The two Protectors looked at each other. "If this is true, if he instructed a Sapiens to carry this on his behalf, he will be fined," the female said.

Neven didn't answer. The only way to save himself was to implicate his boss.

"I'll check to see if he corroborates this Sapiens' story," the female told her partner. She stepped away and took out her comms disc.

"He must have a lot of trust in you to send you to get controlled technology on his behalf," the male Protector said to Neven. "But if he's as smart as his reputation, he'll disavow you now to keep himself out of trouble."

Neven swallowed and watched the other Protector. She returned the disc to her pocket and walked back. She looked surprised. "He confirmed it. We'll take you to him."

They got into an autocarriage outside the market gates, Neven in the caged seat in the back, and sped off toward Mohom.

Mohom was the largest city of eastern Nehomi, a communitarian village scaled to spectacular heights. Graceful skybuildings towered above crowded parks, gardens interspersed between their occupied levels and on their roofs, their paneled facades soaking in the energy from sunlight, pools of water filled with tilapia and supporting broad-leafed vegetables bordering the broad avenues between them. Their residents walked and biked and hopped on and off the ubiquitous rails in the skybuildings' shadows.

Kathu's building was one of the oldest and tallest structures in the city. His condominium was on the second highest floor, just below the penthouse level.

Kathu met them at his door. He was burly even for a Neanderthal, looking more like a korant player than a chronophysicist. His nostrils flared when he saw Neven standing between the Protectors.

The Protectors first handed him the microchip in its plastic sleeve and then a ticket. "This is a fine for four thousand krinth, Kathu Gowan. It must be paid within two moondarks or you will be sent to the worklands for a full rotation. Do you understand?"

"I understand," Kathu rumbled.

Once they were inside and the Protectors were gone, Kathu turned to Neven. He still held the microchip and the ticket in one meaty hand. "If I'd been betrayed by someone who didn't know the project so well, they would have just fried the motherboard or corrupted the RAM sticks. But you wanted me to waste time figuring out what was wrong. This is a reconfigured field-programmable gate array you were planning to swap in?"

"I'm sorry, Gowan." Neven said it automatically. He was telling the truth. Kathu had taken him in, given him a job, placed his faith in him. Granted him access to tools that few Sapiens, even few Neanderthals, would ever have the opportunity to use. But it wasn't the whole truth.

It couldn't overcome the inner voice that was already trying to figure out how to do it again.

"You know better than anyone that it's too late." Kathu closed his fist and split the plastic, bent and snapped the chip with an audible pop. The paperfiber ticket crumpled in his hand. He dropped both onto the foyer table. "If you break the machine, we'll build it again."

They stared at each other. Neven tensed, waiting for Kathu to fire him. For a moment, watching Kathu's hands bunch into fists again, he thought the scientist might strike him. Neven resisted the urge to raise his own hands or step back. "The machine shouldn't exist."

"Maybe. But it does, and now it always will. We know, now, how to make a device that can peer into the past and change that past by looking. Knowledge can't be rolled back."

"It's wrong. Using it to wipe out Sapiens is wrong."

Before today, Kathu would have argued that this was a misunderstanding: *We're not trying to erase Sapiens. We just need to shift the balance a bit.* This time, though, he shook his head. "I understand why this is hard for you, Neven. That is why I'm trying to be patient with you. It's why I didn't let the Protectors take you away."

"Hard for me? When you use the machine, I'll no longer exist."

"We don't know that. There will still be Sapiens. Just fewer." On the foyer table was a model of the solar system, miniature planets affixed to arms of brass. He pushed the tiny Earth and it circled the yellow-painted sun. "Far fewer? Yes. Easier to manage. We won't need all the controls we have now that chafe Sapiens and Neanderthal alike. We won't need separate queues, separate facilities. Once almost everyone is a Neanderthal, we can truly open up our society, share as much as we would, make it as equitable as it should be."

"You'd risk destroying me to get there. And all the other Sapiens on the planet."

Kathu let go of the model and returned his attention to Neven. He sighed and lowered his voice. "You know I don't want you to disappear. I hope you won't. I would protect you, individually, if I could."

"It's not just me. You might be erasing your own existence."

"That's the risk. But this isn't about us. It's about our society."

Neven couldn't prevent his voice from getting louder. "What about Sapiens ingenuity? All the Sapiens engineers and tinkerers who helped lead to chronotechnology in the first place?"

"Yes, of course, we have benefited from Sapiens ingenuity, and even Sapiens rebelliousness. It forces us to try new things that maybe we would not on our own. I readily admit that—and I'm hardly the only Neanderthal to do so. But those Sapiens inventors we sometimes, rightly, celebrate, they've been able to hone and apply their creative intellect because of the stable society we provide. Were it not for us, Sapiens would have used their ingenuity to kill themselves as soon as they discovered gunpowder. Civilization requires both restraint and progress. You've survived long enough to progress because of the restraints we've provided."

"That's not true."

"You're smart enough to know it is true, even if neither of us want it to be. The balance isn't right. There have already been too many Sapiens who have done too much damage. We need to rebalance the scales. That is all."

"Kathu, you know that—"

"Call me Kathu Gowan."

Neven froze.

"I have been too familiar with you. That's how you got into trouble. I see now I wasn't being fully honest and I let you imagine we are equals. It wasn't fair to either of us."

"Kathu Gowan," Neven said slowly, "even if you use the machine, your Parliament team has already mapped hundreds of different Options. It doesn't have to be—"

"When your kind invaded our lands 70,000 years ago, we were too weak to fight them off. This invention can change that."

Neven shook his head. *Your kind?* Kathu had never used those words in front of him before. "Early Sapiens and Neanderthals lived side-by-side, in peace. They didn't have all these modern 'restraints.' We know it's possible."

Kathu stepped away from him and gazed down the hall, unable or unwilling to continue looking Neven in the eye. The living room and kitchen were to the left, bedrooms and a bathroom to the right. Directly in front of them, down the hall, was Kathu's laboratory, where the machine waited behind a closed door.

The machine had started as a prototype Kathu tinkered with to test ideas while the main design and assembly work was performed by teams of engineers and technicians at the huge Parliament of Sciences building overlooking the bay. But it was the first, and so far only, device to successfully demonstrate historical alteration.

"If what we call the Advances had happened earlier, we would have been strong enough to push the Sapiens away. We wouldn't have had to live side-by-side, in ancient Ehomi or anywhere else."

"Gowan—"

Kathu pulled out his comms disc and started stabbing in commands. "Your work here is done. Access to this condo and the building are revoked."

"You're firing me."

"You're a risk I can no longer take. You will be detained if you try to enter the premises again."

"Gowan, Kathu, I've been with you for five rotations. I practically live here."

Kathu shoved the disc back into his pocket and stared at Neven from beneath shaggy brows. "You know how much worse it could have been for you when the Protector called. Consider that your thanks. You'll get your last paycheck in the mail."

Neven took the elevator down. He was just about to exit the building when a female Neanderthal stepped up to the other side of the sliding doors. He recognized her, from the broadcasts and the gazettes, even though she would have no reason to recognize him: Santu the Wise. One of the Deciders. The Deciders weren't meant to come for another week. Kathu must have accelerated the schedule.

Neven ducked away from the doors and made a show of looking at the electronic bulletins on the wall. Out of the corner of his eye, he watched as Santu entered and took a position near a circular couch in the middle of the lobby. She wore a big, practical coat and had unadorned hair, calmly out of place in the midst of the stylish young professionals walking past her.

Soon another three Neanderthals came in off the street and joined Santu. "Santu, Fithi, Nuthi," the last one greeted the others. "Do you know what the hurry is?"

"He's afraid of sabotage," Santu replied.

"Not here," one of the other Deciders said. "We can talk upstairs."

Neven waited until the Deciders had gone up in an elevator, then hurried to the elevator bay and called the next one. When the doors opened on Kathu's floor, he held the door and remained inside until it sounded as though all four Deciders had entered Kathu's apartment. He dashed down the hall. Kathu's door would lock automatically after ten seconds. He reached the door and tried it; still open. He saw the Deciders enter the living room. The lab was in front of him, past the living room, at the end of the hall.

"Thank you for coming at short notice," Kathu said from the living room. "All of you understand what we're trying to accomplish. Some recent events have convinced me that if we're ready to take action, sooner is better than later."

"I am speaking now for the record," one of the guests said. "It has been agreed that the question before us presents too much responsibility for one person, or even one institution, to bear. We Deciders have been appointed by the Parliament to represent our constituent communities."

"I understand and acknowledge."

"To be clear," said one of the other Deciders, "it is Option 234 from the Parliament of Sciences' Survey of Historical Alternatives that you are requesting permission for."

"That is correct."

"To manipulate the ancient environment in a way that accelerates the Advances, so that they occur before the first encounters between Sapiens and Neanderthals."

"Yes. If the ancient Neanderthals have modern language by the time the Sapiens arrive, they will be clearly superior. They will not coexist with the Sapiens invaders; they will conquer them."

Neven's muscles were so tight he didn't think he would be able to move. He had no idea how he would get past the Neanderthals in the living room to break the machine. If he made a sound, they were sure to corner and capture him before he could escape.

Even now, though, a part of his mind was following the conversation about the device whose secrets he had helped Kathu puzzle out. Select the right microscopic change in the past, precisely, and it would cascade into macro effects.

"We have already heard the arguments," one of the Deciders said.

"Then you have an answer?"

"Yes. We all four approve. We are ready to proceed."

"Actually, I do have one question." It was Santu. "We already live in a world in which Neanderthals dominated. If we think the past needs to change, why not change it in the opposite direction? Why not let the Sapiens find the route to Ehomi sooner so they and the Neanderthals start on more equal footing ?"

Another one of the Deciders answered her. "We can't know what other changes that would bring. It's too dangerous."

"However good this world is, it's still built on the subjugation of Sapiens. That's the problem we should be solving. How to live cooperatively. Not taking the most controversial policy of our civilization, our treatment of the Sapiens, and amplifying it."

"Really?" Kathu's voice was impatient and annoyed. "Do you think we're what's been holding Sapiens down? Let Sapiens have their own settlements and they'd just fight themselves. If there were nothing else to fight about, they'd fight over skin tone, and if their skin was the same they'd fight over the color of their eyes."

"They fight because they want to escape. Set them free, and maybe we'll see how generous and peaceful Sapiens can be."

"We can't risk it."

"This is an interesting conversation," the Decider who had spoken first said, "but it's not relevant. We're here to represent the consensus of our constituents."

There was a pause. "I approve with the others. You can proceed," Santu said.

Neven drew in his breath. He realized he had been hoping that somehow Santu's argument would win out. There was nothing left to pin his hopes on. The only way left to stop Kathu's plan was to act now.

He forced himself to move. He left his corner in the foyer and slipped down the hall.

A surprised grunt came from the living room. He had been spotted. He lunged forward, but not quickly enough. Kathu charged out and blocked his way.

"Kathu—"

The back of Kathu's hand smashed into his face and Neven's head snapped to the side. He stumbled and crashed into the wall. The Deciders crowded into the hall around him.

"Block the door!" Kathu bellowed, waving at the Deciders as he pulled out his comms disc. "Don't let him out of the apartment!"

Neven spit blood and gripped the wall to keep from falling. Santu watched him, almost curiously, as the other Deciders scrambled to interpose themselves between Neven and the exit.

Kathu roared into the disc: "This is Kathu the Inventor. There's a Sapiens in my apartment. I need you to take him away."

Neven leaned into the wall and closed his eyes for one long moment, gathering strength. His face throbbed and a tooth shifted painfully when he probed it with his tongue, but he didn't think anything else was broken. He opened his eyes, surveying the hallway around him. He swiped at his bloody mouth with his sleeve. Then he bolted.

He wrenched open the door to the lab, slammed it shut behind him, and locked it. He stood there for a moment, breathing heavily, wiping away the blood that kept flowing, staring at the machine, a stack of hardware-stuffed boxes on a rack in front of a cylinder coiled in a nest of wires and chilled from hoses connected to tanks of liquid nitrogen. Behind that cylinder and its layers of quantum processors was the heart of the device, a larger cylinder filled with lasers, sensors and vacuum chambers, connected by satellite to similar cylinders situated across the planet. Clipped to the rack in front of it all was a lake-blue screen, waiting for input.

Kathu rattled the handle and pounded on the door behind him. "Don't go near the machine! If you touch it, you'll wish you'd been sent to the worklands!"

Neven took a step toward the screen. Other Options had been mapped. Not just the one that Santu had mentioned, that would put Sapiens and Neanderthals on level ground. There were versions of history that gave Sapiens the advantage, instead of their masters.

The rattling stopped. Kathu had gone to get something to open the door. Neven touched the screen, and a command prompt sprang to life.

He could make a new world. For himself, for his parents, for the Sapiens woman he had met in the queue at the market. For all the Sapiens who had been born to servitude through all the ages leading to now.

But Sapiens didn't need to rule for that world to exist. They just needed a fighting chance. Both peoples could coexist.

He typed out his command. He never got to input it. The door flew open, footsteps pounded behind him, and a hand grabbed his collar and yanked him back just before his finger was about to make its final contact with the screen. He stared at the command that he would never be able to enter as he was dragged out of the room and marched out into the hall.

It was Kathu who led him. The Deciders crowded around him. A pair of Protectors waited in the hallway, different ones this time. They bound his hands.

"I treated you well, and you betrayed my hospitality." Kathu's breath was heavy and loud. "You'll never set foot in Mohom again."

"Come with us," one of the Protectors said.

"Are you taking me to the worklands?"

"It's like the worklands, but it's a place no one leaves."

Kathu shouted at him as the Protectors pulled him away. "I didn't want to change the timeline. I'm doing it for my people. But you've confirmed it was the right decision. I'm going to cut off the Sapiens' chances with a clean conscience."

Neven craned his neck to catch one last glimpse of his former boss. Kathu stood in front of the apartment doorway, three Deciders on either side of him.

Three. Santu wasn't there. She was still in the apartment.

What was she doing?

Where else could she be? In his mind he pictured her, standing where he had just been, in front of the machine. She was staring at the command he had typed. Perhaps her finger hovered over the screen, as she decided whether to bring a new world into being.

Meet Aaron Emmel

Aaron Emmel is the author of more than fifty published short stories, as well as the Midnight Legion gamebook trilogy, an historical fiction graphic novel and dozens of articles and essays. He grew up in the mountains of New Mexico and graduated from high school in Central America, before cofounding and selling a record label and an online music store. Aaron lives with his wife and two children in Maryland. His story "The Sword of Bone" appeared in the Inklings Press anthology Tales of Magic & Destiny. Find him online at www.aaronemmel.com.

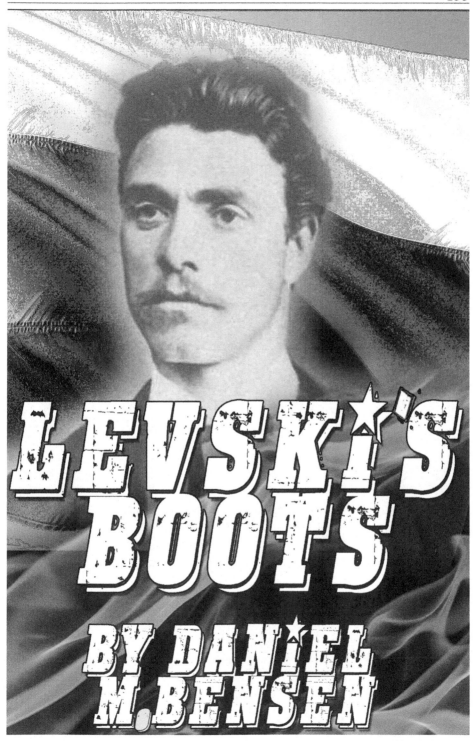

LEVSKI'S BOOTS

BY DANIEL M. BENSEN

Levski's Boots
By Daniel M. Bensen

"Ako Levski beshe s botushi..."
If Levski had boots...

- Bulgarian saying

27 December, 1872 (Old Style)
Kakrina Village, Sanjak of Tarnovo, Danube Vilayet, Ottoman Empire

Levski's boots hit the ground and he kept running.

Away from the inn, through a neighbor's garden, over that wall into a vineyard. Manure flew away from his soles as he churned forward, arms out, warding off vines.

Shouts behind him. The sounds of breaking tomato stakes. Gunshots. Two voices cursed in Turkish. There had been three gendarmes in the raid. The last would be going for his horse.

The road.

Hoofbeats.

Levski sprinted. The nearly full moon cast shadows like trapdoors over ground that might be slick ice, sharp rocks, or potholes of any size. There was no time to imagine what would happen if he stepped on any of them. There. The last house in the village.

Another crack of gunshot. Levski could do nothing but run.

He crossed a field, hit the edge, splashed into an irrigation canal. Icy water clamped around his ankles and another bullet cracked off a tree-trunk. A blackberry bramble tried to claw out his eyes. *Still better than a noose.*

"Ha." He breathed. A chance!

Face buried in his elbow, Levski turned and leaped straight into that bramble. Thorny whips raked over his scalp, but even so the plant was more merciful than the Sultan's justice. Still hung with last summer's leaves, the long purple and brown canes closed around him.

Levski breathed.

Cold air slid like a knife in and out of his ribs. His teeth chattered, his legs burned. His left ear hurt like the very devil.

Levski brought a hand up to the side of his head and found it hot and sticky with blood. There was blood, in fact, all down his face and chest. A bullet must have grazed him, and he hadn't even noticed.

A deep shudder ran through him.

Too close. This was too close!

His hands shook as he patted his sash. He had dropped his dagger, or else he'd never managed to grab it as he'd fled the inn. By some miracle, though, he had his boots. His pistols, both of them. And the *papers*! Thank God the membership rolls were safe.

Vasil Ivanov Kunchev, called *Levski* "the lion" by Bulgarian separatists in three countries, had borne the revolutionary standard in battle, organized dozens of secret committees, and generally humiliated the Ottoman authorities for a decade. He was a *haiduk*, a bandit, and if they caught him this time, they'd hang him.

The scratches stung on Levski's scalp. His head felt as if he'd pressed it into live coals. Blood trickled off his chin. And out there in the moonlight, boots sank almost silently into the stubbly earth.

There, just beyond the curtain of thorns, was the gendarme. He had dismounted, leaving his horse in the middle of the field. His face silhouetted itself against the silvery sky as he looked up and down the brush-choked canal. Hunt the fugitive, or go back? Help with the other two prisoners? Let Levski run north, where all the villages were Turkish, and let him either get captured or freeze to death?

Levski's hands no longer trembled. Even numb with the cold, they knew how to pull free and load the pistols. He would need a disguise. Best not to damage the man's uniform.

Stones and old leaves ground under the balls of his feet.

The gendarme turned back toward his horse and Levski rose behind him.

3 June, 1876
Brăila, Brăila County, Romania, Ottoman Empire (vassal)

The guard released Levski's arm as if flicking an old newspaper into the gutter.

"*Tsk*," he said, and that was all. The prison gate rattled shut, and Levski was free again.

He had not been executed by the Turks. He had escaped, crossed the Danube, returned victorious to his fellow *haidutsi* bandits. Levski even discovered a talent for finances that had pumped resources into the revolutionary cells scattered across his homeland. He organized lines of communication, laid plans. Over four patient years, Levski welded together a mighty engine of war, filled its tank, stoked its boiler, and called forth its flame.

And the Romanians had arrested him.

They had thought they were doing Levski a favor. Romania was still technically a vassal of the Ottoman Empire. If the Sultan forced the issue, they would have to extradite the infamous Bandit-Lion of Bulgaria. Instead, the Romanians had kept Levski safe and relatively comfortable while his revolution messily self-destructed.

It was June, and beautiful. Warm and breezy, with heavy-scented blossoms on the lime trees and young storks gawking on every chimney. The sun smiled down on chestnut trees like boiling green clouds. Somewhere nearby, a cow lowed. The April Uprising was over, and all of Levski's friends were dead.

Levski put his hands on his knees and bent over, fighting the wave of dizziness. He would not be sick. He would not weep.

He rose up, and went back to Bulgaria alone.

19 December 1877
Tashkessen Village, Sanjak of Sofia, Danube Vilayet, Ottoman Empire

It was the night after the first day of battle, and bitterly cold.

Shakir Pasha was long gone, and the detachment he'd left behind was now completely encircled by the Russian army. As with the rest of this war, the question wasn't whether the Turks would withdraw, but how much damage they would do along the way.

Hateful little pins of ice gusted against Levski's face. Heavy clouds veiled the moon, and all the lights in the village had been put out. This meant Levski only had to *smell* the blood and gunpowder. Only hear the occasional moan, mutter, or crack of bullet. The rest he imagined.

The waste. The *pleasure* in waste. Today, we reduced one hundred men, their families, and their homes to sticky gravel. Tomorrow, God willing, we'll do better: one hundred and fifty.

Levski rubbed his hands down the crusty cotton of his looted Ottoman uniform. He'd waded through blood, mud, and filth for the past 15 years, but now it was up to his neck.

The Russo-Turkish war had started with the Herzegovinians. At first, Levski had envied them. *Their* uprising had not misfired and fizzled, it had spread! As little as ten months ago, Levski had been coordinating with *haidutsi* revolutionaries in Bulgaria, Serbia, Greece, and Romania.

He still winced at that memory. "A big enough flock of ravens can scare off the jackal," he'd told them.

Instead, their squabble had attracted a bear.

The Russian army had swept down the Caucuses and the Balkans in two enormous pincers. The flimsy revolutionary network that Levski had so painfully re-knotted had been either swept away or eaten up by this thundering, bellowing war. Levski himself had been reduced to a "volunteer translator." A flea on the back of the Tsar's beast.

The only choice left to him was where and when to bite.

Levski got down on his belly and crawled through the midnight battlefield. Freezing sludge infiltrated the hole in the front of his jacket.

"Help," he croaked in Turkish. "Help me, in God's name!"

The answering voice managed to whisper and bark at the same time. "Shut up! Keep your voice down. Who is that?"

Levski put out his right hand, but kept his left pressed over his stomach. "Help me, brother, please."

The barking whisperer crouch-ran to Levski and grabbed him around the wrist. Levski allowed himself to be hauled up and pulled toward the safety of a broken garden wall.

Levski didn't give the guard time to ask again who he was. "Mehmed?" he said, "is that you, my brother?"

The guard shook his head, the movement more heard than seen in the pitch blackness. "Who's Mehmed? I'm Abdulmejid. Who are you?"

"Abdulmejid, my friend! But don't you know me?"

Levski gave the name and regiment of the man whose uniform this had been, and Abdulmejid seemed to believe him. "Oh, uh, right. Are you injured?"

"Yes, sir!" said Levski. "Grievously!"

"Well, if you've got arms and legs, there's nothing the medics will do for you."

"I've been shot, sir. Gutshot."

Abdulmejid leaned forward, squinting at Levski's left hand and the bloody hole in the jacket around it. In this light, he wouldn't be able to see much. Just smell.

The guard backed away, choking, "God's mercy and peace be on you!"

"Thank you, sir. Is there anywhere I could have something hot to drink?"

"Why bother? It'll just pour out of you again. God, that smell! I would kill for a cigar. Damn this war."

"Please, sir. I have information."

Abdulmejid shook himself out of his muttering trance. "What? Idiot! Why didn't you say sooner? You came from the southeast? What's..." He stood straighter, staring into the freezing blackness over Levski's shoulder. Remembering home? His voice when he spoke again was small. "...what's...going on out there, soldier?"

"Russians." Levski kept the relish out of his voice. "They're dug in, sir. On the high ground on both sides of the road. And they have the road too. Cannon emplacements stand ready to start the bombardment as soon as there's light."

Abdulmejid cursed. "That puts them in range of the munitions stores! We'll have to move them...again." His voice sagged with hopeless exhaustion. "Don't...just don't tell anyone, alright? Don't want to cause...a panic."

It was too dark for Levski's expression to be visible, but still the bandit did not grin. "Please, sir, is there anywhere I can have something hot to drink? I feel so cold."

take both of us hostage. You can't march us through all of Baker's soldiers. Your only choices are to kill us and escape, or else join us."

Levski did not let a muscle twitch. "Join you?"

"Yes! Don't you see what's happening here?" The man leaned over the table, as if crouching to leap. "You're just trading one yoke for another. The Russians have all the vices of the Turks and none of their virtues. Shall the Bulgarians share the fate of the Poles? The Circassians?"

Circassian mercenaries employed by the Sultan had murdered hundreds of Bulgarian women and children last year. Levski spat on the floor at mention of their name.

"Bad move, Burnaby," said Baker Pasha.

"Listen," said the seated man – Burnaby. "If the Tsar is allowed to capture Constantinople, that will only be the beginning of a territorial expansion that will put all of Africa and the Near East in danger of falling into Russian hands! Europe will not allow this, and the war that follows will crack the continent in two."

"You should surrender," advised Levski.

But Burnaby wasn't listening. He was caught up in his own argument, eyes alight with speculation. "An arrangement could be made. As with Egypt, for example. We have similar plans already for Khiva, the Catholic territories, and the Caucasus. Imagine: the Knyazdom of Bulgaria, under British protectorship!" Burnaby nodded to himself. "I swear to you I will make every effort to sway my government in your people's favor, but there's nothing I can do while you're pointing that gun at me."

Shouts from beyond the windows. Baker Pasha seemed to hear them, but Burnaby was staring at Levski. The man's need to be understood was almost painful. No, not understood. Justified. Burnaby could not bear to learn he was on the wrong side of history.

"*Will* you join us?" he asked. "It takes bravery to see the future and march towards it."

"This is not bravery, what you're doing," Levski told Burnaby. "It's cowardice. You don't know what will happen if Russia wins this war, and that uncertainty terrifies you. You know what the Turks are doing to us, yet you support them because you prefer..." what was the English expression? "...*the devil you know.*"

Burnaby shook his head, eyes wide, teeth clenched.

Levski sighed. Botev might have been able to make the right arguments, but Botev had been shot last spring.

The British spy looked away from Levski. He let out a long breath and shook his head. "Shoot me or let me go or take me prisoner, it won't matter. Nothing of importance will be decided in this room."

Levski wagged his head in agreement. "I know that. All I want is to stop you from burning this village."

At the window, Baker Pasha twitched. "Wait a moment. This is all a game. You've been stalling us."

"Well, yes," said Levski. "Haven't you been trying to stall me as well?"

Baker scowled and Burnaby laughed. "I've got to give you credit, sir. Yes, any second Baker's men will rush up those stairs and kill you. But you still have a chance -"

"They won't," said Levski. The shouts from outside had mostly died away. "Because I told them the same thing I told you: you are surrounded. They listened."

Baker swore fluently in Turkish and made a dash for the stairs. Levski let him. He kept his eyes and his gun pointed at the spy. "Come with me, Mr. Burnaby."

26 June, 1879
Tarnovo, Tarnovo okrug, Principality of Bulgaria, Ottoman Empire (vassal)

Vasil Levski stood with the other ministers before the National Assembly, watching the new prince take his oath, thinking about security holes.

Those houses across the street. An assassin could be disguised as a manservant – no, better yet, a maid. Another agent, dressed as a chimney sweep, would deliver to her a rifle disguised as a brush…

And we'll have our freedom.

The prince's name was Alexander Joseph von Battenberg. Born in Verona to a Hessian father and Polish-German mother, but none of that mattered. This vacant-eyed boy with the medals on his chest was the nephew of Tsar Alexander II.

The Russians had indeed won the Russo-Turkish war, but the western Powers had intervened. They'd cut great swaths out of Bulgaria's original territory, accusing Russia of attempting to establish a powerful Slavic puppet on the Balkans. Russia vehemently denied this, then planted a Russian prince on top of what was left.

Levski considered: what if he stepped out of this crowd of respectful politicians, pulled out a revolver, and just shot Battenberg?

His hands trembled where they pressed against his hips. God, what a lovely thought. To be a bandit again. The fingertips of his right hand probed at the edges of his pocket.

But he had left his gun at home.

He could bribe one of the Russian soldiers guarding the prince. Deliver him fox-glove tea in the morning. Surely the upcoming move to the new capital would present an opportunity to slip in a knife.

The coronation ground forward and Levski kept his face blank, waiting.

9 August, 1886
Sofia, Sofia okrug, Principality of Bulgaria, Ottoman Empire (vassal)

How can a man change his mind?

Vasil Levski stood before the window of his office, hands clasped behind his back, watching the clouds break over the hunched back of Mount Vitosha.

The square in front of the new National Assembly bustled with evening business. Apricot light shone on the westward faces of the young buildings.

The tears caught Levski entirely by surprise. Why? This was *good*, what was happening, wasn't it? In accordance with his plans. So why weep? Why lose his vision at this time of all times, when he must see clearly?

There was to be a coup.

Levski shuddered, gasped through the hand he pressed to his mouth. At least he managed to stay silent. No secretaries or distinguished colleagues blundered into the room to see his shame. He was Finance Minister now, but he kept to the habits of his time as Minister of the Interior, when his desk contained state secrets.

Another habit he'd kept was the collection of those secrets.

Levski blinked his eyes open and there they were: accounting tables, records of honors bestowed after the Battle of Slivnitsa, copies of intercepted letters.

The letters contained bribes to several Bulgarian generals.

Join the Russian army and retain your rank. Increase your pay. Remove the inconvenient monarch.

And none of the conspirators told me!

Even more humiliating, Levski hadn't noticed until now. He'd thought the Minister of War was simply stupid, rather than a traitor. That contempt was probably why nobody had asked Levski to join the plot. Or tried to kill him.

Bitter old Levski. Still in the government because nobody could forget his bravery before independence. No one could forget how he'd insulted them, either, when they were trying to build a government. For seven years he'd beaten his head against other people's plans for his country and achieved nothing but damaging his vision.

Except now, just before the end, when God chose to give Levski one last, clear view, just before it became too late.

The troops were already in place. There would be a midnight raid on the Royal Palace. The guardsmen saluting the officers who strode through the gates and doors, all the way to the royal bedchamber. The disrespectful knock. The honeyed threats, the cutting smiles. *No harm will come to you, Your Royal Highness. Just sign this abdication.* Battenberg wouldn't take long to capitulate.

Then the puppet government. The counter-coup, which would weaken the country whether or not it succeeded. Then some new prince to run this little country just like all the other little countries in the shadow of the Powers. They would fight their little wars, draw and re-draw their wrinkled little borders. Every spring, a new map of the Balkans as more men died.

And Levski would survive, just as he always had. Making his plans, playing his part, winning every battle and losing every war.

Levski doubled over with the effort of staying silent. He wanted to howl. *When will I accomplish something?* If he'd been executed at thirty-five, would Bulgarian history have changed in the slightest?

No.

It felt like a weight falling through him. As if some heavy organ had dropped away.

Levski straightened and blinked. People streamed down the dirt roads, and smoke rose from chimneys, white against a sky gone dusty indigo. The mountain had faded from view.

When had Levski's plans ever done him any good? His successes had always been opportunities spotted, moments seized, ways of thinking and acting that put him where he needed to be.

And where he needed to be was not in this office.

Levski did not run toward the palace of the prince. He walked, boots thumping briskly down the rutted boulevard, as if he had important business to attend to.

The air had turned cool, but the heat of the day still radiated off the ground and buildings. The full moon overpowered the gas lamps on the gates of the palace. The *konak*, Sofians still called the building.

"You there. Halt!"

Levski stopped and turned, allowing his own self-doubt to put a bite into his voice. "Who's that? Don't you know who I am?"

The man – the boy – came closer, squinting at Levski's face. "Minister Kunchev?"

"Call me Levski."

The name still carried some weight. The boy swallowed and stood straighter, rifle-tip quivering. "Sir! You, uh, can't go further."

"And why not?"

"State emergency, sir?" He swallowed.

Levski stepped closer, smiling, ducking his chin, and lowering his voice. "You mean the coup?"

The boy sagged. He was so relieved he didn't have to lie to his childhood hero, it was as if his strings had been cut. "You know about it, sir."

"Know about it? Who do you think organized it?"

The plan had unfolded in the minutes it took Levski to leave the National Assembly. A lie centered upon a lovely, glowing wish.

"We will make Bulgaria a great democracy," said Levski, "clean and holy."

The boy licked his lips.

"What's your name, son?"

"Yordan, sir."

"Whose?"

"Angelov."

Levski straightened. "Cadet Angelov, I need your help. Escort me to the prince."

"But, sir! It's too soon, sir! The generals aren't here yet."

"The generals are in the pay of Tsar Nicholas III. You know that, right? Do you want *him* to have our prince, or us?"

Angelov's brows wrinkled. "You said you were organizing this coup."

"Which means I know more than you, doesn't it?" Levski spun on a heel. "Come."

He swept up five cadets on his way to the palace gates, and five palace guards between there and Prince Battenberg's apartments. Any second now, the cadets and the guards would compare stories and realize they were actually on opposite sides.

Quickly, heart thudding, Levski stepped up to the door. Knocked.

"Yes?" came the reply. "Is this an emergency? I was dining." The prince's Bulgarian had become quite good.

"Your Royal Highness." The honorific stank in Levski's mouth. "There is to be a coup."

A pause. The voice when it spoke was clearer, as if the prince was just an inch beyond the door. "And if I shoot you through the keyhole?"

Levski took a breath. Behind him were the loyal palace guards. Behind them, the cadets, who were loyal as well, but to something else.

"Your Royal Highness. If you shoot me, then I won't be able to rescue you."

15 April 1894

Levski tapped down the corridor of the Military School of His Princely Highness in Sofia, surrounded by hatred.

Behind him, the now ex-headmaster was trying to kill Levski with the force of his glare. The teachers and staff ducked their heads as he passed, but the trained eye could see the contempt in their shoulders and fists. *Jumped-up peasant* they were thinking.

And the students. Levski had stopped the political purge, so the young men in the corridor were all still openly socialist. Openly angry, too. Levski didn't need his decades of experience to know what *they* were thinking.

"Dog," they whispered. "Traitor. Boot-licker."

Levski did not respond. He knew they were wrong.

His men saluted as he approached the doors of the school and said, "Mr. Prime Minister."

That was wrong too, in a way. Survive the revolution, make yourself indispensable to the king, trade favors among the powerful, and you too might find yourself called "Mr. Prime Minister."

What was a title, wondered Levski as he returned the salute. What was the ache in the joints of his hand? Surface distractions. Deep down, he wasn't a social climber, or the stooge of the king, or a politician, or an old man. Not really. He was a *haiduk*.

The last haiduk, *if I can help it.*

The rock struck him as he passed through the door. It sailed expertly between two guards and the wall of the building, and hit Levski hard on the hip. He stumbled, cried out. Then, as gloved hands caught him, "Don't kill the boy! Bring him to me." And once he had caught his breath. "Don't hurt him."

Because of course it was a boy. Angry enough to hurl a rock at the Prime Minister, but still unsure. He had aimed low.

They caught the miscreant quickly. Levski's hip ached like the devil, but he had had enough time to compose his list of questions. There were only two.

"Put him in the carriage with me," Levski told his guards.

"Is that safe, sir?" asked the guard in a tone that meant *that is not safe, sir*.

Levski shifted his weight and shot his man a pained look. "I trust you removed any weapons he was carrying?"

The guard saluted. "We haven't disabled him, sir. You told us he was not to be hurt."

"You think I can't defend myself if he comes at me with his bare hands?" Levski reached under his seat, setting off another flare of pain, and extracted his pistol from its cupboard.

"Ah," said the guard. "Very good, sir."

The boy was soon pushed into Levski's carriage. He was large and burly, the collar of his school uniform tight under a face still more petulant than heroic.

Levski set his gun on the seat next to him and said, "Sit."

The boy's eyes flicked to the gun. "So you can shoot me?"

He had a southwestern accent. The Ottoman Empire still controlled this boy's homeland, which explained the anger. "I can shoot you easily enough while you're crouching there on the floor. You missed my hand, after all." Levski jerked his chin up. "Sit. And tell me your name."

"Georgi."

"And your father's name?"

"Nikolov."

"Whose?"

"Delchev."

Levski folded his hands in his lap. The pain had more or less subsided by now. "Well then, young Master Delchev, tell why you threw that rock at me."

A flash of eyes from under those lowered brows. "You're a traitor."

A disappointing answer, but it was what Levski had expected. "And why didn't you aim at my head?"

Delchev glared at the floor.

"Answer!"

"You used to be my hero!"

"Ah." Levski leaned back. "I thought that might be the case."

"Don't pretend to understand me."

Levski met the stare with equanimity. "Boy, I used to be you."

"You betrayed the movement! A federal republic, you said! Democracy clean and holy! And I'm twenty two years old."

Levski turned up his hands. "And now here I am, rather older."

"You're working for a prince! Half of Bulgarian lands still under the Turkish Yoke! You should have died. You should have ended your life while you were still a hero, instead of living to betray everything you believed in."

Delchev said what he thought would do the most damage. Throwing rocks again. But this time, Levski declined to be struck.

"Instead," he said, "I lived to become someone who frightens hotheads in his private carriage."

"I'm not frightened."

"You should be, boy. If I let you continue, you'll repeat my life. Running around, giving angry speeches and destroying things." Levski leaned forward. "Do you know how many of my friends died in the April Uprising? And how many of the rest destroyed themselves? Destroyers. That is what we were."

"That's what our people need!" Levski remembered a certain conversation with a pair of men during the war. Then, he had been the angry one. Now, Levski reined back his anger and considered how to attack Delchev's mistakes in thinking. *Let me do a better job with him than Burnaby did with me.*

"Prisoners must break their prison," he said, "yes. But once we are running our own country, we must stop breaking and start building." Levski swallowed a sudden, unexpected lump in his throat. "It took me thirty years to learn how to build something. Don't you waste so much of your life."

"Go to hell," said Delchev. "Where is our democracy? Where is our Balkan Federation? Where is our freedom and dignity?"

"In your head, where they've always been." Levski turned up his palm. "How would you like to try to make them real?"

"What?"

Levski sighed. "The Prime Minister doesn't generally visit the school when he fires the headmaster, does he? But an old *haiduk* might take an interest when his agents tell him about the correspondence flowing from that school to revolutionary councils scattered all over Ottoman Europe."

Levski waited while Delchev digested that.

"You read my letters."

"You didn't even put them in code," Levski said. "Although I wasn't sure they were yours until just now...oh, don't worry, boy. I'll have someone teach you cryptography."

Delchev looked around, as if preparing to flee this carriage.

"Tell your comrades I have an offer for them. Scholarships."

Delchev sneered. "At a prison?"

"I've been in several prisons." Levski reached out to part the curtain and look out the window. "But not enough schools, I think."

A guard looked in.

Levski signaled him. "Take us home."

Delchev, who had been watching the pistol lying unguarded on the seat next to Levski, looked up. "You're taking me where?"

"Well, you can't go back to school, can you? You threw a damn rock at the prime minister." Levski rubbed his hip. "But there's always space in my household guard. Tosho's been grumbling about the night shift since his daughter was born."

The boy wobbled as the carriage began moving. "You're offering me a job?"

"And in exchange, all I want is a means of contacting your revolutionary friends." Levski smiled. "I have plans for them."

6 September, 1908
Sofia, Sofia okrug, Kingdom of Bulgaria, Yugoslav Monarchy

Levski hobbled down the hall and flung open the door to the prince's study.

Battenberg looked up, scowling, ready to have the intruder dragged out. When he saw Levski's face, he stood so fast he knocked his chair over.

"What's happened? It's Russia and England, isn't it? They've formed another entente, haven't they? They're going to take Constantinople."

That was the scenario they'd discussed most often. England, France, and Russia, united. Why *wouldn't* they tear the Ottoman Empire apart? What had actually happened, though...Levski had never expected this, but he was ready to seize the opportunity.

He jerked his chin up, too out of breath to speak.

"What does that mean?" demanded the prince. "No? Yes?"

"No invasion," Levski gasped. "Turkish. Revolution. But it's time." He swallowed. "Your Majesty."

Battenberg straightened. His face went blank. "Your Majesty," he mouthed.

They had prepared for this. Wait for the moment of weakness. Declare yourself King of Bulgaria. Triple-monarch of Yugoslavia.

Battenberg – King Alexander I – looked around, as if for help. "Your revolutionary net?"

"They have surely already begun, Your Majesty. They have standing orders."

"But, we're not ready," said the new king. "There's so much we haven't done."

Levski placed a hand on his friend's shoulder. "One way or another, this will happen. It's just a matter of how much pain we can avoid."

He caught Levski's expression. "Oh, don't sneer at me so. The Turks came late to this peninsula, I admit, but wasn't there a time, too, before the Bulgars? Before the Serbs and the Romanians? If the Indo-Aryanists are right, even the Greeks were once invaders here."

Levski noted the Colonel didn't mention the Albanians, who had presumably fallen from the moon. "I thought you said you were going to keep this meeting brief," he said.

The Turkish colonel nodded complacently. "My point is we are much alike. We want the same things. What is best for our people. Peace. Prosperity. The respect due to a great nation."

"Which nation?" Levski asked dryly.

"I came here to ask you for advice on how to do it. How did you defeat the Sultan and build a great country?"

Levski had prepared a sarcastic reply, which now turned to dust in his throat. *Defeat the Sultan?*

Kemal Mustafa saw his meaning had been taken. He closed his eyes and dipped his chin. Then, as if commenting on the weather, he said, "The Ottoman navy plans a sneak attack on a Russian base in the Black Sea."

Levski scrabbled for stability. He had not spoken to someone this good in a long time. "Oh, I see," was the best he could manage.

Delchev was even more wrong-footed. "A *what*?" he said, but he'd heard it as clearly as Levski. He could imagine the consequences as well. "But all of Europe will go up in flames!"

Levski wished he could disagree, but he'd spent the last three decades worrying about exactly this eventuality. A war between the Powers. A Great War.

Russia would launch a counter-attack. England and France would be pulled in. Germany, Austria-Hungary, and Italy would join, and smash a path for themselves right down the Balkans to aid their ally Turkey.

Bulgaria would have two choices: either join the Quadruple Alliance and break with Serbia, or else join the Triple Entente and get cracked like a pistachio between Austria-Hungary and the Ottoman Empire.

No. No, there were more than two outcomes here. If Levski telegraphed back to Sofia, told everyone what Mustafa Kemal had told him, spoiled the Turkish navy's element of surprise, kept the disputes between the Powers tied up in diplomatic scandal…

He would give Mustafa Kemal time to do whatever it was he intended to do in Constantinople.

The train slowed as it crossed the bridge over the Tundzha, and the rattling became worse.

"Finally," said Delchev. "It's time."

Levski's eyes narrowed. He looked from the boy to the Turk. "All right," he said. "What is this? What are you two using me for? What do you want from me?"

Mustafa Kemal folded his hands in his lap. "A week."

"A week. A week for what?" asked Levski, although he already knew. He glared at Delchev. "God damn it, boy, you'd make me the midwife to a *Turkish revolution*?"

"Yes," said Mustafa Kemal.

Levski rose from his seat. His chest swelled with deep, red hatred. "No," he said.

Delchev flushed. "Sir, please give this – give us the consideration we deserve."

"You deserve nothing! Traitor!"

"Keep your voice down! And don't be a – Would you rather have a weak enemy or a powerful friend?"

"Friends?" said Levski. "The Turks? What happened to you, boy?"

Delchev looked to Mustafa Kemal for help, but the colonel looked away, as if embarrassed by their argument.

Levski's limbs tensed. Long ago, he would have pulled out a pistol and aimed it as his enemy's forehead. Later, he would have been coldly polite and schemed where to stick in the knife. Now, Levski was too tired for anything but honesty.

"I've spent my life fighting you," he told Mustafa Kemal. "God damn me if I stop now."

A palpable hit. The man's face hardened. Muscles in his jaws tensed. He flicked a chill glance at Delchev. "Are you two testing me?"

"He's testing both of us," Delchev told Mustafa Kemal.

Levski had enjoyed seeing his contempt mirrored in his enemy's face. But to hear it in Delchev's voice? It shamed him how much that hurt.

"How dare you?" Levski snarled at his protégé. "You would turn us into the pawns of this horse-thief? You would sell our homeland *back*?" He choked. There were no words big enough to pull the rage out of him. Action! Action was needed!

Houses rushed past the window as lifted his cane, mouth opening, full of spit ready to fly.

He stopped.

Mustafa Kemal was looking up at him, eyebrow raised.

Fear fought with anger. *How dare this young Turk treat me the way I treated Battenberg? And, when did I become as big a fool as the King?*

Levski looked down at the trembling tendons on the backs of his hands. He lowered the cane. Where was his control?

He stood there, rattling along with the train, feeling hollow. He had bartered himself away. Given himself up to expediency. Compromised again and again until nothing was left.

Tears came to his eyes. *What would my younger self think of me?*

He blinked. *What would I think of him?*

That poor, foolish boy.

The cane thumped on the carpeted floor of the carriage. Levski turned his face away from the other two men. He looked out the window.

The train was slowing. Streets and houses rotated around the enormous wedding-cake pile of the new Saint George Cathedral. They were on the wrong side of the train to see the Selimiye Mosque, but if the cathedral's gleaming, golden domes had been gun-turrets, Levski knew where they'd be aimed.

"God forbid any of us get our way." He realized it as he said it. The only real progress happened when a hundred people bashed their plans against each other and against the world. What came wouldn't be something that anybody could have foreseen, but it worked. Mostly.

"Sir?" asked Delchev.

Levski snorted. "Peace," he said in the language of his enemy. "Wasn't that what you said? Prosperity. Respect. Democracy, clean and holy."

"You've fought for them your whole life, sir," said Delchev, as if Levski might have forgotten.

"I fought," he said. "I beat myself bloody against the world. I made plans, and the world rarely agreed with them." His smile was tight, and tasted of salt. "There are laws in history, gentlemen, and it is not ours

to break them. All we can do is seize opportunities when we see them."
He held up his hand, still a bit sticky from the *sarma*, and closed it.

Mustafa Kemal chuckled. "Spoken like a true bandit." In Turkish,
the word was *haydut*.

How does a man change his mind?

A little bit every day.

Levski looked at Mustafa Kemal. The man had gotten up, perhaps
to make sure Levski didn't fall and break a hip.

"I'll give you your week, Colonel," he grunted.

Mustafa Kemal gave another small bow. "Thank you. I will seize
it."

They shook hands.

The colonel slid the door open. "May you find many more oppor-
tunities, sir. And…" He nodded to Delchev and switched to Bulgarian.
"I beg you to give my very warmest regards to Dimitrina Kovacheva.
And to her father."

He left.

Levski swung around to glare at Delchev. "General Kovachev's
daughter?" he grated. "Is that how you bought this meeting?"

"Don't be crude, sir." Delchev stood, smoothing down his jacket.
"They fell in love at the New Year's ball. It was very romantic. And
you were the one who taught me the importance of political match-
making." He held out his hand. "Where to now, sir? The baths, or the
telegraph office?"

Levski winced as his friend pulled him out the carriage door. "The
telegraph office of course, you smug-faced young rascal."

"Smug?" Delchev blew out his cheeks. "Relieved is more like it."

"Yes, because this stubborn old goat nearly ruined your revolutionary plans again, eh?"

"I'm relieved because I can still respect you, sir," said Delchev.

Levski frowned. "Well, *that's* good to hear. But don't you ever
again–" Levski paused in the corridor to shake a finger at Delchev.
People shoved past him.

"Watch where you're going!" said Delchev. "You damn villagers!
Take a moment, sir. Hold onto me."

Together, they eased their way into the mild October sunlight.

"Thank you, sir," said Delchev. "I'm grateful."

Levski grunted, squinting, secretly pleased. "Oh, enough with your

Meet Daniel M. Bensen

Daniel M. Bensen is an American-Bulgarian author of science fiction, alternate history, and fantasy. His work includes the speculative-biology novel Junction and its sequel Interchange, the optimistic post-apocalyptic comic-book First Knife (with Simon Roy). and the Sidewise Award-winning alternate history short story "Treasure Fleet" (in the Tales from Alternate Earths anthology). These stories have been called "clever, entertaining, and thoughtful" (SFBook Reviews) and "at times poignant" (Big Comic Page).

You may also enjoy his other alternate history short story, "The Goose's Wing" in the Tales from Alternate Earths 2, his novella Petrolea, and his self-published novel *Groom of the Tyrannosaur Queen*. Daniel is represented by Jennie Goloboy of Donald Maass Literary Agency.

Daniel classifies his work as "speculative aspirational fiction," which means that he explores other, better places, and the doors that lead to them. He loves learning about real life and extending from it to build plausible and surprising worlds. At odds with themselves and each other, the people in these worlds struggle to turn themselves the right way around, and so generate stories.

Daniel studied biology and history, teaches English as a foreign language, and has survived cancer. After growing up in Chicago, Maine, California, Montana, Japan, and Boston, he followed his then-fiancée to Sofia, Bulgaria, where he has continued to grow up. He now teaches, writes, and resides with his wife, daughters, and in-laws in the Balkan Tower of Matriarchy.

He says: "This story is dedicated to Emil. Life is full of strange and terrifying choices, but that's better than the alternative. Da rastem, no ne staraem."

NOT MY MONKEY

BY J. L. ROYCE

Not My Monkey
By J.L.Royce

She strolled through the doorway of Harry's Bar and made her way down the long wooden rail. A hunched figure at the end of the bar glanced up from his drink to study her approach from the safety of the shadows.

Her cocktail dress was a deep forest green, straight lines falling from her curves. She moved with a purpose, arrived before the bartender, glanced at the torn leatherette stool, and remained on her feet.

"I was told I could find Will Shakespeare here."

She moved with a purpose, and it occurred to Will that just might mean trouble.

Harry, the bartender and owner, looked up. "What'll you have?"

"Oh—nothing. If you could just point me to Mr. Shakespeare…"

Harry kept wiping the polished wood in silent protest.

The hunched figure in overcoat and fedora stirred and spoke.

"Ahh…let me guess—Sidecar, Harry. On me." He turned, tipping his hat brim up to regard her. "As Harry's fond of saying, *I'm a businessman, not a phone book.*"

The bartender shrugged and turned away to exercise his craft.

She stepped towards the speaker. "Thank you…Mr. Shakespeare?"

"Call me Will. "

"My name is Helena Gibbons. I'm pleased to meet you."

She had a petite, sloe-eyed face of exotic beauty. Whether her blonde curls came naturally or from a bottle, Will liked them.

Will's eyes, dark and soulful, were his best feature. The round, wrinkled face and expansive jaws were an acquired taste. Seeing him, the visitor's mouth became a perfect red ring of surprise, moist and inviting.

"I'm...sorry," she stammered.

"For what? My face, or your lips?" Will extended a long arm, hairy down to the horny nails. After a moment, the woman closed her mouth and accepted it with her gloved hand. "It can be helpful—people underestimate me."

"I've never met one of you before. I'm hoping you can help me."

"Why would you think that?" Will's lower jaw protruded in a lopsided grin, lips peeling back to display gleaming albeit overlarge teeth. He crooked a brown finger towards an empty booth.

"Harry? Bring 'em over—I'll have another Boilermaker."

Will slid off his barstool and straightened, but Helena remained considerably taller. She glided alongside the broad-shouldered, limping figure, Will noticing her as she noticed him. He waited for his guest to be seated before sliding in across from her.

She patted her hair, as if anything could be out of place. "Were you injured?"

"The limp?" Will scowled. "Old injury, old story."

He removed his hat and tossed it on the bench next to him, revealing close-cropped black hair, receding down the midline.

Helena smiled. "I like stories."

Will found it hard to resist that smile.

"If you expect an adventure," he warned, "I'm afraid I'll disappoint you. I was Army, made in the lab at Adelphi—supposed to be an ALFA soldier. During the re-bottling—the cortical transplant—I stroked. They saved me, but I was damaged goods. Medical discharge."

"That's so sad."

He shrugged. "Could have been worse, I guess. I was a ninety-nine percent plus human match. Any less, they'd have called me a chimp, and just put me down. But no—too *pan-human* for that." Bitterness tinged his voice, a pain remembered then dismissed.

"Never mind." Will's expression became placid, watching Harry make his way over. "What can I do for you?"

The barkeep placed a delicate glass with cherry and umbrella in front of Helena. He set the tall beer before Will, tossed in the shot.

"Let me get this." Helena moved to open her clutch, but Harry shook his bald head.

"Mr. Shakespeare's running a tab." He walked away, muttering, "Has been, for some time, seems."

She glanced at Will, who shrugged. "I live upstairs, solve problems for the management. Quid pro quo."

Helena's eyes fell on the black stock of the weapon hanging in the folds of Will's coat. He caught her glance—and the delicate hand falling to her purse—and shrugged it shut to cover the Remington.

"How may I be of service?" His lips quirked into a lopsided smile.

Helena sipped the drink, set it down, pulled off her left glove, displaying a gaudy ring. She twisted it as if it were an unaccustomed burden. "My fiancé's disappeared—at least I think so. The police aren't so sure. A friend thought you might be able to inquire…discreetly."

Will's full lips pursed. "How long?"

"Three days, now."

"Fiancé, not married."

"That's correct."

The PI's dark hands stretched slowly towards her, halfway, pale palms open.

"Standard fee, missing persons, is a grand, plus travel out of town." He'd just made it up; there was very little investigative work for a pan-human except second-story break-ins.

"Has he done this before? Weekend with the boys? With another girl? I have to ask."

"No—never. He's very steady, reliable. And dedicated to his work."

"Which is?"

Helena's face closed. "He works at the Army Lab."

Will pulled back with an indrawn hiss of breath, shaking his head. "Can't do."

"Why not?" Helena challenged.

"Why isn't the government looking into it—Army Intelligence, or FBI?"

"It's personal. I wouldn't want to embarrass him if he's just, just…"

"Gotten cold feet?"

She glared at Will but didn't disagree. Self-confidence fading, she pulled her glove back on.

"I don't think he'd betray me; and he'd be up front with me if something had changed. But if he just wants to break off our engagement, well…"

Her color rose. Helena removed a tissue from her purse and daubed her eyes delicately.

Will couldn't stand tears. "Alrighty—double the fee," he said bluntly.

"Half now," she murmured. She thumbed through a stack of bills, placing some into an envelope before withdrawing it and other papers.

"Here's some information." She slid the thick envelope across the table. "Can you start right away?"

Will glanced inside, took out a snapshot, in color: Helena and a gent, the pair smiling. He stared at it skeptically, but said, "Sure."

The envelope also held a photocopy of a Maryland driver's license: Morris Hewes. He tapped it.

"This his real name?"

Helena did a fair impression of innocent surprise at his question. "Of course!"

"Of course," he echoed. Will slipped his wallet out and placed the white rectangle before her.

"My card. *Work* is my office, the address—there's a service; *Home* is, well…here."

"I'll call when I have something." She examined the card, studied the address. "Know the neighborhood?"

"I can find it." Helena stood, purse clutched before her. "Thank you so much."

She smiled. It was the sort of smile that could get a man to do just about anything. She swiveled and walked away, angelic amongst the cluttered tables and disheveled patrons. Will watched her out the door, staring at the emptiness she left behind. He wondered what she'd gotten *Morris Hewes* to do with that smile.

Harry dropped a tray on the table.

"So." He collected the glasses, waiting.

When Will remained silent, Harry demanded, "Take it, or not?"

The PI slouched, an arm wrapping over his head to scratch the opposite ear. He stared at the photograph.

"You know," Harry observed, "if you ever want to make it with classy dames, you'll have to learn to act a little less like a monkey."

"Chimp," Will growled, but brought down his arm. "Makes no sense."

The couple in the photo was dressed for business, not pleasure. They were smiling—barely—and not touching.

"Why?"

"Nobody wants to get married *this* bad." Will lifted the envelope, dropped it. "She could have any Joe she wanted. Every Cracker Jack box she opens must come with a fiancé inside."

Harry chuckled.

Will tapped the photo with a horny nail. "Why *this* guy?"

"Rich?" Harry suggested.

Will snorted. "Working for the Army?"

He slid the license photocopy over, adding a hundred from the envelope. "Check this out for me—NCIC, IAFIS, you know?"

Harry nodded, folding and slipping them into his pocket. The former Philadelphia cop still had connections.

Will shook his head. "Something doesn't square."

"Well," Harry opined, lifting the tray, "if anybody can figure it out…"

• • •

The bus ride to the complex at Adelphi was an hour and a half. To avoid the morning crowd, Will took the earliest departure from downtown. He sat in the back with the brim of his hat drawn down, reading a tattered copy of *Hell's Angels*. The sun appeared through the rear window, casting his long shadow down the aisle.

It was early for his quarterly check-up, government-mandated as one of the terms of his release. Will had left the Remington at home (the Army not approving of his right to bear arms) but had a baseball in his coat pocket.

Will hoped he would not have to use it.

"ID."

The MP at the gate, a familiar face, didn't give him a second glance. He handed the ID back with a scowl. Will returned it to his wallet.

"As if I could recognize you lot from a photo. What d'you want, you hairy little devil?"

"Check-up."

"Early, ain't it?" The guard frowned down at him. "Something wrong?"

"Your old lady—wearin' me out." It was an old routine, but the MP grinned.

"Know where to go?"

"Straight to hell."

"You got it. No straying, no socializing with the other little bastards."

"Sure." Will casually pulled out the photo.

"Say…ask you something?" He passed it up to the guard. "Ever see this guy?"

The ten-spot folded beneath it dropped out of the guard's hand and into his pocket with a practiced gesture.

"Yeah; a regular here, for some months."

"Regular?"

The guard nodded and grinned. "*And* the dame, just recently, once or twice."

Will tensed. "Her?"

"Kind of hard to forget, you know? Well, maybe you wouldn't."

Will gritted his teeth, suppressing an urge to howl in frustration. "Well, he wasn't here for his de-worming."

"Come to think, the doc hasn't been around for a week or so."

"Doctor?"

"Doctor, vet, whatever—he worked on your sort." He passed the photo back.

"Anything else?" Will knew what to do; another bill went under the photo. "Take another look."

The MP nodded. "Sure. He's cozy with Sakura, in ALFA."

When Will greeted the information with a blank stare, the guard rolled his eyes.

"For a regular visitor you don't know much. The big-shot Japanese doctor. Changed his name after the war, what I heard. MacArthur got him and his crew of mooks out of Japan. Some top-secret weapons development."

"What sort of weapons?"

The uniformed man grinned again. "Look at your ugly face in the mirror? The Commies got the V-2's, and the Moon, and we got…" He waved at the pan-human.

"Aw, what's the Moon good for, anyway?" Will replied. "Let the Russkies have it."

Will walked away, then slowed and said, "Word to the wise—you might not want to repeat that story where anybody with a GS-1 or above can hear you."

"Have a nice procto exam," the guard called after him. "And don't be thinking about my girl, while your pants are down."

Will bared his teeth in a crooked grin, and with an obscene gesture, made to leave.

"Ain't you gonna ask about the babe?" the guard teased.

Will paused. "What about her?"

"You should really pay for this; but seeing as how we're such pals…"

"Go on, then."

"Thought I'd give you fair warning, in case you were thinking of hitting on her. She's FBI." He winked.

Will nodded and forced himself to stroll away towards the labs. On a training field, a squad of ALFAs loped along at an easy run, chanting a cadence. He ambled by, hiding his limp, his long arms swinging casually. Will wanted to fling them into the air, and shriek.

His mind gnawed restlessly at the insights, and the lies, and the image of the blonde at the center of it all.

• • •

At Harry's place, the bartender could add little from his police sources. "Security clearance—can't find out what he's doing. But he was a neurosurgeon at Massachusetts General before the Army got him."

Will grunted and took his place at the bar. "Okay; the ALFA project. Makes sense. What about this Dr. Sakura?"

"Another one under wraps. Ever hear of Unit 731?"

"No. What's that—FBI?"

"Naw—Japanese Army."

"Didn't think they had an Army anymore."

"During the *war*," Harry said. "This guy Sakura is continuing research done by Unit 731. That's all I could find out."

"And Miss Gibbons?"

Acne had put out the cigarette and was holding a pistol pointed at the pan-human. His opponent aimed a last kick at Will, who dodged it easily.

The gunman stood. "Message delivered. Next time, you won't hear us coming. Keep your flat nose out of this one, monkey. There won't be another warning."

The speaker circled around Will, the gun never wavering, and led his somewhat battered muscle out the back.

The fog of pain settled onto Will like an unwanted cat and prepared to spend the night. Fists clenching and unclenching, Will thought about the tall blonde with the lying smile.

• • •

The morning was as gray as the ache in Will's head. He was in the park working out on the monkey bars when Helena strolled up. Will ignored her, like the pain in his bruised body.

"Can we talk?"

Swinging around the outside of the steel cage by his strong, uninjured arm, Will dropped and rolled, grunting at the tenderness of the opposite shoulder. He sprang to his feet before her.

Helena peered at him. "I saw the note on your door—what happened?"

"It's why I called—somebody wants me off your case. Said you were trouble. Well, problem solved, right? But watch yourself."

She noticed his swollen face. "So, you *can* get a black eye."

"If I don't move fast enough, yeah. Or I'm jumped from behind. Towel?"

Helena stretched behind her, pulled it from the swing set, and handed it over. "You're barefoot. I guess you don't care to wear shoes."

He gingerly wiped his tender face, then the thick fur on his arms, grimacing as he ran the towel across his back. "Doesn't matter for walking. But for climbing, shoes would be like wearing boxing gloves. Do you wear heels when you're out catching the criminals?"

The agent considered her practical flats. "Point taken."

Will started off towards his office, Helena trailing.

"The sign says the playground is only for children and adult supervision," she pointed out.

"Signs can lie. *Appearances* lie."

She didn't rise to the bait, and he continued. "Special dispensation from the Monsignor. They had a pest problem; I took care of it."

"Pests?"

"Druggies, prostitutes, deadbeats. We chatted. They moved down the street to the public park."

She caught up with him, easily outpacing his limp. "You do a lot of bartering, don't you?"

"You scratch my back, I scratch yours. Why? You with the IRS now?"

"Just wondering…maybe I should have tried that approach. Quid pro quo."

It was his turn to remain silent.

At the blank steel door off the alley, Will tore the Post-It from the keypad and threw it to the ground, tapping in the code. He pulled open the heavy door and motioned her in.

Helena first stooped to pick up the crumpled paper, folding at her knees and rising again with a dancer's grace. Will watched her with a mixture of resentment and longing.

The fluorescent lights revealed a short hall with all the charm an industrial park could offer. A scant distance along they came to a door with the hand-lettered sign: Shakespeare Investigations.

Beneath it, some wit had scrawled, *Hear No Evil, See No Evil, Do No Evil.*

"Been meaning to replace that," Will muttered. "Though, maybe it's appropriate."

Retrieving a key from his gym shorts, he unlocked the door and invited Helena in.

A small reception area buffered his office itself from the hallway. It lay in the building's corner, a narrow window revealing the alley entrance.

Helena glanced around. "What is this?" she asked.

He blinked. "My office?"

"The building."

"Veterinary hospital. I keep an eye on the place."

Helena nodded, looking at the few personal touches with a trace of a smile. She peered through a half-open doorway to another room. There was a cot, the sheet tightly fitted with military precision.

"What's that?"

"Sometimes if I'm working late, it's a place to flop."

Will stepped past her and yanked the door shut. He gestured expansively.

"A tire swing and a bunch of bananas would really make the place feel like home."

He opened a supply cabinet, taking out a stack of fresh clothes. Glancing from his shorts to the long pants in his hand, he thought better of it, and collapsed with a grunt into the chair behind the desk. "Sit?"

Helena did, and Will studied her, a pleasant enough task. "I'm pretty pig-headed, for a monkey; so, if somebody tells me to piss off I piss back, instead."

He opened the file drawer of his desk, taking out a bottle and two glasses. "Drink?"

Helena shook her head.

Will poured and sipped the rye, set it down, picked up the scuffed baseball from his desktop.

"Do you like the game?" she asked.

"Sure, I guess. Phillies are awful, but the rest of the division is mostly worse. And I'm a decent pitcher."

He tossed it from hand to hand. "Lucky baseball."

"What's lucky about it?"

"Stick around; you'll see."

She opened her purse, again displaying the envelope. "Does this mean you'll help me?"

"Only if I like the story—the real story—of what's going on."

Helena placed the envelope on the desk, lips tight. "Very well. Straight story—my personal story. Have you heard of Unit 731?"

He peered into her face—an easy face to watch. "Something about the Japanese Army."

"Surprised you know that much—it's a topic the government prefers to avoid. Unit 731 was a Japanese research division, their ARL. They studied battlefield issues like hypothermia, blood loss, wound contamination. When MacArthur brought their scientists out of Japan after the war, it's natural they'd end up at Adelphi.

"I followed clues to ARL, rumors about war crimes committed by Unit 731—and didn't get anywhere. Morris—Doctor Hewes—approached me later. He'd been working with Dr. Sakura, the Director of the ALFA project, on new surgical techniques. Morris overheard a conversation Sakura had with Security—about an FBI agent getting 'too close'—and that 'something had to be done'."

"Our Morris figured they didn't mean harsh language at your next personnel review."

"No. And Morris claimed there was evidence in the Army archive, a report prepared for MacArthur after the surrender, detailing Unit 731 operations—all of them. He was sure Sakura meant to destroy it—so Morris stole it before he could."

Will grunted in surprise. "That's a hanging offense. I'm guessing you've lost Hewes and this report. Must have been some story you told him."

"My story is my father's story." A smile quirked her lips, then vanished.

"He was a physician in China before the war. The Japanese captured him when they overran Harbin, forced him to care for the prisoners at their 'Epidemic Prevention Department'—Unit 731. He saw what happened...the experiments..."

The daughter's face recalled the father's pain.

"At the end of the war he escaped, made his way to the American Army, and emigrated to the States. He married my mother, they settled in a little California town, he practiced medicine, they raised me. He just wanted a quiet life.

"For years he'd told himself that the monsters from the war had been imprisoned, punished, because he'd heard nothing more of the Japanese crimes. But he happened to attend a medical conference in San Francisco. There was a Japanese speaker, presenting on infectious diseases, and father recognized him—from Harbin, Unit 731."

Will frowned, rolling his left shoulder absently.

She stood and placed her hand over his: cool and soft. "Take off your shirt."

Will's dark eyes went round. "I don't think—"

"Lean on the desk. You're no use to me groaning and complaining." He did as he was told.

"I learned first aid, from my father. There was usually a scuffle in town, on a Saturday night." Helena expertly followed the ribs down his back. "Nothing broken, or you wouldn't tolerate this. Think you might

river!"

She silenced him with a hand on his shoulder, stretching out a slender finger.

"There." It was obvious: the closest of the black doorways. "And if I were you, I wouldn't talk about *smell*."

Will couldn't help but grin. "Okay; let's see." He crept around the corner and into the shadow of some rusting machinery.

"Will!" she hissed, but kept up.

It wasn't difficult to find Hewes: they just followed the moaning, far into the structure.

The doctor lay on a dingy cot in a damp, low-ceilinged chamber. A bare bulb in a utility lamp clamped to a chair illuminated his pallid face, bruised and bloodied.

"Morris!" Helena moved his face side to side, eliciting a moan, then checked him for other injuries. "Can you walk?"

Hewes opened a swollen eye and groaned. "FBI—hello. Not on my own, no."

Will prowled the concrete-walled perimeter. A power cord snaked from the lamp into the darkness.

"Let's get moving," he insisted.

"Did they find out about the report?" Helena asked.

Hewes tried to shake his head but grimaced. "Still think I got it out of Adelphi."

"Wait—you didn't?"

The man's gaze wandered to Will, and a slight smile appeared.

"Hello, Mr. Shakespeare. Told her to find you."

"Charmed. Why?"

"The report—you'll know where to look. I put it where you spent all your free time, during your recovery. Yes?"

Will reared back, baring his teeth. "How would you know that?"

Morris chuckled, a liquid sound that degenerated into a cough. "Videos. I was doing research on surgical techniques, your case…" He coughed again, too loudly, and Helena tried to calm him.

"Do you know what he means?" she asked Will.

He stared into her hazel eyes. "Yeah, if I can get back into ARL in time. Let's get moving!"

They had gathered Hewes into a sitting position on the edge of the filthy cot when the light went out. Will grunted a curse, then asked,

"You should consider your position." He paused and leaned over her. "A young, healthy body like yours—I'm sure we could find a use for it..."

Helena twisted her face away from his. "You can try."

"You're wasting my time." Sakura straightened and glanced around. "Your monkey—where is he?—does he know where the report is?"

Helena didn't get a chance to answer. The baseball, thrown flat and hard, hit Sakura squarely in the forehead. He remained standing for a moment, a surprised look on his face, then collapsed.

The two thugs swept their pistols around, searching the darkness beyond their circle of light. A smile twisted Helena's bleeding lips.

"Not my monkey..."

From behind her came the sharp, sweet snick of the Remington's action.

"...not my circus."

"Got a match?"

Footsteps approached. Helena snarled a challenge, cut short by the sounds of a struggle.

• • •

A hand gently stroked Helena's cheek. Her eyes fluttered open, revealing a man's silhouette bent over her. She jerked away. "Who?"

He was tall and darkly handsome, not much older than Helena. His concerned look spread into a smile.

"There you are! So pleased to make your acquaintance, Agent Gibbons."

"Sakura?"

The man withdrew his hand and bowed, smirking. "At your service."

He was fashionably dressed, projecting a youthful vigor, with longish black hair swept back from a regular face. Sakura studied her.

"So beautiful…your father married well. The Nazis, of course, would never have approved—no appreciation of hybrid strengths."

Helena struggled, found herself tied to a chair, at ankles and wrists.

"I must apologize for my associates' precautions, but you have caused a bit of trouble." He gestured behind him to a pair, one badly complected, the other over-muscled. "We'll clear everything up shortly."

The thugs watched her with unhealthy interest.

Helena looked at her bared arm, a bandage covering a tender spot. "What have you done to me?"

"Ether, in the other room—can cause nausea—and a mild-altering substance, by injection. One of my research interests; it reduces inhibitions of all kinds."

One of the hoods snickered.

Sakura continued. "I've assured my associates that if you're unable to satisfy my needs, I'm certain you'll be ready to satisfy *theirs*."

"What needs?"

"Answers, to simple questions. Our friend Hewes was unwilling to disclose where has taken certain materials stolen from Army archives. Sad case, that: he is a skilled surgeon. It would be truly unfortunate if he were to lose the use of his hands…"

"I don't know," Helena answered.

Realizing his error, Sakura asked, "Where is the report?"

"What report?"

Sakura cast a disappointed look at her. "Now, now—the report prepared for General Douglas MacArthur, detailing the activities of a certain Imperial Japanese Army Unit 731 during World War Two…"

"A report describing the war crimes of Unit 731?"

"Research projects," Sakura corrected. "Now tell me, where did Hewes leave it?"

"At ARL."

"Yes, yes—he removed it from the archive, he had it at ARL…and then where?"

"At ARL."

Reaching out, Sakura spread her eyelids, left then right, peering at her pupils. "Did you know that I met your father?"

Frowning, he straightened and slapped her hard, backhanded. "Stay awake, please." The muscle behind him chuckled in expectation of a show, but the doctor frowned at them.

"Shiro Ishu didn't trust him, but I insisted we needed his help. I kept him alive. So, you see, in a way, you wouldn't be here if it weren't for me."

Helena's expression was dull, the drug leveling her emotions. "That's impossible. You're too young."

Sakura asked, "Why do you think I am at ARL?"

"*Adelphi Laboratory Fighting Animal* project."

"ALFA," he scoffed. "All that genetic manipulation, for talking monkeys. We don't need to waste time creating these pan-humans—human soldiers are cheaper and live longer. Merely a subterfuge, disguising our actual objective." He spread his arms, smiled, and bowed: *voila*.

Her eyes grew wide. "*Human* transplantation. *You've* been re-bottled."

"Fully—personality, memories and all. Now do you see how important it is for the work to continue? Why this report must never be disclosed?"

He resumed pacing, a forceful figure. "We can have as much life as we want!"

"You're mad."

Meet J.L.Royce

J. L. Royce is a published author of science fiction, the macabre, and whatever else strikes him. He lives in the northern reaches of the American Midwest. His work appears in Allegory, Ghostlight, Little Demon, Love Letters to Poe, Mysterion, parABnormal, Sci Phi, Utopia, Wyldblood, etc. He is a member of HWA and GLAHW. Some of his anthologized stories may be found at:

amazon.com/author/jlroyce.

Twitter: @authorJLRoyce

Facebook: AuthorJLRoyce

'Not My Monkey' was a Finalist in the Q3 2020 Writers of the Future competition.

Unit 731 was a real unit in the Second World War, that undertook lethal human experimentation. A number of researchers were given immunity by the United States secretly in exchange for the data they gathered.

HEAVEN ABOVE HELL BELOW

BY LEO McBRIDE

Heaven Above, Hell Below
By Leo McBride

The manmade island was quite a sight from the air. Two islands would be a more accurate description – an outer ring around the central island. Four long roadways connected the two as if they were spokes, making it look somewhat like a wheel. The outer rings had the most construction going on, with vehicles and workers buzzing around putting up hotels, while groynes extended into the sea to help to create the beaches shown on the glossy cover of the brochure on Ellie's lap. But it was the central island that was her business.

"Make the most of it, no one will get a view like this soon," said the man sitting across from Ellie, a slim older white man dressed in the clothes of a pastor, complete with white collar and crucifix around his neck.

Without looking away from the window, Ellie replied: "I know. Anyone tries to get this close, two F15EX2 Eagle 2 jets will blow them out of the sky. If that's not enough, the tower has Sea Sparrows mounted on all corners able to take anything down far enough away not to worry about fragmentation."

The man coughed. "I'm sorry," he said, "Clearly you know far more about the defenses of Shinar than I do. Allow me to introduce myself,

I'm Bishop John Wilson. And you are?"

He extended his hand across the space between them, and Ellie took it, his pale skin a contrast to her own black skin.

"Ellie Floyd," she replied, "and yeah, I guess you could say I do - I designed the defenses. You here with the religious advisory body?"

"That I am. Although I do fear my opinion might not matter much, I'm not sure how much I can offer to a project as ambitious as Shinar."

Ellie paused. "That's the second time you've called it Shinar. So far, it's just Pacific Base while the marketing teams do all the brand testing. Why are you calling it Shinar?"

The pastor raised his hands. "Oh, you know what they say, if you want something try to speak it into being. I figure if I keep on using it, it might stick in someone's mind and might just make it to the final list. My own little contribution."

Ellie smiled. "Well, clearly you know far more about where that comes from than I do. I'm afraid my days of learning scripture are a long while back. What's Shinar?"

"Ah," he said, "well, Shinar was once—"

He was interrupted by the chopper pilot calling back. "On final approach, buckle up, we'll be touching down in a moment."

Ellie smiled. "Something to tell me over lunch," she called, as she buckled her belt and the helicopter banked and descended to the central island.

As she straightened up after getting off the helicopter and away from its whirring blades, Ellie took a chance to look at the tower. The ground structures were broadly complete – certainly the bulwark around the anchor point.

Some work was still being carried out on the concourses and security areas further out, but there were fewer construction workers on Pacific Base Central now and more of the science teams. Badges from both NASA and JAXA dominated instead.

She tossed her bag in an electric cart as it pulled up and nodded to Jackson, her number two on Pacific Base in the driver seat.

"How was the flight?" he shouted over the sound of the helicopter.

"Screw the flight," she said as she sat down, "get me to Mother so we can make sure this place doesn't get blown to shit."

Mother was the best security hub money could buy. A wall covered with monitors cycling through the hundreds of cameras around Pacific Base, and dozens of computer terminals, each logging one activity or another across the artificial island.

Ellie put Jackson to work showing her everything. Every blip in the camera network, every manifest of deliveries, every ID card from the newly arriving science teams. If there was anything that had changed recently, she wanted to know it. Touchdown was less than 24 hours away and she'd be damned if anything was going to happen on her watch.

By the time the morning was over, Jackson was probably wishing she'd stayed on the other end of a video link. Still, she set him to recheck the port stops for every ship delivering supplies in the past month while she headed for some lunch.

The cafeteria area was dominated by a large glass wall that gave a view of the anchor point. For now, there was little to see. She grabbed a salad to keep it light and a juice and was headed for an empty table when a voice called out her name.

"Miss Floyd! I believe we have a lunch date."

It was the bishop. Wilson. *Why not?* She sat down across from him in his seat by the window.

"It really is a fabulous feat of engineering," he said. "Or will be, tomorrow."

She acknowledged the comment half with a tilt of the head, half with a slight frown.

"Something wrong?" Bishop Wilson asked.

"These kinds of projects there's always a dozen things wrong until everything is right. Just last-minute hustle, ah… Reverend?"

"Call me John," said the bishop. "Sounds like you've got enough to worry about without fretting about what to call me."

"I do at that," she sighed.

"And you're wrong about one thing," he said.

"I am?" Her answer was a little on edge. She didn't like it when people put her on the defensive.

"You say these kinds of projects. There's never been this kind of project before, Miss Floyd. You're breaking all kinds of new ground."

"Yeah," she said, sparing a glance out at the anchor point. "I guess we are at that. And if I'm calling you John, you're calling me Ellie, deal?"

"Deal," he nodded, then gulped another spoonful of the soup he had in front of him.

They both ate quietly for a few moments, then he set down his spoon and looked again at the anchor point.

"You know, they say that tomorrow will be a remarkable day, but it occurs to me that we are here thanks to a succession of remarkable days."

"And tragic days," Ellie replied.

The bishop looked at her peculiarly. "How do you mean?"

"All of this," she gestured out the window. "It might not have happened at all. After Challenger…"

"The shuttle?" asked the bishop.

"Yeah. I was only a kid then. There was an astronaut on there by the name of Ron McNair. He was one of the first black astronauts. I kinda dug that when I was a kid. He was even going to take part in a concert live from space, he played sax. He just made everything seem… possible, y'know?"

The bishop nodded.

"I was watching on TV when Challenger exploded. I thought it was fake. Some special effect or something. But then they cut to the expressions in mission control and… I knew. It was one of those moments. Where were you when this happened? The kind of thing that unites everyone. You remember it, don't you?"

"Yes," said the bishop. "I'd just finished a service when my housekeeper called to say something had happened. We watched it together on the TV."

"Those kind of moments can go either way," said Ellie. "With NASA, it provoked a lot of debate. What were they even doing with the shuttles, that kind of thing. One expert said they realised what they'd been doing for years was just throwing junk into space. One shuttle after another, one satellite after another, with little real reason for doing it that way except habit. After Challenger, there was a push to do things differently. It took a while but they came up with the Marshall plan – named after a workshop at the Marshall Flight Center. Out of that came… well, this."

"And Challenger," said the bishop, "that brought you here too."

"Yeah," said Ellie, "that and 15 years in the military, all the usual conflict zones. Then this project came calling, and I got transferred.

Recruited the security teams, trained them, so it's on me if anything goes wrong. Project like this has a big target painted on it. Every day we get threats – some credible, most not. This close to completion, we've got to treat them all as credible, and be ready to move on them as fast as we can. Challenger was an accident, sure, but it showed it only takes a moment, to go from a world where everything is possible, to a world where we stop believing in what we can do. We could so easily have gone another way, could have stopped reaching for the next big thing."

She nodded toward the anchor point, adding: "There was a writer, Arthur C Clarke, who said this would be built about 50 years after people stopped laughing. Well, Challenger made people stop laughing. We were a bit faster than he guessed, though."

"An elevator to the stars," said the bishop. "Even saying it now, it sounds fanciful, like some impossible thing I will wake up to discover was a dream all along. Like something out of that fairy tale..."

"Jack and the Beanstalk," said Ellie, "Yeah. Except the Beanstalk is growing down from space. And tomorrow it makes contact."

The bishop smiled. "One more for our succession of remarkable days, I think."

"What about you?" she asked as she ate some more of her salad, "What are you filling your time with while you're here?"

The bishop gave her a withering gaze. "Some would say I'm wasting my time and the religious advisory body is nothing more than a PR effort."

"Are you one of those?"

The bishop took his time answering, finishing the last of his soup before replying.

"There are a lot of people who find this a hard sell," he said. "There is the crowd who say oh you mustn't spend the money on this, you should spend it on feeding the poor or housing the homeless."

"Are you one of those?"

"No... I mean, I want that money spent on those who need it but all this costs a fraction of the money we spend on going to war with one another and the people who complain about this kind of thing seldom seem to complain about that. No, this is just a big shiny object they can point at to complain while they really worry about whether it's putting up their taxes. This isn't the cause of such ills.

"But that's just one group. Then there are those who complain about this being built on an artificial island because 'why not build it right here in America?'."

At that, the bishop swelled his frame as if he were a taller man and put on a voice far less eloquent than his own. Ellie laughed.

"I know the type," she said.

"And so it goes on. The whatabouters, the whataboutus crew, the whataboutGod folks who wonder whether it's against God's divine purpose to dare to reach for the stars as if we haven't already been there. And while some of those are so far to the extreme you can let them go about their business and not fret, there are others who hear those kinds of complaints and wonder if there's something to what's being said. I think that's where we come in, the religious advisory body. If we give it our blessing, we can steer some of our congregations away from some of the doubts. Maybe there's someone in my congregation that might say 'well, if it's alright with Bishop Wilson, it's alright by me'. I don't know if you call that PR, I don't know if you call it a waste of time, but well... here I am."

"You know," said Ellie, "my mom used to drag us all to church every Sunday, and I think I know what she'd have said about you."

"Oh?" prompted the bishop.

"Yeah, she'd have said you were alright by her."

The bishop smiled.

"I can't ask for anything more than that," he said.

"I can, though, you owe me an answer," said Ellie.

"I do?"

"Yeah," said Ellie, looking at the twinkle in the bishop's eye, "and you know you do. You remember."

"Shinar," he said, matter of factly, not a question.

"Yeah, what is it?"

"Well," said the bishop, folding his napkin and putting it on the table, "at the risk of pushing my luck, perhaps I can tell you that this evening over dinner. I have a few interminable meetings to go to and then the good part, a tour of all these marvels. After that, though, perhaps we can catch up here?"

Ellie smiled. "Sure, John, I'll let you get away with that. I gotta go too really. Tomorrow is a big day, lots to do today, but gotta eat. What time's your tour finish?"

"Six, I believe, if there's no overruns. Meet you here at seven?"

"Seven, it is. And you owe me an answer, y'hear?"

"I do indeed hear."

The rest of the day was one hassle after another. First there was the latest briefing from the intelligence communities – as if they were ever much use. There was talk of "chatter" from one terror group or another, but while Ellie listened and duly ticked off one risk or another, she knew any assault was far less likely to be an external attack than an individual on the island with a grudge or a cause or an overblown sense of screw you. They were the worst to plan for. Bigger attacks took infrastructure, support, planning. The lone attacker was the one you never saw coming – no message intercepts, no trail of intelligence, just the hope you got lucky with enough time to stop them.

If ever there came a day when the island was subject to an attack, those Eagle fighter planes were probably still going to be cooling their jets on the runway rather than up in the air in response. The pilots regularly sent gripes up the chain about having the dullest duty on the air force and being of better use elsewhere. They weren't wrong, but their value was as much in deterrence as anything else.

After the briefing, Ellie went back to Mother and ran through everything Jackson had prepared earlier. She looked through inspection logs, looked for any way a stowaway might have gotten in, but everything looked secure.

On it went. Checking logs on security routes, inspections of the armories, check-ins with mission control on the progress of the descent plan.

She was in the middle of dealing with a contractor complaining his guys had left behind some equipment in the anchor point zone and he needed access to get it back when she noticed the time, almost seven. She cut the contractor off, telling him his equipment would have to wait until after touchdown, grabbed her jacket and headed to the cafeteria.

"I'm late," she said as she crunched down into the seat opposite the bishop – the same seat with the same view, this time with the anchor point illuminated by spotlights pointing toward the sky.

Ellie noticed the empty plate in front of the bishop.

"Wait, I'm… very late?" she asked.

"No, no," said the bishop. "Have no fear. I was somewhat early, the meetings overran, but the tour sadly underran. We didn't get to see as much as we hoped."

"Oh," said Ellie. "Okay. I mean, I'm sorry about that. Wait, why am I apologizing, it was nothing to do with me…"

"As I said, have no fear. Now eat some of your food, you sound… hassled. Been a day, I take it?"

"It feels like it's been three days," she said. "But… we're good, I think. I mean, I won't be happy until it's done. And then when it's done there'll be a thousand more things. But the things that are supposed to be working are working."

She took a moment to take a bite of the casserole she'd grabbed for dinner, then pointed her fork menacingly at the bishop.

"But you, John, you owe me. Talk."

The bishop smiled.

"Shinar," he said.

"You know I could have just Googled it, right?"

"But then you wouldn't have had an excuse for dinner. I'm sure I'm just a good way of getting out of talking to people about those thousands of things that need doing, but I'll take it. You give me a good excuse to avoid being cooped up with boring old men like me talking about scripture."

"Okay," she said as she wolfed down some more food. "So what are we going to talk about instead?"

"Scripture, of course," smiled the bishop.

"Well, God damn," muttered Ellie.

"I hope He doesn't."

"Shinar. Spill it."

"Eat your food and don't roll your eyes when I say 'As it says in the Bible'."

"Yes, John."

The bishop arched his fingers and began.

"As it says in the Bible… Genesis actually, there was once a time when the whole world had one language. But as people moved eastward they decided to build a tower. A tower, as they said, 'that reaches to the heavens, so that we may make a name for ourselves'. You know of it as the tower of Babel. And when God saw them trying to build a tower that reached heaven, he confounded their speech and scattered them over the face of the Earth.

"People talk of the tower of Babel falling, but there's actually no record of its destruction. There are suggestions of it being a parallel to the Sumerian tale of Enmerkar who built a massive ziggurat, or the Great Pyramid of Cholula in Mexico – a Cherokee story here, a Greek story there. In many different cultures, however, there is this story of an attempt to build a tower to heaven."

"But, John," said Ellie, putting down her fork. "The attempt failed. So what's that about?"

"The attempt failed," answered the bishop, "because people were divided. When they were united, it was possible – but when divided, it was not. They didn't speak with one voice any more. What stopped them from reaching their goal was that they could no longer under-stand one another. Sometimes, as I look around today, I think we have never understood one another less – with all the hoaxes and conspiracy theories and so on getting passed around as if they were the Gospel itself. When that first block was set down, and the next block on top of it, and the next and the next to build this tower, people were united. In the Bible, it says 'they said, Go to, let us build us a city and a tower'. When they were united, humanity could achieve so much together. When divided, they could achieve nothing. I would so dearly love this endeavor to bring us all together. United, I believe we could achieve so much. It is too easy to let what divides us bring us all tumbling down."

Ellie thought for a moment, leaning her head to one side as she did.

"A nice thought," she said, "though I don't buy your story. No of-fense."

"None taken."

"And you still didn't answer the question."

"Ah, you noticed that. Well, that united people had travelled to a place, the place they decided to build their tower, and that place was called…"

"Shinar!" exclaimed Ellie.

The bishop raised his glass of water in salute. Ellie laughed and clinked hers in return.

"Okay, okay, but why name here after the place where the tower of Babel fell… or was never finished, or whatever?"

"We're not naming it after that," said the bishop, "rather we would name it after the last place that we were united in the goal of building a tower with its top in the heavens."

Ellie harrumphed, then smiled, then harrumphed again. "Okay," she said eventually, "I kind of like it. But no one else will, I bet you."

The bishop shrugged. "It may be an impossible dream," he said, then pointed out the window at the anchor point, "but then so was this at one time. Sometimes, all it takes for our dreams to become reality is the determination to try."

"I'm not going to fault you there, John, go right ahead," said Ellie. "So did you manage to convince any of the rest of your advisory group? And what didn't you get to see on the tour?"

"Oh, to be able to convince people, they have to be open to the idea that someone other than themselves is right, and I'm afraid that doesn't describe some of my colleagues. But no matter. I'll freely admit that one or two of them are here entirely for that PR we were talking about earlier. I'll keep prodding."

"And the tour?"

"That was frustrating. We weren't able to go into the anchor point."

"Why not?" asked Ellie as she ate a little more.

"The area was taped off and there was construction equipment in the way. Rather frustrating but…"

"Damn," said Ellie, "I was just talking to a contractor about that, he said some of his guys had left stuff behind."

"Well," said the bishop, "you'll forgive me for saying so, but one of his guys was rather a loudmouth and kept yelling at us that we couldn't come in his area, and…"

"Wait," said Ellie. "There was a guy there? The construction crews have cleared out from the anchor area…"

"Well, there he was, big mouth, hard hat and not listening to a word of sense. I believe you said earlier you know the type."

"I know the type? Wait, yeah, you said the 'build it in America' kind, right?"

"That's the sort. He even had one of those little lapel buttons saying 'America First' on it… Ellie?"

The last was a call from the bishop to Ellie as she rose quickly from the table. But by then, she was gone.

She broke into a full run after leaving the cafeteria, while she got on the radio and started yelling to Jackson to get to Mother and check the cameras around the anchor point.

By the time he got back with a reply, she had commandeered one of the electric carts and was making her way to the tower.

There was nothing to see on any of the cameras, Jackson reported. There was a "but", though. One of the cameras was out of action. "Could be nothing," he said. "Want me to get a tech over to check it?"

"No," snarled Ellie into the radio. "Give me the location. I'm on my way over there now."

"Base level, quadrant D3."

"I'll be there in three minutes. I want a security team right behind me. Get on it."

She shut off the radio and urged the cart to go faster.

When she arrived, the location was eerily quiet. Spotlights shone up towards the tower, spilling light into the sky above. High above, a small dot of light marked where the space station held geosynchronous orbit over Pacific Base. Even now, the tether was already slowly being lowered down into the atmosphere, ready for tomorrow's touchdown. Beyond the station, another tether extended the other direction, fastened at its end to an asteroid used as an anchor. Centrifugal force would keep the line taut once secured.

Unless someone stopped it, and sent the whole project crashing down.

"Not on my watch," muttered Ellie.

A portion of the tower's quadrant here was designated as a cargo loading space. Outside a half-open shutter door stood a small forklift truck with a contractor's logo emblazoned on it. A few cases of equipment stood nearby. It was the same contractor as Ellie had been talking to earlier.

She clicked the radio. "Where's that security team?"

"Five minutes out," answered Jackson.

"Five minutes? Too long. I'm going in."

"They'll be right…"

"I said I'm going in," she answered, and clicked off the radio.

Quietly, she moved up to the shutter and ducked inside.

Inside was dark, especially after the spill from the spotlights outside. She thought of her phone in her pocket for a moment and the flashlight on it, but decided against it for now. She paused while her eyes adjusted.

Much of this area was empty. It was designed to be where the freight would be stored prior to being loaded onto the elevator and sent to the stars. What that freight would be, she didn't know, but lifting it by elevator instead of by rocket gave so much more potential. The tether, however, was not yet anchored. Tomorrow had not yet arrived. Instead, this space was full of empty pallets, and unused loaders. Shiny and new, waiting for the future.

Ellie couldn't make out much at first, but as her eyes adjusted, she could see a faint glow from further into the complex. She felt her way forward to begin with, her hand tangling in some tape strung across the room. Probably warning tape saying "Under Construction", she guessed. She ducked under it and kept moving.

The glow from the light up ahead soon showed her more details, and she was able to move more surely. The light came from a powerful LED construction lamp, the kind used for working at night. Someone was using it to work, too. Hunched over a table next to the lamp was a large man in jeans and a yellow jacket. White guy. Middle aged. Scruffy in appearance, hair wild, a few days growth of beard. His hard hat was on the table. She couldn't see what he was working on, not from this distance, so she kept moving, as quietly as she could. She was still ten yards away from him when he turned from what he was working on for a moment. And saw her.

Things happened in a rush. Ellie opened her mouth to say something, but the man roared over whatever she had to say. He grabbed a wrench from his tool kit and charged.

For a second, Ellie thought about where that damn security team was, but then he was on her. He swung the wrench at her head, and she ducked to one side, pushing him past her and letting his momentum carry him away from her. It sent her off balance too, though, and she hit the floor before rolling and getting back on her feet. He had turned by then and looked at her with contempt, hefting the wrench as he started to walk steadily towards her. Two things locked in Ellie's mind. One was the little America First button she saw on the man's lapel. The other was the fact he was between her and the exit.

"Made a mistake coming in here, missy," drawled the man. "Shouldn'ta done that. Oh no. Coulda just left me to my business. But oh no. No. Not. You."

He punctuated each short sentence by thumping the wrench into the palm of his other hand.

"You haven't got any business in here," said Ellie. "You shouldn't be here at all."

"No, missy, you got it wrong," he said. "No one should be here at all. Coulda built this elevator at home but no, had to do a deal with foreigners and build a whole island to try to keep the likes of me out. It ain' right. And I ain' gonna let it happen."

Ellie stole a glance at the table where the man had been working. A bunch of tubes, with wires protruding from them. Pipe bombs. Crude. Simple. Effective if put in the right place, or at the right time. An explosion as the tether made contact – as the world united to watch a moment in history.

The man took advantage of the glance and charged again. Ellie cursed as he swung the wrench. She leaned back just beyond its swing, but that meant giving ground and the man came forward again. He was at least twice her weight, and he put every ounce of it behind the next swing. She ducked that one, the wrench slicing through the air just a couple of millimetres above her head, and she kicked at his knee in return. He yelped, but it didn't stop him, and the next swing she didn't have time to get entirely out of the way.

The wrench caught her just above the elbow and she felt and heard the crack as it reverberated around the cargo bay. It knocked her to the ground, and there he was, towering over her, wrench raised high above his head for a deadly swing. She saw it come, then rolled aside at the last, grunting in pain as she did, and using her legs to scissor around one of his and twist.

The man came crunching to the ground beside her. She was on him in an instant, knocking the wrench out of his grip with her good hand, then punching him hard in the face once, twice, three times. Blood spattered from his nose over his yellow jacket and that lapel pin. He whimpered and tried to push her off but she gave another punch with all her strength and he went quiet.

She rolled off him and shuffled back along the floor, feeling the pain flooding her arm. Somewhere behind her, she heard the noise of the shutter door being pulled fully open, and flashlights started to illuminate the area.

"Over here," she called. Then the security team was there, putting the man in zip tie restraints, while a medical crew was called to come and see to Ellie. Someone gave her a shot and everything faded.

"I thought they might postpone after last night," said the bishop as they sat in the cafeteria looking out the window.

Ellie sat across from him, her arm in a sling. She shook her head.

"Too important to stop. Everything was secure. I made sure of that."

"Even with your arm like that? Is it…"

"Fractured," she said. "They put it in a cast, but I wasn't about to let that stop me."

The bishop nodded, then glanced back at the tower. "You could have watched this from a better spot, I'm sure."

"So could you," answered Ellie. Again, the bishop nodded.

"How did the man get in?" asked the bishop.

"Got himself a job on a contractor crew and just hid when they were clearing out. They didn't bother checking properly until they noticed they had some gear missing. Gear gets noticed before people, I guess."

"And who was he?"

Ellie fought an urge to scratch the itch under her cast. It ached too. "Just some asshole," she said. "Same as it always is. They're the ones that are hardest to spot. Some guy who bought all the conspiracy theories, bought all the people telling him those in charge were trying to screw him over. Someone who hated others and found an excuse in what people said to justify it. Doesn't matter, he's gone. Just got to watch out for the next one. Because there's always a next one."

In the sky above the anchor point, a slim thread was slowly edging down, flanked by helicopters on all sides monitoring its descent.

The bishop wasn't looking at the thread, but at Ellie. "You were very brave. And if it wasn't for you, it could have been a disaster."

Ellie shook her head firmly then returned her gaze to the descending cable. Closer. Closer. Closer.

Her reply was a whisper, but a whisper with steel in it.

"Not on my watch."

Meet Leo McBride

Leo McBride is a journalist, editor and fiction writer. He has been published previously in each of the Inklings Press anthologies, along with collections from the Sci-Fi Roundtable, Rhetoric Askew, Starklight Press and elsewhere. He has also self-published his own short story collection Quartet, available on Amazon, and ghost written and edited a number of biographies. You can find more of his work on his blog, **www.alteredinstinct.com**, on Twitter as @AlteredInstinct and on **www.facebook.com/leomcbrideauthor**.

This Tale looks at how things might have turned out differently after the Challenger disaster. There was indeed a description after the disaster that NASA was "throwing junk into space" and the Marshall workshop did take place - though there the hopes of a space elevator ended. At least... for now. There are still talks, still discussions, and still technical hurdles to overcome. At least, in our world.

STEEL SERPENTS

BY RICARDO VICTORIA

Steel Serpents
By Ricardo Victoria

Why does it always have to be this early in the morning? Can't these summons be at a more appropriate time, such as after dinner? When I'm not being punished by Liber Pater?

Agricola was a thin Roman man with long beard. Serious to a fault, he was known to be a master of metalwork and applications. Agricola claimed to have been taught in dreams by Vulcan himself and his works supported that boast. He had been the one to improve the metal used in the legions' gladii, saving a disastrous campaign against rebellious Thebans. And right now he had one Hades of hangover.

Some days, Agricola just hated to be one of the lead engineers of the legions of the Great Roman-Hellenic Empire research corps. Because, more often than not, it meant he had to answer his boss's summons really early in the morning, usually after spending the previous night in a bacchanal. The inevitable hangover generally caused a migraine. His boss was not only an early rising person, but very demanding as well: Julius Alexander Augustus, the twelfth divine emperor of the Julia-Alexandrina family, descendant of the famous conqueror Alexander the Great and through him, carrier of the divine blood of the gods. Also known as the "most difficult client in the Empire". His lack of patience when progress wasn't made was well-known. He was a forward thinker always looking to improve the lives of his subjects. On the other hand, Agricola preferred dealing with him over his predecessors, whose infamous exploits — such as starting a fire across the whole capital to "make room" for a landing pad for incoming "chariots

"If only," the emperor replied. "You know I'm a realistic man. As much as the legions are ready to beat anyone, there are some problems brute force can't solve and my power can only do so much. I face the same problem now that my ancestor The Great faced through all the years of his long, long, long life."

"Apologies, my liege, but I fail to understand."

"The problem is logistics," Cornelius interjected.

"Logistics?"

"Have you heard the legend of what The Great said when he reached the edge of the world?" Theo asked.

"Yes, that he, and I apologize my liege for the word, wept for he said that there were no more lands to conquer," Agricola replied. It was a well-known story taught at the Lyceums as part of the philosophy lectures.

"No need to apologize, Agricola," the Emperor said. "He wept, but I doubt that it was because he ran out of lands to conquer. After all, he turned back, survived several attempts on his life and then moved westward to conquer the Latins, where he fell in love with his third wife, Julianna, descendant of Aeneas and my other ancestor. I believe the reason he wept is that he realized in his zeal to conquer and unify the world, he had forged an empire so vast, with distances so great that it had become unmanageable; impossible even to maintain communication, let alone rulership."

"Hence logistics," Cornelius said. "The absence of which allowed the Ptolemaic Dynasty to secede."

"Seleucus the 15th, the governor of our eastern lands, last communicated with me two months ago. Since then I haven't heard from him," the emperor held a bejeweled cup as a servant poured him Corinthian wine in a golden goblet. "But now… show him."

Cornelius grabbed a filthy bag from under the table and dropped it on the surface. With a loud thud, a head rolled out of the bag.

"Agricola, meet Seleucus the 15th," the emperor said.

Agricola stared at the head, undecided if his headache was planning to turn into a stomach ache. The head was that of a bearded man, the eyes rolled back to show the sclera.

"A messenger brought it last night with a note from Hannibal, saying I wasn't capable of keeping my friends or my lands safe. I took it personally. I mean, I didn't even like Seleucus as a friend. He was annoying as the Hades. That said, I wouldn't take off his head without a good reason," the emperor quipped.

"Nonetheless," Theo interjected. "Hannibal is right in one thing: it's becoming hard to keep in touch with far-off provinces, to keep commercial routes safe and…"

"More to the point," Cornelius added. "Mobilize the legions in an expedite manner."

"I see the problem, my liege," Agricola replied. "But I'm not sure how I can be of help. My expertise in military logistics is limited to building siege engines and bridges."

"Well, like Daedalus and Icarus, it's time to expand your wings and reach for the sky," the emperor said.

Except that Icarus died a gruesome death when he thought a pair of wings made of wax would support his weight flying that high, Agricola thought.

"Hereby," Cornelius said, reading aloud a parchment. "Agricola, son of Flavius, you are tasked by his divine grace, emperor Julius Alexander Augustus, to form a research and development team with the most emeritus inventor and designer of the Lyceum, and his team, to find faster routes across the empire to connect all the provinces, so their roads can help us move our armies with ease."

"No matter how short the road," Theo added, moving a few carved wood figurines around the map, "armies can only travel as fast as their slowest element. And that is usually the food and other… amenities, shall we say. And the sea is out of contention, as Hannibal's fleet is there and will attack soon."

Oh great, Agricola thought. As if he wasn't busy enough working on that new reinforced metal alloy structure mixed with concrete to make bridges more resistant. But he couldn't refuse or his head would join that of Seleucus the 15th. And he knew the emperor kind of liked him. Agricola sighed and extended his hand to receive the parchment.

"I humbly accept the commission, my liege. How long have we to find a solution to your trouble?"

"Before next spring, when I'm sure Hannibal will attack by land," the emperor replied as he examined a carved wooded elephant. "The Celts have been losing territory to him and soon he will be able to launch an attack from the north."

"I'm sorry, my liege, but even Hannibal knows trying to cross the

Alps with his army is a foolish task," Agricola said. "And I'm sure he won't try a frontal assault on our coasts."

"Foolishness, as that head staring at you can attest, Agricola, hasn't stopped him before," Theo countered. "It's as if Ulysses himself had returned from Tartarus and inhabited that pirate's body to haunt any Aeneas descendant once more."

"And let's not start with those snakes from Egypt and their summonses," Cornelius said, "We are close to finding ourselves fighting a war on two or three fronts. Even The Great learned it was unwise to do that – even if he learned it the hard way."

"The point is," the emperor mused. "We need to find a way to move our troops to any point of the empire and deploy them fast. Our roads are the best of the Known World, Roman engineering and Greek inventions have made sure of that. Your new concrete mix is working better than ever. But even Hermes would be hard-pressed to use them to ferry our soldiers. I don't want to lose more territory. The senators are still reminding me about the eastern provinces and that was my grandfather's fault! Stupid old men."

"I see your point, my liege," Agricola replied.

"That said, any works you do with your new associate must be kept secret," Theo said.

"May I ask why?" Agricola said. "An enterprise of this undertaking will surely raise attention. It might even be impossible to avoid unwanted attention after a while."

"At this stage, secrecy is of the upmost importance! Do I need to remind you of the assassination attempt on the emperor during the past Saturnalia?" Cornelius replied. "Or the one during the Ides of March? By Hades, Hannibal even tried the Wooden Horse. Who does he think we are? Trojans? I will take care of Hannibal's spy network. You do what our Emperor says."

"Weren't you Romans the ones claiming to be descendants of Aeneas of Troy?" Theo countered, smiling.

"That... that doesn't count," Cornelius waved his hand, dismissing the comment.

"How convenient."

"Enough, both of you!" Julius yelled, breaking his silence. "Theo, Cornelius, arrange that Agricola and his new associate receive all the resources and guards needed. Let's get this over with."

Agricola bowed once more and walked towards the exit, when he realized he had forgotten to ask the most germane of questions.

"Forgive me, my liege, but who is this new associate?" Somehow, a pitch in his stomach told Agricola that he wouldn't like the answer.

"Hero, of course" Theo replied with a smile.

"Hero!" Agricola said, wanting to roll his eyes. "The man is too gr…"

"Be careful about what you are about to say about the Greeks, Agricola, or should I remind you that I'm part Greek?" the emperor said, clearly not amused.

Although Agricola was tempted to point that the emperor's ancestry was more Macedonian than Greek, he was not that interested in parting with his head just yet, regardless of the headache he was suffering. Seleucus the 15th would remain alone for the time being.

"I was about to say that he is too absent minded. The man might be creative, but would be hard to keep him focused on the task at hand," Agricola said. *Nice save*, he thought.

The emperor squinted at him.

"That's why you will be there with him. Your Roman pragmatism will keep him focused. Now begone! I still need to think what I'm going to do with this head," the emperor waved.

Agricola left the residence wondering if there was still time to become a shepherd. Maybe dealing with wolves and robbers was a less stomach-churning job.

• • •

A month later, and the life of the shepherd still called to him. Herding sheep had to be easier than herding scientists. Agricola squared his shoulders before entering the lion's den – almost literally, the secret laboratory under the Coliseum used to be animal pens that occasionally held lions. Now it held something far more daunting. Not for the first time, he wondered why the gods had created two similar yet opposed civilizations so close to each other. Even more, he wondered how The Great's family had managed to unite them. It must have been a nightmare. One he had been living in the flesh for the better part of the month. And it was driving him crazy.

It was true Roman engineering and pragmatism had combined well

slaps. Soldiers they were not. Hero pushed Agricola away who in turn crashed into the wood table, making Hero's engine crack. From one of its chambers, a tiny Ifrit escaped, looked around, bowed before both men and ran away, leaving a trail of flames behind, soon spreading and engulfing the nearby bushes.

The cylinders gave out and the engine exploded, pushing the table away. It crashed into a wall, demolishing it. Agricola and Hero barely had a chance to dodge the flying debris from the engine. Soon, the whole stable was a mess of fire, smoke, broken stones, scared people and a dancing Ifrit looking for wine. The guards tried to put out the fire.

Both Agricola and Hero stood there admiring the chaos, as Amphitrite led Cornelius to them.

"Ahem," Cornelius said. "While I'm glad you are having fun at the expense of the emperor's coffers, I have an urgent message from him: You better show some results in the next fortnight."

"Why the hurry?" Hero asked. "Science can't be rushed."

Agricola could swear that if looks could kill, Cornelius' stare at Hero would have turned his colleague into a bloody salad.

"What my colleague is trying to say, in that typical manner of his people, is that we had till next spring. We have been working for only a couple of weeks. What changed?" Agricola asked.

"Hannibal decided to strike at several Celt towns in what is a clear declaration of war. If the Celts fall to him, or worse, decide being allied to the Hellenics wasn't worth the hassle, his rival would have the gates to the north open for his armies. That, coupled with the disloyal Mamertine mercenaries from Messene playing both us and the Carthaginians. Hannibal is flexing his muscles."

"That's bad," Amphitrite whispered.

"Indeed, Amphitrite," Cornelius said. "How do you manage to do any work with these two around? You are too good to be a slave."

"I find the way, my lord," she replied.

"Anyways, our emperor is considering taking a Celt queen as bride to bring them into the fold, but diplomacy takes time we don't have. So you better hurry. You don't want to pass into history as the men that failed their emperor and brought down the dynasty created by The Great."

"We will try our best," Agricola replied.

"You better," Cornelius said. "Remember poor Seleucus the 15th. And the emperor does like you."

. . .

After Cornelius left, and he and Hero were left alone in the stable, Agricola put his elbows on the remains of the table and held his head. He stared blankly at what was left of Hero's engine; his eyes swelling with contained tears. He muffled his cries by biting his lower lip. Their suppressed echoes thickened his throat.

Hero brought him a parchment to wipe his tears.

Agricola stared at the offering, as that was absolutely not a use for parchment. Especially not one depicting a map of the Empire and its roads. They were expensive to come by. Agricola's desperation was turning into irritation, and it showed as his face turned red.

"I've never seen you like this, Agricola," Hero offered. "I apologize for being so difficult to work with. I... I... just can't make my mind to stop and work the kinks of my ideas. I'm not like you. I'm sure that by now you have worked out all the kinks of your Steel Carriage.

"It's not your fault alone. And I haven't thought of the carriage in years. It is my greatest shame," Agricola said as he stared at the parchment and the roads depicted on it. He remembered The Table at the emperor's residence and an inkling of an idea came to him. "Amphitrite, bring us a candle!"

Amphitrite ran with a candle, as Agricola extended the parchment on what was left of the table. He, Hero, Amphitrite and even the tiny Ifrit looked at it.

"Are you seeing what I'm seeing?"

"A parchment smeared in your snot?" Hero replied unsure.

"A map of the Great Empire," Amphitrite said. "With the most used roads in red."

"Exactly!" Agricola replied. "Roads!"

"I don't think that's the solution the emperor is looking for," Hero said. "He already has them."

"Yes, the legwork has been already done," Agricola said, as his mind raced through the possibilities, deep in thought.

"What's wrong with him?" Amphitrite asked Hero.

"I think he is having a Eureka moment, as we say in my homeland,"

Hero replied with a smile.

Where other men would only see disparate ideas, separate people, Agricola was seeing a connection between dots, a system. Hero looked at him and then to the remains of his engines. Both men's gaze met as the same idea dawned on both of them.

Design meets engineering. Both sides of the same coin, landing on the edge. The connection of ideas in concerted chaos to create a solution to a need.

"Are you thinking what I'm thinking?" Agricola said.

"That the Emperor will be mad at us for damaging the Colosseum a third time this month? He was furious that we blasted a whole section last time. He is not fond of asymmetry." Hero replied.

"Yes... No! Not that," Agricola said. "What we have here: roads. Roads reinforced with my steel, the same steel I used in that carriage. The one that can withstand the pressure from..."

"My steam engine!" Hero started to dance. "No more explosions!"

"No more dead horses!" Agricola exclaimed, joining the dance

"Well," Hero interjected. "Only if we found a way to maintain the direction of the carriage regardless of the speed.

"Carriages, plural. I'm thinking of a chain of them, like..."

"Steel Serpents!" Hero yelled, pumping his fist into the air.

Before them, in their minds, steel serpents raced through those red lines, connecting all the cities and regions of The Great Empire. Soon they grew to cover all the territory, carrying troops, uniting cultures, trading goods. The Emperor would be pleased. And if he allowed for the use of the priest of Chronos – which was always risky since it involved affecting the flow of time - the whole network project could be concluded in a timely manner.

"Exactly," Agricola replied regaining his composure.

"And we will still need to think of a way to stop it once it reaches its destination."

"I'm thinking ceramic disk brakes and they might be able to withstand the heat." Agricola mused as he stared into the void. "We need to create a prototype!"

"And convince the Ifrit to help us!"

"You are the man for the job!"

"We are, partner!" Hero said as he embraced Agricola.

Amphitrite looked at the tiny Ifrit standing next to her.

"I think you have a new job, little spirit."

• • •

Hannibal sat atop Asterah, his eldest elephant, looking at the valley below through a tube whose ends held magnifying glasses. The landscape crossed by strange metallic lines. The unsuspecting towns ready to be taken and not a single legion in sight. The Egyptians had held their side of the bargain by keeping Julius Alexander Augustus and most part of the legions busy at the Dardanelles. He, after much travail had managed to cross the Alps with his army. It had only been doable after imposing his will upon his army and the world itself. The Old Gods may be gone, but they had left a proper heir behind. Or so he thought about himself.

Of course by sea would have been easier, but those damned Hellenic had stationed all their fleet along the coast. They even called in favors from Triton's brood. Yet, they wouldn't expect this. And even if they did...

"What in the name of Ba'al is that?" Hannibal exclaimed, passing the tube to one of his generals. Something in the distance moved at incredible speed over those metal lines. A column of white clouds emerged from a cylinder on top of the head. A screech echoed through the air, scaring most of the animals. His spy network had been quiet for the past months, which unto itself clued him in that his bitter rival was planning something, given how many of his spies became suddenly indisposed to keep living. The few whispers that had reached him, told tales about the Roman-Hellenic slaves and engineers working on some kind of metal roads, but no one had clear what they were for... until now. It had to be seen to be believed.

"It looks like a giant metal serpent my liege. And troops are coming from its innards. It's Julius Alexander Augustus! But he was seen at the Dardanelles last month. There is no way he can be here on such short notice. Unless his gods have granted him a boon!"

"Yes, they have," Hannibal smiled. He believed in gods, like his forefathers. But he put more stock in human audacity than in divine solutions. He had to give it to the Roman-Hellenic. They were resourceful. They had always been. And these "steel serpents" of theirs confirmed the whispers from his spy network. Yet Hannibal wanted to witness it.

"Well played Julius Alexander Augustus, well played," Hannibal whispered.

He felt invigorated. Adrenaline ran through his veins and a smile appeared on his face, startling his advisors. His muscles bulged with energy; tiny flames burst from his fingertips: he finally had a rival to match wits. Hannibal would gladly fight against these steel serpents and their divinely empowered liege.

Meet Ricardo Victoria

Ricardo Victoria is a Mexican writer with a Ph.D. in Design — with emphasis in sustainability — from Loughborough University, and a love of fiction, board games, comic books, and action figures. He lives in Toluca, Mexico with his wife and pets, working works as a full-time lecturer and researcher at the local university. He writes mainly science fantasy.

His first novel, Tempest Blades: The Withered King, was released in August 2019 by Shadow Dragon Press, an imprint of Artemesia Publishing. The sequel, Tempest Blades: Cursed Titans, published in July 2021. He has a number of stories published by Inklings Press, and other indie outlets.

His short story Twilight of the Mesozoic Moon, jointly written with Brent A. Harris, was nominated for a Sidewise Award for short form alternative history.

You can find out more at his website, http://ricardovictoriau.com, or follow him on Twitter, @Winged_Leo.

GOING OVER THE TOP

THE TOP

BY JEFF PROVINE

Going Over The Top
By Jeff Provine

"Two."

"Eight."

"Jack."

"Ace."

"Seven."

"Seven! War!"

The marines laid out their cards onto the makeshift table of an overturned crate lid. Before they could flip to reveal their next ranks, a rumble of manmade thunder shook the ground. The loose cards scattered out of place.

"Incoming!" The shout came too late.

The marines held still, waiting for the next one. It didn't come. There was only the lingering smell of overturned earth, acrid gunpowder smoke, and the old-leather stench of the men in the trench.

Finally, they breathed.

Thompson, the taller of the two, who had first laid the seven, straightened his helmet. His arms were lanky, and his body thin, like he had been stretched out on the rack in Brooklyn before they stuffed him in a uniform and shipped him across the Atlantic. "That was a close one."

"Them Huns're bringing more artillery up," Michaels, who had matched the seven, muttered. Shorter than Thompson, his body was thick, the mark of a man well fed and thoroughly worked his whole life on the farm in the heartland. He turned his head to peek out of the alcove dug into the trench wall, as if the gray-brown sky would give him a hint at what was over the top. "Must be lining up their sights. Think they're getting ready for a counterattack?"

"Is it really a counterattack if we stopped their advance back on the third? Really, if we went out, that would make a counterattack. This would just be another advance for them."

Michaels pulled his head back into the alcove. "What're you tryin'? To become general or something?"

"I don't see why I couldn't be a general."

"We already have generals, all the way up to Black Jack Pershing." Michaels took a moment to snort. "And good luck making officer anyhow."

"Depending on how long they're going to let this war run, I might work my way up to general anyways."

"You got a long way to go from enlisted, friend."

"All it takes is time, and time I have," Thompson told him. He leaned back and unbuttoned his breast pocket, showing the steel flask inside. "I'm packing my own luxovy. So long as I keep my helmet on and my head down, I'm in for the long haul."

Michaels grinned. "Well, that must've cost you."

"My brother-in-law bought it for me. He said it wasn't a 'going away' present so much as a 'come back safe' present."

Michaels's grin turned to a laugh. "Mighty fine family to have, professor. I'll let Uncle Sam foot the bill for my luxovy if I get hit."

Now Thompson laughed, not with the cheer from the belly as Michaels had, but a throaty snort. "Sure, ideally, but I like having a bit of self-help instead of relying on government work. Besides, you know why they say this whole war started, don't you?"

"That fella from Austria got shot, wasn't it?"

"Yeah, at the beginning. That was the spark to set off the powder keg of Europe." Thompson leaned forward over the crate-table. It wobbled under his elbow. "Some people say it's all a conspiracy."

"Do they now?"

"Think about it: we have, what, thirteen billion people on the planet? Things are getting overcrowded!"

"Oh, sure, in most places. Back home in Bigsby, it's still pretty quiet."

"Yeah. And how many people live out there?"

"A few hundred, I guess."

"And mostly farmers?"

"Sure! Somebody's got to feed them ten-odd billion people."

"Thirteen. So why aren't you back there doing farming, then?"

Michaels shrugged and sniffed. He wiped some dirt from his face with his dirty hand. "Well, the Huns sent out that telegram to Mexico trying to get them to pick a fight with us, and I'm one to agree with Mr. Wilson that we can't abide that."

"Of course. But you told me you signed up *after* you were already living in St. Louis doing that factory work. How long has it been since you've been in Bigsby?"

"I went back last Christmas."

"But when did you move away?"

"Probably three or four years ago... what was it, 1914? Yeah, that'd be four years."

"Why'd you leave?"

"Well, y'know, it was getting pretty crowded on the farm."

Thompson clapped his hands and then held them out, palms up, like a stage magician inviting Michaels to awaken from a trance.

Michaels laughed and shook his head. "Oh, I see what you did there! That wasn't what I meant. It's not overpopulated."

"Couldn't you say it is, though? Family farm, right? How many people did you have living there together?"

"Most of the whole family, about thirty or so from five generations."

"Enough so that all the work that needs doing can be done."

"Well, sure! My great-great-grandpappy cleared the trees for the first field. He had some fine stories about the old days, working with horses instead of tractors."

"And what happened once tractors came in?"

"There were more hands than work. Quite a few of us headed into St. Louis looking for something to do."

"Precisely. We've had an agricultural revolution. One man can produce far more food than he needs. People are living so long, aging down with a dose of luxovy once they get gray, and then they keeping on having children. The children do the same, and so we have more and more people. What are we going to do with all these people?"

Michaels shrugged. "There's always more work to do someplace. Building roads, dams, that kind of thing. Besides, they're always inventing new things to make in factories. That's what I did: made windows for houses."

"Houses for people moving in off the farm."

"Yep! St. Louis's growing like gangbusters. They're opening new neighborhoods all the time. They say we'll have over three mill—"

A soft whistle drowned out Michaels, ringing louder by the second. Without a word, both marines shrank to the bottom of the trench. The whistle turned to a scream louder and louder until it gave way to a roaring boom. Dirt fell from the rough edges of the earthen wall.

They held still for a moment, listening to the shouts from the others along the trench. No one was shrieking in pain.

Michaels picked himself up first. "Still falling short."

He helped Thompson up. The two men brushed the loose dirt off their long coats. They sat back at the makeshift table. The lid had fallen, and their cards lay scattered across the loosely nailed bits of wood.

Both marines leaned down to collect the cards.

"Just picking up where we left off," Thompson mumbled. "How true it is."

Michaels just grunted and sighed.

"That's what people are saying about this war. There hadn't been a good, long war in mainland Europe since Napoleon's legions were finally stopped. Instead, the Europeans used all that manpower to conquer everybody else. Now that they've run out of other places to take, they're turning on each other to keep the ranks thin."

Michaels sat up. "What on earth are you going on about?"

"The war conspiracy," Thompson said, putting the cards he gathered in numerical order as he found them. "There are farms filled out just about everywhere on the planet we could put a farm, so people go to the cities. What happens when we run out of space in the cities?"

"What college'd you go to, again, professor?"

"New York City Public Library," Thompson said. "Can't afford the real thing, not yet. But I'm helping my brother buy real estate up the river, and that's going to give us a foothold. Real estate: that's the money with earth filling up."

"I reckon so. I wouldn't mind owning a little piece of property myself."

"So you know it! But it isn't easy to get your own piece with folks not dying."

"People die."

"I know, of course, violent deaths or starvation, all that, but not like they should. That luxovy changed things. Humans are piling up, growing old, taking a sip, and going back to the peak of life. And now that China and Africa are all carved into colonies, Europe's run out of places to stick the overflow. That's why we're having ourselves a war."

"I don't know that's how this all happened."

"Isn't it? Look at the people in charge: Billy the Third in Britain's been ruling for two hundred years. Freddy's been running Germany for almost as long, even if he got chased out for a few years by Napoleon. And France, the only republic around, is caught in the middle. Now somehow America's mixed up in it, oddly right about the same time we ran out of territories to become states. We're just the rabble to them. Everybody's nervous there'll be another round of guillotines come chopping, like they did to King Louie."

Michaels leaned over Thompson and whispered, "I better not be hearing any of that red talk. You saw what that did to the Russian folks. Turned their whole country on its head!"

Thompson retreated, holding up his hands. "Right, right. Of course! It's just a story they tell. But then…"

"What?"

"Well, if it's true, I want to be on the right side of that decision-making. That's why I want real estate, and the military's the only one really hiring."

Michaels squinted at him. "So you're not a red, you're a… What's the word for you?"

"Red-blooded American," Thompson said with a smirk. "Pulling myself up by whatever bootstraps I can find."

"Opportunist," Michaels added, stressing the many syllables to hiss and then end with a spit.

Whistling rang in the air again. They both looked up. It didn't grow any louder. When the thunder finally rang from the shells hitting, it was far away.

A deep voice roared over the thuds. "Thompson! Michaels!"

The marines jumped to their feet and saluted even before their sergeant came up, walking sideways through the narrow trench.

"Yes, sir!" both rang.

The sergeant turned. His face was hard, serious, chin jutted out even with the end of his nose. His uniform read "Daly." The hair that peeked under his helmet was the color of steel. "I have a job for you boys." He returned their salute and then jerked his thumb to the man behind him. "Go with Corporal Henry here to get a medical restock crate."

Henry stood behind the sergeant, his ruddy uniform almost clean but for the mud stains up to the knees. Red crosses stood out in bright white patches. His nose was long, his brow tall, his chin prominent, and his eyes a deep blue that seemed they had seen endless years, yet he looked no older than a man in his forties.

"Sir, anybody injured?" Michaels asked.

Daly shook his head. "No, just a restock."

Thompson gasped. He slapped his hand over his mouth and mumbled through the fingers, "T-that means we're going over the top."

Daly stopped shaking his head and glared. "We've received no orders on that, only to re-stock." His voice turned to a shout. "And what are you still doing here?"

Without another word, Daly marched past them, crowding them in the narrow trench. Without another word, the marines turned to Corporal Henry standing in his medic's uniform, bold red crosses like medals on his arm and helmet. They shouldered their rifles and saluted.

Thompson's eyes were wide.

Michaels elbowed him. "After you, sir. We're with you."

"Right ho," Henry agreed, saluting back. He turned and led them deep into the network of open ditches that crisscrossed what had once been lush French fields. Now it was something else entirely. Beyond the lip of the trench, this was No Man's Land: too wet to be a desert, too scorched to be a bog. It was an ocean of mud that sucked at your boots as you tried to walk over it, as if it were made of a million tiny mouths each trying to draw you in. The marines were familiar with every stone and burned-out tree now from their turns on watch. They shot at anything that moved out there, killing even the bloated rats and the spies that tried to lurk through the muck.

"I'm going to ask him," Thompson whispered.

Michaels winced. "Leave it."

Thompson smiled.

"Corporal Henry, sir?" Thompson called.

Michaels grunted. He tried to fall back a step, but Thompson caught him by the shoulder.

"What is it, private?" Henry called back without losing pace.

"Well, a few of us were talking the other day, around the mess, you know, and I heard a rumor."

Henry made a sound something between a chuckle and a sigh. "I shall save us further discomfort! Yes, I am Patrick Henry, *the* and *that* Patrick Henry."

"Ah, I knew it!" Thompson clapped his hand on Michaels's arm. "I recognized you from your portrait in the history book! I mean, the hair is different. No curlers around your ears, but, you know, it's you."

"We kept much more prodigious locks about ourselves then, didn't we?" Henry shrugged. They walked on a few more thudding steps before he asked. "Are you going to ask me to say the line? 'Give me liberty' and what?"

Thompson opened his mouth with a grin, but Michaels glared at him. The thin man slapped his lips together, pursed them, and then opened again. "Oh, nah, I think we've all heard it. I mean, do it if you want, but what really gets me curious is… what are you doing out on the front of all places?"

"He's tryin' to serve his country!" Michaels cried.

Thompson bit his tongue and fell back behind Michaels.

Michaels grunted at him and scowled. "Sir, it's an honor to fight alongside you. I've long admired your service."

"And I yours. We must all do our parts."

They stepped around a group of soldiers huddled over a game of checkers. The men were waiting in silence, several with their lips tucked into their mouths to keep from slipping. One marine had his hand over the board, hovering as he chose while his opponent stared. He picked up a piece, and half the group growled with outrage.

"Something to pass the time, I suppose," Henry commented.

"Is it much different?" Thompson asked.

Henry peeked back over his shoulder. His 180-year-old eyes were sharp blue. "What do you mean?"

"Fighting here," Thompson said. "Much different than the Revolution? I mean, we were fighting the English back then, I guess, instead of being allies."

Henry fully laughed now, tossing his head back. "Oh, we fought

Germans, then, as well! The Hessians, I mean. Curious how things repeat themselves. Alas, I was not a soldier myself like Washington or Harry Lee. No, I was serving a different course far behind the desk in those days."

The marines behind him glanced at one another. Thompson scratched his head under his helmet.

Michaels mumbled, "But you fought for liberty, didn't you?"

"Sir, I argued for it. That's the fighting lawyers know. Although I may have been overdramatic in my youth asking for death. Things change."

"Change?" Michaels blurted. "W-what do you mean 'change?'"

Henry shrugged. "Things do change."

"But liberty is liberty," Michaels protested. "You meant that, didn't you?"

Henry stopped and turned about face. He raised a fist. His blue eyes looked like jets of flame. "I meant my shout for freedom with every ounce of my soul!" His mouth hung open a moment, and his eyes moved, staring long past them. Then Henry closed his mouth and turned back to walking.

It was several yards of sloshing steps before Henry spoke again. "I should have realized my hypocrisy at defying a king yet holding slaves myself. It took another war for me to learn that."

The marines didn't say anything. Thompson nodded, and Michaels shook his head, but neither said anything.

"I did fight in that one," Henry went on. "My fortunes had not grown as I would have liked after my service as governor and representative. Arguing for manumission proved unpopular in Virginia. Secession was more in agreement, so I ultimately placed my voice behind that. Freedom. Isn't that what we yearned for with the Revolution? But, then, popularity is a tricky friend, as we know. It deserts you as quickly as your fortunes do. My arguments were not met with kind ears by the Reconstruction bureaus. My land-holdings were gone, ruined as they were anyway. I spent much of the last I had on enough luxovy to start over."

"I don't know half of what he's talking about," Michaels whispered.

Thompson glared at him. "He is pouring out his heart."

"Shouldn't've gotten him started." Michaels snorted. "Those old-timers just love getting into their rants."

"I went west, as we did in those days," Corporal Henry continued. "There was always work in the law to be found somewhere. And there was novelty from my name to stir up some business. Even so, novelty rarely lasted, and I often thought best to move on to another frontier."

Henry went on until they at last climbed out of the trench network to the flatlands far enough back that the German artillery couldn't hit them. Plants grew here, although their patches were framed by broad tracks of mud where trucks went by, their engines roaring and brakes squealing. Tents and makeshift huts were neatly lined up, making a village too square to be real. Between them, the world swarmed with soldiers in drab-colored uniforms that matched the drab gray of the smoky sky. Men called and shouted, not at all like the quiet of the trenches between the test-shots of the enemy.

Their course took them to the munitions quartermaster, a plump man with red hair. He sat behind a desk placed in an open-air office outside a broad supply tent. Piles of papers were weighted down by old artillery shells embossed with screwdrivers into the shapes of stars and eagles. Trench-art, they called it.

Henry fished a folded paper out of his pocket. "Medical resupply request from the 3rd Battalion 6th Marines."

"Ho boy!" The quartermaster groaned. He struggled off his chair and slinked into the tent behind him.

None of the men spoke while they waited. Thompson and Michaels exchanged a look but couldn't find any meaning between them.

With a groan as he bent past the tent flap, the quartermaster returned with a loose-lidded wooden crate. The side was branded with, "Luxovy - Elixir of Life! From Johnson & Johnson."

He set it on the desk. "There it is! That's all I have for you."

Thompson opened his mouth to ask something, but Michaels stepped on his foot.

Henry lifted the lid. "Why, this is half-emptied already!"

The other marines leaned forward. The feathery bits of packing straw had been pulled back. There were a dozen brown-glass bottles with the silvery liquid inside, but stamped spaces in the straw showed where there should have been a dozen more.

"That's all I have!" the quartermaster said, throwing up his hands. "Had to fish out of it already for someone else. The trucks haven't made their deliveries yet. Should be more tomorrow morning."

"Yeah, right," Thompson said sing-song.

"Enough! We shall make do," Henry said. "Privates, if you will."

Thompson and Michaels hefted the crate between them and followed Henry back into the trenches. They slipped on the muddy wooden planks laid down to make the ramp. The marines held the crate tightly with both hands, taking on weight as the other faltered, keeping the crate balanced. When they were finally down inside the earthen walls, they both took deep breaths.

"Did you hear, a few months back?" Thompson mumbled when he could. "The French just about mutinied when their commanders ordered them over the top even though they'd run out of luxovy." He hummed. "Strange to think the French running out, what with old Nicky Flamel inventing the stuff. *Elixir de vie*, they called it then."

"We have some," Michaels assured him, lifting his end of the crate an inch. "Besides, you packed your own, prof."

"For me. But what are we going to say to everybody else?"

"Nothing to say. We're United States Marines. We don't have to worry about patching ourselves up. It's the Huns that'll need to worry!"

"Sometimes I wonder," Henry called back.

The marines bit their lips, wondering how much he'd heard.

Yet Henry went on, "if it might be better to face our foes without luxovy as a crutch. Would we be so willing to begin advances..." He swallowed under his long chin and started again as if it were a different conversation. "We do our duty as we receive it. You've heard about what the Black companies have accomplished despite being wildly undersupplied. Harlem hellfighters, the papers call them."

"But can you blame those French boys for cracking?" Thompson said anyway. "How many times since '14 have they been sent over the top, mowed down and raked up by medics who dump enough luxovy down their throats to heal them up, all so they can go back over the top and do it all again?"

"And you said we were havin' us a war to thin us out," Michaels said with a laugh.

Thompson hummed. "Right, right, of course it doesn't make any sense if they keep turning us over with luxovy."

"Maybe it ain't so bad," Michaels said. "Sir, you've had luxovy. What was it like?"

The corporal looked back over his shoulder to smile. There was a glimmer in his eye before it went away. "Remember those summers as a youth, running fast through the sunlight? There you have it. I had my last draught in 1900. My hands and eyesight were beginning to go, you see, but then they came back, strong as ever!"

Michaels smiled at Thompson.

Thompson hummed again. "I saw a truckload of French soldiers as we were coming in, our company relieving theirs. The whole gang of them had the thousand-yard stare, everybody twitching with shellshock."

"We knew this as 'the soldier's heart' in the War Between the States," Henry called from in front of them. "That was when they quite stepped up mass-production of luxovy."

Michaels didn't say anything. His face faltered.

Thompson sighed.

They marched on, coming to the crowd around the checkerboard. The players had changed, but the game went on. Everyone looked up, eyed the crate, and then pressed themselves into alcoves to let them pass.

The air began whistling again, louder and louder. Then there was a different sound, a huff of air as wind pressed heavy on them. This shell wasn't going to pass overhead or go short.

Thompson dropped his end of the crate, but Michaels held onto his, peering up at the sky. The marine from Brooklyn tackled him, throwing them all to the muddy floor of the trench.

"Protect our lux—" was all Henry could cry before the shell hit.

The world became a barrage on all the senses. The blast was so loud none of them could understand hearing it. Heat and pressure pushed on them. There was a blinding flash of light and then brutal darkness as the trench wall collapsed. Wet dirt flooded the air, making anyone who could breathe gag.

There was a moment of silence, and then they all began coughing and shouting.

Thompson worked his way to his feet first, wobbling with his hands on his knees. He imagined it was night now, somehow. His ears rang, but he could make out concerned cries from other soldiers. They sounded so distant. When he was able to see again, he found them right beside him.

Two of the marines who had been playing checkers helped Michaels up. Thompson slapped his trench coat, knocking off mud as well as checking for shrapnel. The Missourian coughed and wheezed and finally fought them all off. "I'm fine! I'm fine!"

It was a circus of everyone moving at once, crawling over each other, except for Patrick Henry.

The patriot lay on his side with his brown uniform turned to burgundy with blood. His face was white, and his mouth hung open. Still his brilliant red crosses showed on his sleeves.

"Did it get him?" Michaels cried.

Thompson bent over him, placing his ear next to the injured man's mouth.

Rasping breaths slipped out over pale lips.

"He's alive, but he's not by much!" Thompson called. "Help me with him!"

The marines rolled the body onto its back. Beneath Henry was the overturned crate, its white wooden sides cracked at all angles. The bottles inside had shattered, spilling the sliver elixir onto the packing straw, which had turned green and supple, giving the smell of fresh cut hay alongside warm cedar.

"It's gone," Michaels growled. "He tried to protect it."

The other marines began shouting again. "Gone?"

"What are we going to do?"

"He's dead, bud. He's a goner."

Thompson bit hard on his lip, feeling the pain as something he could control. His stomach lurched. He swallowed and then dug into his pocket for the steel flask.

"Out of the way!" Thompson called, elbowing his way to Henry as he unscrewed the lid. He took Henry's head in one hand and poured out the shiny, smooth luxovy into his mouth.

"That's yours!" Michaels cried.

"I know," Thompson said, "and I get to do with it what I want." He kept on pouring, draining the whole dose. It smelled sweet, and it made Thompson's nose itch.

Henry swallowed, belched, and then swallowed again. The color came back into his face so quickly it seemed like a shadow passing over him. The thin wrinkles that had formed around his eyes pulled tight as his skin grew plump. His hair, a light brown on the edge of turning gray, became dark again as if brushed with paint. The blood-stained uniform shifted, his waist shrinking and his shoulders broadening. The years fell away until he looked twenty-five and strong.

Henry heaved so violently it made him sit up when he coughed. He spat dirt and blood.

The marines all retreated, stared, and then rushed back to his side. Several patted him on the back. Others worked on straightening his legs for him.

"What?" was all Henry could say at first.

Then his blue eyes went wide. He patted himself over the chest where the blood stain was thickest. Long, trembling fingers undid the buttons, revealing a layer of scabs sloughing off fresh skin below.

"You were hit," Michaels told him.

"I recall," Henry replied. Then he turned to the ruined crate. "The luxovy! It's gone?"

"Huns got a lucky shot," Michaels said.

"But then," Henry mumbled, touching himself over, "how am I not...? One didn't break?"

Thompson was at the edge of the ring of marines. He had his steel flask in his hand, lolling it left and right as he watched it, sighing. Finally he tipped up the flask and shook free two last drops into his own mouth. Then he tucked it back into his pocket. "Looks like we're all out here, too."

"I have lived three lifetimes already!" Henry cried. He crawled to Thompson's side, who now looked older than he did. "Why would you do this for me? Don't think that because I gave some speech all those years ago that I'm worth more than you!"

Thompson shook his head. "Those past lives don't matter. What matters is you're one of us now, a soldier halfway across the world. And how could I live with myself if I held onto some luxovy while someone died at my feet?"

Michaels clapped both soldiers on the shoulder. "Some things'll never change. We help them folks who need it."

"I could not have spoken any better," Henry said, then his speech turned to a coughing fit. When he cleared his lungs of blood clots leftover from the healing frenzy, he finished, "words myself."

The marines crowding around them parted. Louder shouts were coming through now in Sgt. Daly's deep voice. He climbed through the brown-coated marines like rubble. "Who's hurt?"

"No one now," Michaels told him.

Thompson pointed at the broken crate. "But we lost our luxovy supply."

Daly took three slow steps to the pile of glass, wood, and straw, some yellow, some green.

"Damn sorry to see that," Daly said with a growl. He squeezed his hand into a fist. "Orders just came in. We're going over to run those Germans out of the woods to the north. Spread the word, affix bayonets, and be ready to move in three minutes!"

The marines stared at him. They were panting, coughing against the putrid air. Then they all turned away, most looking down at the shattered bottles.

"Sir, the luxovy," Thompson mumbled.

A wave of grumbles broke over the soldiers.

Daly drew his gun and pointed toward the far lip of the trench. "For Christ's sake, men, come on! Do you want to live forever?"

Then he pointed his other hand down at Patrick Henry, fallen from where he had stood in oratory before the Virginia legislature to lying in his own blood on the muddy floor of a trench somewhere near the Belleau Woods. The marines looked down at him. He looked at his hands, young again, and touched his face.

Michaels grabbed his rifle and presented. "Hoorah!"

Thompson smiled and took his own rifle up. "Hoorah!"

Now a new wave rolled over the marines as they gave the cry that cannot be translated into any language. Weapons in hand, they charged toward destiny.

Meet Jeff Provine

Jeff Provine is a Professor of English in Oklahoma, USA, tackling topics such as Charles Chaplin, mythology and the history of comic books. He collects local folklore and has created three walking tours of ghost stories in the Oklahoma City metro. His fictional works include YA adventure Dawn on the Infinity, steampunk Celestial Voyages, and alternate history Hellfire.

Check him out on Twitter @JeffProvine, follow his updates at **http://www.facebook.com/AuthorJeffProvine**, and read some of his twists on history at **http://thisdayinalternatehistory.blogspot.com**.

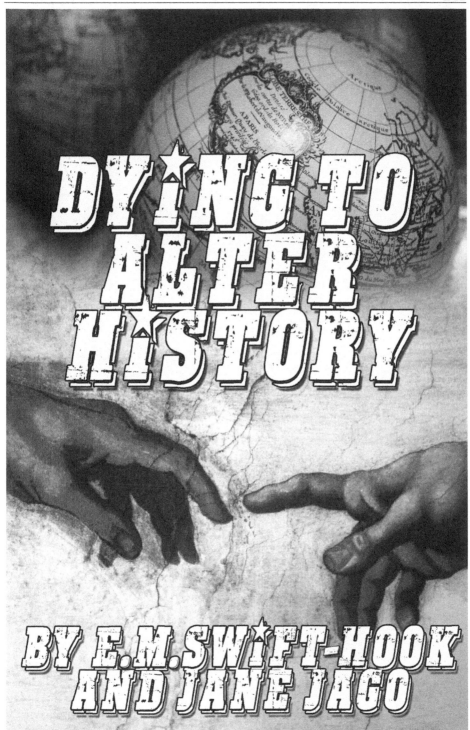

DYING TO ALTER HISTORY

BY E.M. SWIFT-HOOK AND JANE JAGO

Dying to Alter History
By E.M.Swift-Hook
and Jane Jago

I

"Blueprints for a plough?" Bryn Cartival, decanus to Dai Llewellyn, vigiles investigator, sounded incredulous. "Let me get this straight, Bard, you're saying we are being assigned to find some old sketches of a horse-drawn plough?"

Dai nodded.

"Ox-drawn. Except you're missing the point. These are not designs of any old plough - these were the original designs of Lugh Tasgo."

There was a silence and Dai realized the puzzled look on Bryn's face was not lifting.

"Who's he when he's at home?" Bryn sounded as if he thought Dai was playing some joke on him. Dai gaped and shook his head. "Didn't you learn anything when you were at school?"

Bryn shrugged. "Enough to get by. I was the kid sitting at the back of the room playing games on me wristphone or listening to music on my IXI."

"They had wristphones when you were at school?"

That produced an odd snort from the decanus whose greying hair betrayed his middle-age in a way his tough body still did not. "So who was he? Someone famous? Sounds British..."

Dai shook his head in mock despair. "He was British. He was an agricultural engineer back in the time of the Divine Diocletian. He invented the heavy wheeled plaumoratum and was hailed as a hero. He saved the Empire."

Bryn laughed. "Now I know you're joshing me. How could a ploughmaker save the Empire? Besides, Romans don't make farmers into heroes. Not even clever farmers. And never if he were a Briton."

"The Divine Diocletian had a passion for gardening. Even a spado like you must have learned that. And Tasgo's plough is what saved the Empire. Because of it, places like Britannia and Gallia could grow enough to feed the people living in our towns and cities. Without it, they would have starved and civilization broken down, taking the Empire with it over a thousand years ago."

Miming a yawn, Bryn cut to the chase. "So, ancient history aside, who would want the designs of his plough nowadays? We have hydroponics and automated combine harvesters today. So not like it's exactly cutting-edge technology."

"No. But they are unique historical documents. Extremely valuable historical documents. In fact, priceless historical documents. They were on loan from a private collection somewhere to the Bibliotheca Britannica. Theft was reported by the courier about twenty minutes before she died from the stab wounds she received in the robbery. No info on her attacker — not even gender as he or she was wearing an obscuring helmet and a hoverbike outfit."

"We're investigating a murder then?"

"You'd think." Dai made no attempt to keep the wry note from his voice. "But we got the budget for this from Antiquities. Our masters value the stolen document, 'an artefact of Roman significance', more than the life of the courier — but then she was only a Briton."

His mood was not improved when they went to interview the owner of the stolen document, a Roman Citizen and an official who also owned the chump half of Valentia in northern Britain. Claudius Albus Balbus. Balbus refused a polite invitation to come to the vigiles headquarters, so they tracked him down to his plush hotel.

It was a shimmering construction built beside the skyliner ascent, convenient to transport access for visiting Romans. Dai noted the stylized eagle, wings spread, hovering over the door 'SPQR' clutched in its ceramic talons. He was not surprised this building was sub aquila — Roman only. He was also not surprised when he and Bryn had to show their ID before being allowed past by the discreet security guard in the porticus. He was surprised, however, when Bryn nudged him in the ribs and nodded at the retreating back of a man who had just walked out of the building.

"Atty Brickenden. Thug for hire. How could scum like him even get let into this place?"

"Maybe he was providing drugs for one of the visitors." Dai suggested.

"True. Or fixing them up with a girl."

Asking after Balbus, once inside, Dai was told the magistratus could be found in the atrium. Dai led the way until he was brought to a halt at the door of the open courtyard. An elegant woman, wearing a stylish stola, daringly cut and in this season's colours, stood occupying the entrance.

"Oh, there you are. At last." She lifted a languid hand imperiously and pointed to her feet. "Crinitia needs to visit the little girl's room."

Dani's gaze followed her pointing finger down to what appeared to be a perfect sphere of fluff, from which emerged a leash that was looped over her arm. By the time he had registered that 'Crinitia' had to be some variety of canine, the woman was pressing the end of the lead into his hand and, as he opened his mouth to explain, she walked away.

Behind him, Bryn was suffering an inexplicable fit of coughing and wore an unrepentant grin when Dai spun round.

"I don't know how you do it. Your Celtic charm wins the ladies every time, Bard."

Dai returned the grin, but with an edge of irritation behind it. He held out the lead.

"Looks like you get to take Fluffy here for a *mingo* and *merda*, Decanus Cartivel."

Bryn's smile faded suddenly. "You don't seriously mean— "

"Oh but I do."

The grin Dai wore as he walked into the atrium was much more genuine and it was still there as he approached the corpulent figure of Balbus, spreadeagled over a lounger, beside two other far less portly, middle-aged Romans. They were unmistakably patrician breed, each with an over-exaggerated aquiline nose, the high bridges jutting out from their faces almost laterally, before plunging in a vertical line towards their respective, respectable upper lips.

Where the serving staff were being careful to approach the small tables from behind, Dai strode up between their couches and stopped, the sun behind him, right in front of Balbus. The Roman had to use one hand to shield his eyes from the brilliant light streaming in through the glass roof of the atrium, as he peered at Dai with an expression of outrage.

"Who the—?

Dai flicked out his ID just long enough for the three to see it was genuine.

"Investigator Llewellyn. Just a moment of your time, dominus, I wanted to ask about a woman who worked for you, Grainne Cathan."

The expression of outrage developed into a frown of confusion, which then vanished abruptly.

"Oh, Grania? Yes. Incompetent *moecha*. Thanks to her I have lost one of the most precious items from my collection. Handing it over to some thief — she was probably in league with them."

"Dominus, your courier was murdered trying to protect your precious diagrams. They had to stab her and almost hacked her hand off to get them away from her."

Balbus lifted a hand dismissively.

"That was not my understanding. It seemed more a falling out of thieves from the description I had. But it hardly matters. The parchment is lost and I have already put in my insurance claim. The matter is closed."

Dai felt his hard-won self-control give way. For a moment, he imagined he had seized the fat patrician and head-butted his over-sized nose back into his skull, spraying blood over the delicate mosaic of the Divine Diocletian, whose gracious reforms had laid the foundations for an empire that had endured nearly two millennia. Then someone seized his shoulders and the red mist lifted. He was looking into Bryn's face, and it was Bryn's hands that gripped solidly, while beyond him Balbus was shouting.

"Did you see that? He was going to attack me!"

Dai managed to answer the silent question on Bryn's face, and his decanus turned to the irate Roman.

"You were mistaken, dominus, I assure you, he was simply trying to grab this dog before it — uh — had an accident on the hem of your toga."

Bryn reached down to pick up the squirming ball of fluff, which willingly colluded in the lie by urinating over the lavish dishes laid out on the side table…

• • •

"The case is closed, Llewellyn. Magistratus Claudius Albus Balbus has decided he has no wish to pursue the matter further since we have no strong leads on the whereabouts of his antiquity. And you should consider yourself very fortunate that he has decided not to press any charges against you."

The prefect in charge of the vigiles did not even raise her voice or bother to look up from her work as she delivered the news. Which was probably as well or she would have seen Dai's fury. It was written plainly on his face and he struggled to keep it in check in his voice.

"But, domina, a woman was killed — murdered, we can't just —"

She looked up then, with a cold frown.

"Closed, Llewellyn."

Dai swallowed back the sudden taste of bitter bile which rose in his throat and snapped a half-hearted salute.

Bryn was waiting outside, leaning against the wall. He fell into step beside Dai.

"There is one thing I do remember from history at school. It's why his Divineness Diocletian took back the grant of automatic citizenship from all those born outside Italia. It's 'cos we provincials just don't have their natural, inner nobility." He broke off as they passed a group of vigiles and picked up again as they stood waiting for a lift. "You see these Romans, they really are a virtuous lot — born that way, it's in the genes. They have *gravitas, dignitas, humanitas…*"

"*Veritas?*"

Bryn shrugged.

"It's a *conceptivae*, Bard — a movable feast — Balbus just forgot to announce it this year."

"Bastards. Bastards the lot of them." Dai hit the wall with his fist hard enough to bruise the knuckles. "I'll never trust one. Never."

A hand gripped his shoulder for a moment.

"Never say never, Bard. You don't know when you might meet your fate." Bryn squinted at his boss. "You hafta be more philosophical. You can't challenge Rome…"

II

Just less than a year later, Rome was having the last laugh. Dai was lodged in the home of a prominent Roman Citizen, betrothed to the tiny, determined Julia Lucia Maxilla and wore a silver ring of Citizenship on his index finger.

It was an unseasonably cold, wet August morning, and Julia was in her sitting room watching the sun try to break through a veil of black cloud, with her two wolfhounds Canis and Lupo asleep in a twitching heap by a small simmering fire. Their usual keeper, her personal bodyguard Edbert, was busy about some other business, so the dogs stayed close to her. Julia was breaking her fast in the British manner, seated on a chair with both feet on the floor. As she had a sneaking preference for that manner of dining, she wasn't making an issue of it. Instead, she smiled sunnily at her beloved who sat opposite her eating bread and honey.

"You," she remarked with mock severity "have honey on your chin."

"Do I?" he asked. "It's probably because I was looking as well as eating." His startling blue eyes met hers. "Isn't the love of my life sitting opposite me dressed in silk and looking good enough to eat?"

She felt the blush running up from her throat to her face and he leaned across the table and placed a chaste kiss on one burning cheek, then he chuckled.

To his intense irritation, the sitting room door banged open and the burly, hook-nosed figure of Decimus Lucius Didero, Tribune in charge of the praetorian guard in Britain, stomped into the room.

"Do come in, Decimus," Julia said coolly.

"I appear to be in," the big man spoke mildly. "And now I am, I will have some of that bread and honey and some words with your man."

Julia gave up the attempt to bring her foster brother to a sense of his own impropriety and spread honey on a hunk of crusty bread. She handed Decimus the bread and grinned at him.

"What do you want with my betrothed?"

Decimus masticated carefully before answering her.

"I'm in the nature of a supplicant. Being as how your man is now, thanks to his deeds of extraordinary valour, a Roman Citizen and a submagistratus-in-waiting to boot, the civilian authorities in general, and that stupid *cunnus* of a prefect in particular, can't just order him to look into something. They have to ask. And it goes against the grain. They'd sooner lick my arse than his. So I get to ask."

"Ask what?" Julia didn't like the sound of this at all. "Today and tomorrow are public holidays and Dai and I had plans on how we wanted to spend them."

Dai patted her hand.

"Hush, love. Let the man explain."

She snarled at him, but subsided.

"Dai, do you remember Lugh Tasgo's designs?"

Julia looked into Dai's eyes and saw a slow flare of anger in their depths.

"Oh yes. I remember. I remember a dead Briton and a fat Roman bastard. And an investigation called off because nobody cared that a woman died."

Decimus met his eyes.

"So you wouldn't mind another look at the case?"

"That depends."

"On what?"

Dai got up and went around the table to where Julia sat. He lifted her out of her chair and sat down with her in his lap. She could feel the tension in his lean body and turned her face into his neck. He wrapped his arms around her and hugged tightly.

"Grainne Cathan died trying to protect those designs for her employer and he called the investigation off. So it depends," he said harshly, "on me being permitted to actually investigate no matter what the outcome."

"Absolutely," Decimus nodded. "I already made that point. And just to be sure, Bryn and your boys are waiting outside, I can spare you a handful of praetorians," he added, licking a dribble of honey from his thumb, "but not as many as I'd like because we're on security detail today for the big civic events. And I'm going to be toga'd up with the rest of the dignitaries out in the rain all afternoon." He paused and took a deep breath before ploughing on. "Before you decide though, you need to know why Rome wants the investigation reopened. An hour ago, the curatrix of the Bibliotheca Britannica was found dead in her office and copies of those plough designs were found sitting on her desk. She was Roman, with patronage in high places, so now the comms centre is buzzing with indignation. And that stinks. But maybe, just maybe, if you take this on you will be able to finally get justice for a girl who died trying to protect a fat bastard's bit of parchment. I have a couple of my lads guarding the crime scene and its dead occupant just to make sure nobody muddies the water."

Julia looked up at Dai's set jaw.

"You going to do it, love?"

"I am," he grated "and I'm not even going to pretend not to want Decimus' praetorians."

She lifted her hands to cradle that jaw.

"We'll do it together then."

He looked down into her face and his eyes softened. "Would you really?"

"I will. I have to protect my investment." She looked down at her clinging silk stola in some disgust. "At least I get the chance to wear something a bit less bloody girlie."

Sliding off Dai's lap, she ran into the bedchamber.

• • •

It was only about half an hour later when three hovercars filled with various enforcement officers headed for the Bibliotheca Britannica. The journey took longer than usual because they were diverted to avoid the route of the planned Londinium Amburbium parade, due to occur that afternoon. All the civic dignitaries would be taking part, splashing water from the Tamesis over the crowds who would turn up to watch, cheer and enjoy the various floats and displays.

The cars disgorged their passengers under the elaborate portico of the building that housed the finest collection of British documents and artefacts in the Empire. A closed sign on the door was causing some consternation among a group of tourists and more than a little curiosity among a growing group of local journalists and hangers-on. At a subtle signal from Dai, a couple of his men peeled off to deal.

The largest of them bulked his shoulders as he spoke. "Move along, ladies and gents. Nothing to see here. Just a precautionary measure. The Bibliotheca will reopen very soon."

The rest of the party was admitted by a uniformed doorman who looked deeply uncomfortable. Another nod and two more of Dai's posse stopped for a vape and a chat.

"Your man's command is very smooth," one of the praetorians bent to whisper in Julia's ear. He did not add "for a shower of Britons" but it hung in the air all the same.

Julia looked up to find the man's smile was benign, so she smiled back tightly but said nothing.

They climbed a noble staircase of dark, heavily carved wood and trod a thickly carpeted corridor towards a set of equally elaborate double doors, where two praetorians stood guard. These saw Dai and saluted before opening the doors.

As soon as the heavy wooden leaves were parted, Julia could smell the iron-rich tang of blood; she threw Dai a grim smile before walking into the office with her head held high and her back straight. From the corner of her eye, she saw Dai gesture for the praetorians who had been on guard to exit the room, before he and Bryn followed her in and closed the doors firmly behind them.

The curatrix's office was spacious and graciously appointed, with whitened stone walls paneled to above the height of a man's head with dark wood. The dead woman sprawled across her desk, and the cause of her death was obvious. Somebody had seen fit to cave the side of her head in with a cheap marble bust of the Divine Diocletian. Julia was sure there was an irony there somewhere and in searching for it recovered her own equilibrium. She strode forward for a closer look.

At first glance, the curatrix seemed to be just an ordinary woman of middle years — if a bit too thin, rather overdressed and possessed of a nose that was most definitely Roman. The first anomaly that struck Julia was an embroidered leather protector on the woman's left wrist. It certainly didn't sit well with the fashionable stola and overabundance of jewellery. The thought had obviously occurred to Dai, too, as he leaned forwards and unfastened the wide strap.

"What have we here?"

On the inside of the woman's wrist, there was a small tattoo. It depicted a heart with a heptagon inside it. One segment of the heptagon was coloured purple.

"Oh," Julia said. "Oh *merda*."

"Oh *merda* what?"

"Oh *merda*, I know what this is. It is the sign of the Seven. There are just seven patrician families who can claim to trace their bloodlines back to the Divine Diocletian without any dilution. That is to say, for the last few centuries they have never bred outside of their own seven families. Which hasn't done them a lot of good. They tend to be physically weak and there are whispers that they have a mental problem which is passed down from generation to generation."

Bryn ambled across the room and spat into the embers of a rapidly cooling hearth.

"Huh. They only need to look at horse breeding to see that new blood is essential for health."

Julia laughed. "They wouldn't admit that there can be any correlation between humans and horses. From what I heard, they don't think Romans can breed proper human offspring if they mate with non-Romans. The real irony is they are so conservative they won't even use modern genetic manipulation methods to ensure healthy children. Bryn, you take a picture of her tattoo, central comms should be able to tell you which family she comes from."

The decanus grinned. "According to this here plaque on her desk, she is Lilia Cornelia Fecunda."

"Well, she ain't. That isn't a name from the seven families."

He looked doubtful, but flicked at his wristphone to run the check .

"Central says the tattoo is from the Antonine family. There are, the computer states, only two women this could be. And one of them is actually called Lilia."

He angled his wrist to photograph the undamaged side of the deceased's face. Seconds later, he got a response.

"Yup. That's her. Though I dunno how much further that gets us."

Julia sighed. "Dai is right when he calls you a *spado*. It gets us towards motive." Nobody seemed to know what she was talking about, so she shook her head and explained. "Every child born and raised in Rome knows and fears the Seven. Slum kids get told that they do weird experiments. On children. Whether or not that is true I dunno. But what is fact is that the families have some pretty fixed ideas about what it means to be Roman, and a group of them — called with patrician lack of imagination The Seven — has pretty much spent the last century trying to rewrite history. They refuse to believe that anything good can come from anyone not Roman. And not only that, they don't believe that anyone who isn't of patrician stock is fully human."

She let that sink in and went back to her study of the dead body. She soon found another anomaly. Among the strings of beads and bright enameled amulets around Lilia's neck, there was a thin platinum chain with a strange, unadorned pendant attached to it. Carefully undoing the clasp, she unwound the chain from among the jumble of dross.

"Come look at this, Dai."

He turned away from the low-voiced conversation he was having with Bryn.

"What have you got there?"

"I don't know for sure, but I think it is some sort of electronic key."

"So it is. Probably coded to our corpse. Shame, as I'd very much like to know what it opens."

"Me too," Bryn interjected brightly. "So let's hope it don't know dead from alive."

He twitched the key out of Julia's grasp and stared at it for a moment. Then he grinned and picked up the corpse's left hand.

"Good job rigor ain't reached her hands yet," he remarked in a conversational tone as he wrapped the dead fingers around the pendant, aligning the digits with grooves in the metal. A small red light blinked and one of the wooden panels beside the fireplace slid silently to one side.

"*Spado* is it?" he chuckled as he dropped the flaccid hand back onto the desk.

III

Dai was the first into the small room beyond and he stopped a pace inside releasing his breath in a low whistle.

"You should see this, beloved."

"I'm right behind you darling," Bryn said sweetly, sidestepping the sharp elbow his words evoked.

"*Spado!*"

This time it was said in chorus by Dai and Julia.

"You know, Bard, you could come up with a new insult. That one is getting old and you are the man with all that pure poetic Celtic heritage, not like me with a Romano-Gallic taint in my veins. So I'm sure you could be a bit more inventive than just '*spado*' all the time."

But Dai was not paying his friend any attention. He was marveling at the contents of the small room. It had no external windows and two walls were lined with shelves holding a small library of books, most by ancient authors as far as Dai could tell: Caesar, Cicero, Tacitus, Plutarch. The other two walls were simple paneled wood, with the door from the office opening invisibly in one.

The centerpiece was a round table sculpted from black marble, around which were seven matching ebony chairs. Above the center of the table, suspended as if in flight was, what looked like a solid gold eagle, gripping the SPQR scroll in diamond tipped talons whilst glaring at Dai in accusation with the single ruby eye that faced them.

Resting on the mantlepiece above the ornate and gilded, black marble fireplace, was a bust of the Divine Diocletian. The wall behind had been scooped out to make an alcove and decorated with his traditional halo, surrounded by the emblems of Rome. It was, Dai reflected, something that would not have been out of place in a small local temple.

In a niche set in the plinth of the bust, something glittered and Dai carefully extracted one of seven medallions he found placed there. It was engraved on one side with the profile of the Divine Diocletian and on the other with the words:

"Pridius Idus Augustus— "

"That's today's date," Julia agreed, frowning slightly. She took the medallion from him and examined it. "This looks like a pilgrim's token, you know, the kind they sell in Rome for those attending the sacred rituals at big festivals there — but those are made of base metal or silver, these are —"

"Solid gold," Dai confirmed, feeling the weight as she gave it back to him. He took a final look and slid the medallion back into the small niche with the others. "Some big festival event, for a select few due to take place in this room — today."

"But, what and why?" Julia asked, puzzled. "Today is the festival of the purification of the city of Londinium. The only 'rites' are very public and very civic."

"So maybe our more important question is who?" Dai suggested. "And I think I can guess at least one 'who'."

Julia interrogated him with her eyes.

"Claudius Albus Balbus," Dai snapped his mouth shut on the last syllable of the name. "He is the one responsible for setting the local *conceptivae* — the movable feasts of which the Amburbium is one."

With that unpleasant thought front and center in his mind, Dai continued looking around.

The fireplace was fitted with a modern incinerator, which was capable of achieving much higher temperatures than any regular fire. And the reason for that was clear.

On two tables, set as votive offerings placed before an altar, were stacks of high-tech, atmospherically adjustable scroll cases and a heap of assorted small artefacts. With a frisson of shock, Dai realized he recognized one of the items. He crossed to the table and picked it up, shaking his head in awe before setting it down again and turning to the scroll cases, reading their labels.

"What— ?" Julia was looking wide-eyed.

"British history." Dai told her without looking up.

"British history?"

"Well Romano-British if you want to be precise. For example, that odd-looking thing is Swan's original light bulb. And this," he held up the artefact that had first caught his attention, speaking reverently, "is the prototype for the IXI — the music machine that everyone used to listen to before they upgraded wristphones to do that as well — and here," he pulled out a scroll case, "are those missing designs the courier died for. Half this stuff is supposedly on display to the public elsewhere in the building."

Julia met his gaze and he saw the moment she understood the implications.

"So this," she gestured to include the whole room, "is some sort of shrine to the glory of Rome and its conquest of all things British?"

"It's even been consecrated, if you look at the bust."

"Their planned 'purification' ritual? If they'd completed the offering—"

"Maybe a thousand years of British achievements and inventions, lost. The remaining artefacts on display are provable forgeries, so doubt is cast on their real origins, then convincing and expert-authenticated Roman 'originals' gradually start coming to light and—"

"What are two you on about? You seen this?"

Dai looked over to where Bryn was pointing to a small panel on the wall opposite the one they had entered. Without waiting for permission, the decanus pushed on the panel and the wall opened in much the same way as the one from the office. He put his head through and then lifted his wrist to use the light on his phone to see.

"Executive bathroom," he said and turned back. "Gold plated bog-roll holders and all." He paused and peered at the glass panel which formed the outside of the door. "Looks like this mirror has facial recognition built in."

Dai nodded. This whole thing was going to go higher and deeper into Roman society than he cared to consider.

"Close it," he said and the decanus obliged, easing the panel back to its original place. "This room is our secret for now. And I mean ours — tell no one else." He waited until the other two nodded agreement, noticing the tightening of Julia's expression. She didn't like it, that much was clear. Her trust in the praetorians they had been assigned, some from families of the highest social strata, was probably considerably greater than his own, but she did not challenge his judgment. Relieved, Dai went on, quickly: "Bryn, I want you out of here, keep the praetorians and our boys busy with the basics. Searches, interviews — the works. Lots of song and dance for anyone watching. Julia, get the forensics people in to finish up with the body and move it out as fast as possible, then search the place. I'm going to speak with Decimus to set something up to surprise our Secret Seven."

"What do you think I might find?" Julia asked.

"There has to be something about this place. Right now, we don't know if Lilia was one of the worshippers or just their caretaker. My money is that she is not part of this inner circle — I'm kind of afraid she isn't important enough in her family. For a start, she's a woman and these people are going to be extreme traditionalists. That means they aren't accepting of changes from the last century or two of liberalisation. Makes it that much tougher for someone like me to bring them down."

Julia reached out and squeezed his hand, then held it up to display the silver ring he wore. "You're a Citizen now, Dai — their equal in the eyes of the law. You have every right to challenge even a Senator who is guilty of a crime."

Dai found it hard to meet her serene gaze.

"Yeah. Right. Equal. Maybe they didn't get the memo."

He couldn't tell her that even her foster brother, the Tribune, still gave him the odd condescending look when it came to anything outside their professional relationship.

IV

Julia watched as he strode from the room and sighed. Bryn interpreted her sigh correctly and held up a finger.

"Minute," he said and dived out after Dai.

Julia wandered back through the panel to the office and relieved her feelings by kicking the ornate desk with one small, booted foot. To her surprised delight, a drawer popped out from under the edge of the leather writing surface. She bent to see what it might contain.

"Nice view," Bryn even managed a good approximation of a patrician drawl.

Julia offered him a ferocious mock scowl. Then her face became serious. "Dai is going to take this hard, I think."

"The Bard takes everything hard. But why specially today?"

"Because he has gone to see Decimus with visions of show trials in his head, and he's going to be educated. Told that the only approximation of justice we can hope to obtain will come from killing The Seven. He'll think Decimus is patronising him, and Decimus will think he's a romantic fool. And it will be made worse because Dai already thinks Decimus snarks at him for being a Briton."

"And does he?"

"No. He snarks at him because he don't like the idea of anybody being with me." Julia blushed fiery red and Bryn looked at her with some sympathy.

"Families, eh? So who is right about this ambush?"

"Neither of them. Or both of them. It ain't as simple as either would like it to be. My heart is with Dai, but my head knows that if we let any of The Seven escape death tonight that's the last we'll hear of them."

"What? They will just poof?"

"Yes."

"Okay. Don't argue with him. You leave that to me."

"Will he listen, Bryn?"

"Eventually. But more important, is he right? Will they still come tonight?"

"Oh, I think so. The death of their gofer makes it even more important to complete their mission and they are arrogant enough to believe we will never find their secret room."

Bryn grinned a feral grin. "I'll go and share around some busy work. And I'll send SOCO to get the corpse. You better see what's in madam's secret drawer."

Julia bent to her task, finding a significant quantity of gold coins, a letter from the Senate in Rome recalling Lilia Julia Antonina to a position in the Senate Librarium, and a sleek little palmtop computer. Putting aside the letter and the gold, Julia concentrated on the personal data unit.

"I hope you don't have facial recognition," she muttered under her breath as she stared at the inert device. There was no palm plate she could recognize and no obvious means of entering a password or code. She turned her attention back to the dead woman. Mentally rejecting hand or face recognition, she started to paw through the jangling jewels that adorned the scrawny neck when she had a thought. Kneeling back down, she looked closer at the drawer. Sure enough, there was a docking station for the palmtop and nestled in the center of the docking plate there was a tiny piece of metal. It looked almost like a key. She levered it out with a fingernail and almost immediately found the minute slot in the edge of the computer. The screen lit up, but nothing else happened. Julia laughed and flexed her small fingers.

"Okay Lilia, let's see what you were made of."

The codes were almost laughably simple and, once she had a handle on the dead woman's mind, it was like opening Aladdin's cave. She worked through the contents with such concentration that she was unaware of SOCO removing the corpse. She didn't come back to herself until Dai came into the room, shutting the door behind him with a bang. She looked up.

"Do you have a moment?"

She stood up. "I have several."

He swooped on her and picked her up, holding her close and murmuring brokenly. She put up with it for a while, then wriggled, so he set her on her feet.

"What?"

"Between them, Decimus and Bryn have just about wrecked my day."

"How so?"

He managed a crooked smile. "I, my love, have just been handed what they would call 'a lesson in the realities of life'. And I didn't much enjoy it.

"I don't suppose you did. Are you taking any notice?"

"I have to. If you will tell me just one thing."

"I'll tell you many things, but which particular thing are you after?"

He looked into her eyes. "Have I been as big a *spado* as Bryn?"

"Probably," she said serenely. "Did you have anything specific in mind?"

"Decimus. I kind of thought he looked at me strangely because I'm a Briton. But Bryn says it's far more likely that he gives me the stink eye because he thinks I'm bedding you."

Julia found herself blushing, but she got herself together and nodded fiercely. "He's right. Decimus is just a bit over-protective. But he means well. Even tells me that if I have to sleep with someone, at least I had sense enough to choose a man of integrity."

Dai picked her up in a hug again, rubbed his face in her unruly black curls and groaned. Julia laughed and he set her back on her feet.

"You may be all sorts of idiot," she said smilingly, "but at least you are my idiot." She punched his shoulder lightly. "Don't dwell on it. Come and see what I found. Lilia's palmtop. I got it working and it is a treasure trove." She sobered. "We now know who killed Grainne Cathan and at the behest of whom."

"We do?"

"Yes. And you're probably not going to like it too much. Lilia was the instigator, but the killer was a Briton."

To Julia's surprise, Dai didn't even frown.

"Atty Brickenden?"

"Yes. But how…"

"You remember the jittery doorman when we came in? My people questioned him and seems he saw Atty coming out of the staff exit this morning. But Atty put the frighteners on him to keep his mouth shut. And I can link Atty with Balbus." Dai whistled loudly and Bryn poked his head around the door.

"You want to send some people to pick up Atty?"

"Consider it done."

Dai turned his attention back to Julia. He fingered the palmtop. "How much of this do I need to know right now?"

"Actually nothing. Though it all goes to proof if you are having any qualms."

"I was. But between Decimus and Bryn, I've had a snap education and if these men are either dead or scot-free, I'd prefer the former. I just find it difficult to accept that Decimus can order a massacre with a snap of his fingers."

"Me too. But that's the power of the praetorians. So, hadn't we better stop avoiding the issue and set a trap?"

Dai's grin was positively vicious. "We had."

By the time the sun was setting over the puddles in the regal squares and avenues around the Bibliotheca Britannica, the trap was set. Julia, her bodyguard Edbert, who had returned from whatever his business was, Canis and Lupo waited in the relative comfort of the curatrix's office. Dai, Bryn, and half a dozen praetorians waited with them, less comfortably as they were squashed hard by the wall-panel door observing the covert surveillance set up in the hidden room. A handful more praetorians waited to secure the other entrance as soon as all The Seven were inside, and another score of men ringed the upper floor of the Bibliotheca with steel. Julia pulled a face at Edbert.

"Now we wait."

"That's always the hardest part," he rumbled before settling himself on the floor and closing his eyes.

V

"Game on," Dai murmured almost reverently as six of the seven patricians appeared one by one to take their seats at the black marble table. There had not been time to set up anything too sophisticated, so the eagle flying over the table had a tiny lens and microphone. But the mic seemed to be broken since there was no sound to go with the images on the screen of his wristphone.

"You can't trust Roman technology," Bryn muttered, breaking the tension. But his voice was louder than intended because a couple of the praetorians glared at him. The decanus smiled back at them. He was the only man not armed in their group, the only non-Citizen and Dai knew how he must be feeling. He touched the cold handle of the nerve-whip he wore at his own belt, a weapon that would put anyone on the floor in writhing agony. It was not something he liked the thought of, but he was living in a society where kill or be killed was not just a metaphor. Politics and power at the highest level was survival of the fittest and justice was as much a *conceptivae* — a movable feast — as any of the others in the calendar, there to serve the needs of the powerful. He looked briefly across the room at the tiny woman who held his heart in her hands and mentally saluted her courage, stiffening his resolve in an unconscious echo of her unconventional morality.

The last man had joined the group at the table. Balbus himself, and suddenly Dai felt less negative about the thought of killing. Atty Brickenden, knowing his life was forfeit for murdering a Roman Citizen, had coughed up the truth in exchange for a promise of 'Mercy' before his grisly execution.

"It were that *futatrix*, hired me," he had whined, speaking of Lilia, "but I figured who she were working for when I nicked the plans from that woman."

"The one you killed?" Bryn had been leading the interrogation, Dai arrived near the end.

"Not my fault the *lupa* fought back."

It took all Dai's self-control not to hit him.

Atty had kept copies of the scrolls and recordings of conversations he had with Lilia leading up to Grainne's murder, stored in a place they would be released to public view in the case of his own demise. "Then I knew they couldn't touch me — if I went down, dead or alive, I'd drag them with me."

But Atty was a very greedy man. Insurance turned into blackmail. He started extorting large amounts of gold from the curatrix who was convinced she would have been sent home in disgrace had details of the blunder come out. Atty had even tried to put the screws on Balbus himself first, but the Roman had laughed and told Atty he would die screaming if he ever tried to use the evidence he held.

He told Bryn that he visited Lilia first thing that morning because she had persuaded him she would pay out one more time before leaving for Rome, if he returned the copy of the plough designs.

"But the *cunnus* snatched them off me, said she weren't paying me another dupondius." In Rome, she had told Atty scathingly, no one cared what you got up to in the Provinces. At which point, Atty hit her with the bust of Diocletian that sat on her desk.

The amount of sheer greed involved in it all brought bile to the back of Dai's throat. Balbus wanted to destroy the documents with his fellow conspirators in The Seven, but wasn't prepared to lose money over it so had set up a scheme to claim insurance for them. Lilia was willing to do anything to ensure she kept her status with the Seven and Atty was more than happy to sink to any depths if it paid.

Dai gagged mentally before dragging his attention back to The Seven, who seemed to be saying some kind of prayers, Without sound, it was hard to be sure, but they had their eyes closed as if in pious contemplation. It seemed the perfect opportunity so Dai gave the nod and eased the nerve whip into his hand as the panel door swung open.

He went for Balbus, aware of the chaos around him, shouts of protest, furniture falling, arms flailing. But Balbus was not in the chair he had been occupying a moment before. The empty seat stood slightly pushed back from the table, almost touching the bookcase behind it. Spinning round, Dai scanned the small room. The praetorians had already killed three of the Romans and as he watched a fourth went down shrieking. Bryn was doing his assigned job and placing himself between the killing and the precious artefacts, making sure they were not removed or damaged.

A slight cold breeze touched the back of Dai's neck, impossible in the sealed room. He turned and stepped back. Then opened his mouth to shout a warning as he tried to use the nerve-whip. But the blow to his head was too fast and too hard and he fell back into the darkness.

• • •

Bryn saw Dai being dragged through the hidden doorway but he was on the other side of a very crowded room.

"Guard alert," he bellowed, "they've got Llewelyn."

The praetorians, who had finished their work, stared at him as Julia hurtled out of the office as if fired by a gun. She had Edbert and the dogs hot on her heels.

"Who? Where?"

"Balbus and some goon. Dragged the Bard through a door behind that bookcase.

With six of The Seven dead or dying, Julia didn't waste any time on them. Instead she started hurling volumes off the bookcase at break-neck speed.

"Aha," she grunted. "Got it. Facial recognition pad. Drag one of them dead bodies over here will you?"

Edbert picked up the skinniest as if he was a doll and pressed his face to the small screen. The bookcase slid aside, with a protesting screech.

"Somebody chock that door," Julia said crisply "we don't want to be trapped inside wherever."

Bryn stuck his head through the aperture and looked down the worn stone steps to where a torch burned in a bracket at the entrance to a brick-built tunnel.

"If I'm not mistaken, it's the *via cloaca*. Been disused for centuries but I'd always heard bits of it still survive. It's going to be difficult to sneak up on them from here."

Julia was already immersed in her wrist unit. "Good thinking, Bryn. This stretch is even on the map. Just no mention of the staircase. But there should be a personnel entrance just down the street."

The praetorian in command saluted.

"On that, Domina."

"In the meantime," Julia snapped her fingers, "Canis, Lupo. Find Dai. Silent." The dogs looked at her with intelligent, dark eyes before slipping down the staircase like grey ghosts.

• • •

Dai came round almost choking as someone forced a ball of cloth into his mouth. He knew he couldn't have been out for long because he could hear Balbus gasping for breath like a broken bellows, but whoever had manhandled him was anything but unfit. The face was Roman, but not patrician. More the hard-man, street-rat look of those he had seen on TV in crime documentaries about the Suburra. Whoever he was, he was good at his job. He had taken Balbus out of the death trap and dragged Dai with them.

"Keep him alive. He's my ticket out of here. For some reason, the Tribune values his worthless British carcass."

The other man grunted and drove a fist into Dai's stomach hard enough to make him double over. He stopped his attempt at freeing his hands. They must have needed to make do with cloth, the same cloth that gagged him It had some stretch in it and, given enough unsupervised time, Dai was sure he could free himself. This time it was a knife point that drove into muscle. Dai gasped as it was twisted.

"Don't try it, scum. I can do you a lot of damage and still keep you alive."

"Shut up, you fool! They will hear you." Balbus wheezed, his own breathing twice as loud as the low-growled threat of his bodyguard.

Dai wondered where they were and then — remembering his conversation with Decimus about the importance of eliminating the Seven and the one with Julia about how little the Tribune liked the idea of any man touching her — he wondered just how much his own life would weigh in the balance against the need to ensure Balbus never made it to freedom. Free, the magistrate could summon the support of the Emperor himself — and then it would be Tribune Decimus Lucius Didero whose life would be forfeit.

• • •

Edbert, Bryn, Julia, and two praetorians followed the dogs down the worn stone steps, moving silently but with speed. One of the praetorians wore an earpiece and he gave Julia a thumb indicating that there were men coming the other way along the tunnel. She showed him her teeth in a grateful grin, just as Canis and Lupo reappeared wagging.

"We are very close," Edbert whispered.

"Let's make some noise then."

At a signal from their mistress the wolfhounds gave tongue and lit out running, followed by five humans yelling war cries, echoed by the praetorians coming from the other direction — although it would be some time before they reached the action. Julia and company rounded a bend in the tunnel just in time to hear a gunshot. Lupo went down screaming as Canis leapt, taking Balbus down, ripping the Roman's scrawny throat with his powerful teeth.

Against the wall of the tunnel, a competent-looking heavy held Dai in front of his body with a needle-pointed dagger pressed up under the Briton's chin.

Julia's heart leapt into her throat and, for a moment, she struggled to pull breath into her lungs.

"Let him go. You are surrounded." Bryn signaled Julia to hold her peace, as he spoke in carefully emotionless tones, his face drained of color.

"Let him go?" the tough laughed scornfully. "What kind of a fool do you think I am? He's my ticket out of here. Which one of you is the boss?"

The biggest of the two praetorians stepped forward, screening Julia from the man's gaze.

"What do you want?"

"Just keep your lot out of my way. I might even let the pretty boy live if nobody tries to stop me leaving."

"Well, we have Balbus so we don't need you." The praetorian spread his hands as if in defeat and the thug made to move away creeping crab-wise along the wall with his human shield in front of him. Dai must have resisted because his captor slashed viciously down his rib-cage leaving a long bleeding cut deep enough to show rib-bone. Julia heard Dai's hiss of indrawn breath.

"Behave yourself, pretty boy. Or the next cut is your scrotum."

The ill-assorted duo continued to edge along the wall, as Julia furiously cast about in her mind for some way to get the thug's attention, before Dai got hurt any worse. But in the end, she needed to do nothing. At a low sound from Edbert, Canis looked up from the throat of Balbus and he growled deep in his own throat.

"Keep that dog away from me."

Nobody moved, or spoke and Canis growled again.

"Keep it away from me, it's a killer." There was a real edge of desperation in the hard man's voice and he stole a sidelong glance at the huge rough-haired hound.

And that was all the diversion Julia needed. She sighted around the praetorian's torso and shot him neatly through the head.

She was at Dai's side before his assailant hit the ground. As soon as she removed his gag, he spoke urgently.

"Never mind me. See to Lupo."

Julia turned huge, haunted eyes to where Edbert knelt by the fallen animal. He looked up and smiled.

"He will be all right, luckily for him Balbus was a useless shot, and the bullet is lodged in his shoulder. He won't enjoy me getting it out but it hasn't touched bone or any vital organ. But you had better call Canis off that corpse."

Julia whistled and Canis came to heel. She bent and wiped the blood from around his mouth. "Good boy." Then her face crumpled like a child's. Fortunately, Bryn had untied Dai's hands in time for him to hold her while she cried.

VI

September came with the warmth of summer that had passed Augustus by and Dai was able to recuperate in the walled garden of Decimus' personal lodgings, attached to the main praetorian barracks.

Lupo lay beside him, not so much recovering as sulking. The wolf-hound had a large plastic cone enclosing his head to stop him chewing at the healing stitches on his shoulder. He heaved heavy sighs now and again to express his displeasure at the device and at having to stay home whilst Canis was out with Edbert. Dai reached out a hand and petted the huge dog.

"You and me both, bro."

He heard voices and, shielding his eyes against the sun, he saw two women walking towards him. One, well rounded and mature, bearing a tray of drinks, the other, small and slender, carrying a folding table. He was smiling as Julia unfolded the table so her companion could place the tray on it.

"Freshly squeezed fruit juice," Dai took a glass and sipped appreciatively, the ice cubes tinkling against the side as he did so. "Now that is what the medicus ordered."

The two women settled on the garden loungers beside him, Julia petting Lupo.

"Is Decimus due back from Rome soon, Boudicca?" Dai addressed his question to the older woman. Officially, she was Decimus' housekeeper, but unofficially it was a much more intimate arrangement. The tragedy, in Dai's opinion, was it could never be formalized without the Tribune risking losing his career. But he had never heard Boudicca complain.

"Hopefully tomorrow. He had an audience with the Emperor himself and he's still got his balls, so all should be well."

Dai smiled and reached out to capture Julia's hand.

"Good. I'd hate for him to miss the wedding."

Glossary of Latin terms

Please note these are not always accurate translations, they are how these terms are used in Dai and Julia's world.

Amburbium - festival for purifying the city

Bibliotheca Britannica - British Library/Museum

Conceptivae - movable feasts

Cunnus - literally 'female genitalia', metaphorically as we might use 'bastard'.

Curatrix - Manager (f.) in charge of a building/organisation.

Dignitas - dignity, self-pride. A Roman virtue

Diocletian - the reforming emperor who established the foundations of a new empire

Dupondius - low value coin

Futatrix - literally 'one who is fucked', metaphorically 'bitch'

Gravitas - serious manner, decorum. A Roman virtue

Humanitas - humanity, kindness. A Roman virtue

Lupa - whore

Merda - shit

Mingo - piss

Moecha - literally 'adulteress' metaphorically: 'slut' or 'tart'

Pridius Idus Augustus - August 12th

SPQR (Senātus Populusque Rōmānus) -The Senate and People of Rome.

Spado - literally 'eunuch', metaphorically 'stupid fool'

Sub aquila - literally 'under the eagle'. An eagle above the entrance of any building means it is Citizen access only - aside for those who might work there of course

Via cloaca - sewers

Veritas - honesty. A Roman virtue

Meet E.M.Swift-Hook
and Jane Jago

The writing team of E.M.Swift-Hook and Jane Jago has produced a number of books following the characters of Dai and Julia in a world where the Roman empire never faded.

E.M.Swift-Hook has had a number of different careers, before settling in the North-East of England with family, three dogs, cats and a small flock of rescued chickens.

You can find her on twitter @emswifthook, and you can also catch up with her Fortune's Fools series of space opera.

The term genre-hopper could have been coined to describe Jane Jago and her books, modern-day thrillers sitting side by side with sword and sorcery, wicked dragons, and short stories and verse. You can find her on Twitter at @JaneJago1.

You can also catch up with both authors at workingtitleblogspot. com.

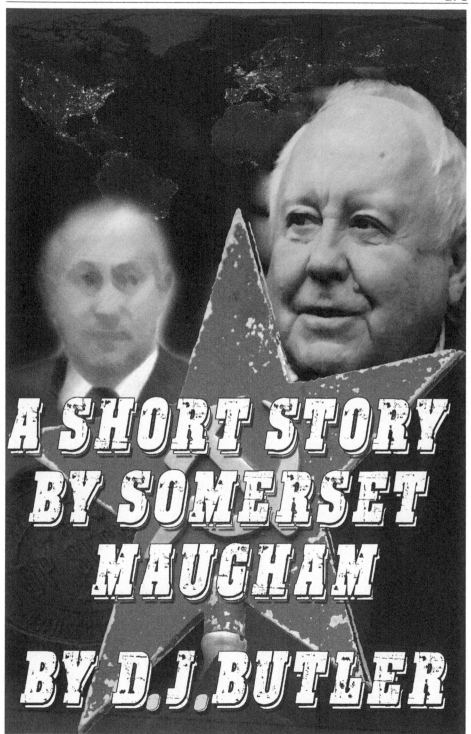

A SHORT STORY BY SOMERSET MAUGHAM

BY D. J. BUTLER

A Short Story by Somerset Maugham
By D.J.Butler

Mikhail Lyubimov answered the phone on the second ring. "Yes."

"Mikhail, this is Oleg."

"Gordievsky, my friend. Don't tell me if you're calling to cancel the visit to my dacha."

"I'm not going to tell you that." Did Oleg's voice sound shaky? Gordievsky, once a rising star in the KGB and the resident of the KGB's London station, had raised eyebrows as a young man with his abstemiousness around alcohol. Lately, though, he'd been drinking. A lot.

"But you're not coming. You don't want to tell me, but you're going to tell me instead how much work you have to do or how you must spend time with Leila and the girls. Which you should do, by the way. She's a gorgeous woman, your Leila. But you'll let me infer that you feel pressed for time, in the hope that I'll let you out of the invitation. Well, I won't. Bring Leila and the girls, if you must."

"I don't want out of the invitation, Mikhail." Did Gordievsky sound rueful? It was late in the evening, and he was probably just tired. "I'm coming to visit you at your dacha."

"Monday," Lyubimov said. "Tanya will be here. I want you to meet her. She's also a lovely woman. If she's as beautiful as your Leila, neither you nor I are impartial enough to judge, but since I'm sleeping with Tanya—"

"I'll be there, Mikhail," Gordievsky said. "Leila has taken the girls to Azerbaijan."

"To visit her parents? I had forgotten she was Azeri. Very good, no wonder she's such a handsome woman. Monday at 11:53, then."

"At Zvenigorod Station. I've called to tell you how much I'm looking forward to the visit."

"Excellent. Tanya and I also."

"Mikhail," Gordievsky said. "Have you ever read 'Mr. Harrington's Washing'?"

Lyubimov tried to remember whether he had.

"It's a short story by Somerset Maugham," Gordievsky added. There was a hint of emotion in his voice. What was it? Glee? Fear?

"Then of course I've read it. I have his complete works." Lyubimov snorted. "I introduced you to Maugham."

"I remember. That's a good story, Mikhail. You might want to read it again. It's in volume four of your collection. Read it, you'll see what I mean."

They chatted a little longer, a few more lines each, and then Lyubimov hung up the phone. He poured himself a drink, a Glenfiddich 40 Year Single Malt that he had because of his Party membership, his diplomatic service, and his own former employment in the KGB. He walked to the glass doors of his dacha's study and looked out at the lights of Zvenigorod, twinkling just a few miles away through the forest.

He had been a KGB man for years, but he was now making a living as a writer. Or rather, he was trying to make a living. He had found words easy to come by, but readers very scarce. He published nothing that wasn't approved by the Party, but some whispered that Mikhail Lyubimov's stories lacked romance and adventure.

Gordievsky had also been a diplomat, and a KGB man, and a member of the Party. In addition to his beautiful family, he had risen to higher status than Lyubimov ever had. He wrote no stories, but his life seemed to contain the romance and adventure that Lyubimov's tales were said to lack.

But was Oleg Gordievsky a member in good standing?

He had been recalled from London under some suspicion. An MI5 officer had offered to spy for the KGB, but had been arrested by the British before the offer could be taken up. And agents in Scandinavia had been arrested by their local counterintelligence agencies, as well. Gordievsky had been posted to Denmark, a decade earlier. Was it possible that Oleg had betrayed the Soviet Union? That he had betrayed Arne Treholt of Norway and Stig Bergling of Sweden?

Mikhail rattled himself like a dog emerging from water, trying to shake off the unease and the suspicion.

Lyubimov and Gordievsky had been posted to Denmark at the same time. They had met there. It was in Denmark that Mikhail had introduced Oleg to the English writer Somerset Maugham. Maugham had had plenty of romance and adventure in his own life, having been a secret operative for the British in Russia, before the Revolution.

Lyubimov finished his whisky in a gulp, poured himself a second, and took volume four of Maugham's collected works down from the shelf. He settled himself into a frayed and slouching armchair in the yellow puddle of light from the study's desk lamp and found the short story Gordievsky had indicated.

As he read, his heart beat faster. He remembered this story now, with its tale of the traveler waiting for his laundry to be finished in Moscow.

Oleg was telling him something.

Mikhail Lyubimov left the story unfinished and volume four cracked open, spine up, on the desk, when he ran to get into his car to drive to Moscow.

• • •

The apartment would be under surveillance. Even if there were not a cloud of suspicion hanging over Oleg Gordievsky—suspicion the substance of which Oleg himself seemed to have just validated—he was an officer of the KGB, and such men were often watched.

Lyubimov had had the presence of mind to bring a bottle of wine with him. He would say that he had an unexpected reason to come to Moscow this evening, and decided to anticipate next week's holidays by cracking open the bottle with his friend Oleg. He had a packet of cigarettes in his coat pocket, but his hands shook too much to be able to smoke them on the drive. They shook so much, he could barely keep control of the car.

It was nearly midnight when he parked in front of Gordievsky's building. One light was on in the Gordievsky apartment—the kitchen? He imagined Oleg eating alone, or perhaps drinking to soothe his conscience and quiet his nerves, as he climbed the stairs to rap on the door.

Gordievsky answered slowly. Oleg was as handsome as ever, fit as a much younger man. The bastard. He smiled quickly at Mikhail, but the smile looked practiced, false.

"Lyubimov," he said. "This is a surprise."

Mikhail raised the bottle of wine. Why were his hands shaking? "I thought we could get started on the drinking early."

Oleg stepped aside to let him in. "Did you bring Tanya?"

"Just wine and cigarettes," Lyubimov said.

"Ah, a feast."

As Gordievsky shut the door, Lyubimov noticed that his shirtsleeves were rolled up and his hands were wet. "Cleaning the house?"

Oleg pointed to the kitchen sink, which was full of dirty clothes in soapy water. "Leila and the girls are away, and I must have clean shirts for the office."

"'Mr. Harrington's Washing'." Lyubimov nodded. "Let me open this bottle so we can get started." He pantomimed writing.

Gordievsky frowned, but produced a pen from a bookcase near the door. Mikhail found the bottle opener, uncorked the wine—an indifferent bottle of Sovetskoye Shampanskoye—and poured two glasses. As he did, he looked around the apartment's living room, noting that it was impeccable. Gordievsky had been tidying up.

In order to leave the place.

Lyubimov took the pen without a word, sat at the square wooden kitchen table, and tore open one of his cigarettes. On the edge of the paper, he wrote: *You're defecting. You're going to Finland. Who will meet you there?*

"This is delicious wine," Gordievsky said. He hadn't touched his glass. He took the paper and pen from Lyubimov and wrote, in a line beneath his friend's words, *I only meant to say goodbye. You must have a drink and go home.*

Mikhail took a drink. *In the story, the man who stays in Moscow is killed. I'm coming with you.* "It's hard to believe it's just shampanskoye."

Gordievsky: *You're in no danger here. If you come with me, you might die.* His words filled the cigarette paper's last blank space, so after Lyubimov saw his writing, Oleg took the cigarette paper back and ate it.

Mikhail carefully opened a second cigarette and drank more wine. While Gordievsky swept the dried tobacco into a wastebasket, Lyubimov wrote: *Your escape plan must have room for a second person.*

Oleg: *Only me.* "This is much better than any drink that can be had in England, for instance."

Mikhail: *There was never a plan to take Leila?*

Gordievsky sighed and took a drink. *What do you want, Mikhail?* he wrote.

To help the west, Lyubimov answered. The words on the tiny scrap of paper were so damning, he showed them to Oleg and then immediately tore the cigarette paper in two, chewing the scrap into quick oblivion.

Gordievsky: *You're not that ideological.*

"I should have brought a second bottle." Lyubimov thought for a minute, then wrote: *A better life. Freedom.* "Two bottles are always better than one."

Gordievsky arched his eyebrows. "Sometimes a second bottle is too much."

Also adventure, Lyubimov wrote. "That doesn't sound very Russian of you, comrade."

Oleg sighed again. *Are you threatening to expose me?*

Mikhail: *Let's not find out. Let me come.*

Gordievsky sucked at his teeth. "In any case, one bottle is enough for us both tonight. Don't drive this evening, my friend. Sleep on my sofa, and you can travel home tomorrow. Then on Monday, I'll come to your dacha, and we can drink all the wine you like."

Lyubimov reached for the last scrap of cigarette paper, but Gordievsky thrust it into his mouth and ate it.

• • •

"These new shoes hurt my feet," Lyubimov grumbled.

"You wanted to come," Gordievsky muttered. "Now keep quiet."

It was afternoon, and they were entering Moscow's Leningrad

Station together. The station was mobbed with young socialists from foreign countries, come to Moscow for the Twelfth World Festival of Youth and Students. The air was thick with the smell of unwashed bodies and unbrushed teeth. Both Gordievsky and Lyubimov wore light jackets; neither man had a travel bag.

In the morning, Mikhail had driven away from Oleg's apartment with loud and ostentatious goodbyes, for the benefit of whoever was surveilling the Gordievsky home, and precise instructions. As Gordievsky had insisted, Lyubimov had begun by purchasing a new pair of shoes. Then he had ditched his car and traveled in a criss-crossing, apparently aimless web across Moscow, sometimes taking the Metro train and sometimes walking. He changed hats twice and his jacket once while doing so, and now he had met up again with Oleg at the front entrance of the station.

"But why new shoes?" Lyubimov pressed.

"In case the KGB has put radioactive dust on the soles of your old ones," Gordievsky said. "We must not be followed. I, too, am wearing new shoes. Perhaps you have forgotten these techniques."

He hadn't. But Mikhail felt uncomfortable at the thought that the KGB might try to follow him with a Geiger counter. "And what have *you* done this morning?"

"Bought new shoes and wandered back and forth across Moscow." Oleg smiled. "And wondered whether my friend Mikhail would be joining me on my cross-country trip."

Gordievsky passed Lyubimov his ticket. "It's an overnight passage to Leningrad. We should buy bread and sausages for the journey."

"I'll pay." Mikhail slipped the ticket into his jacket pocket. It felt as heavy as a ship's anchor.

"In a few days, we'll be spending pounds Sterling and U.S. dollars, never to see a ruble again in our lives." Gordievsky grinned, and care seemed to fall away from him like rain off an oiled slicker. "I'm happy to use some of the last of my money to buy food for my friend Mikhail."

He turned to stand in line at the stall, and Lyubimov saw a subtle weight tugging at Gordievsky's coat pocket. The shape of the bulge and the motion it made as the coat swung around Oleg's hip might have meant nothing to another man, but Lyubimov was a trained KGB officer, and he knew immediately what he had seen.

Oleg was carrying a pistol.

Mikhail was unarmed.

When Gordievsky returned with bread and sausages wrapped in two pages of an edition of Pravda from the week before, Lyubimov smiled.

• • •

They sat facing opposite directions on the same bench and waited for the train's 5:30 departure. Mikhail knew that he should keep quiet, perhaps pretend to doze, and certainly give no indication that he and Gordievsky were traveling together. But questions rankled, and he had to ask them. He chewed at his bread and sausages to mask the movements of his mouth.

"Treholt?" he murmured. "Was that you?"

Gordievsky was silent for a long time. "Yes," he finally said.

"Bergling?"

"Also yes. And, before you ask, also Haavik."

"Is that what you did?" Mikhail felt as if he were wading through a curtain of aspic. His thoughts and his heartbeats were slowed and his balance was off. "Betray Soviet agents to their death?"

"Mikhail," Gordievsky said slowly, "the Soviet Union is a betrayal. It's a sick system that crushes its own people. You know this. You were in Denmark, you know what life can be."

"Life is more than full grocery stores."

"It isn't when you're starving. And you say nothing of the free press, the flowering of literature, the explosion of music."

"You can hear symphonies anywhere in the Soviet Union." But his heart sank, and Lyubimov knew that Gordievsky had a point.

But if Oleg had been willing to betray Scandinavian spies to be arrested and imprisoned, would he also be willing to betray Mikhail? To be arrested, or worse? Mikhail thought of Oleg's concealed weapon.

As if he had read Lyubimov's thoughts, Gordievsky then murmured, "I have done what I have done for more than culture. For more than the West's idea of freedom. I have acted for peace."

Defeat of the Soviet Union by the West would bring a kind of peace, but Mikhail held his tongue.

"Gorbachev," Gordievsky said.

"Is a good socialist," Lyubimov said reflexively, and then regretted it. "What about Gorbachev?"

"He's a good socialist." Gordievsky nodded toward a slew of young people pouring out of an arriving train. "All the students coming to see him will be pleased with his idealism and his words. And he's also not insane, like Andropov. He's not a warmonger who demands that his people give him the proof he wants so that he can launch nuclear war against the West."

"You should not say such things."

"Soon, we'll be in a place where we can both say anything we want, with no fear."

"If you like Gorbachev so much, why are you leaving the country, just as he becomes General Secretary?"

"In 1984," Gordievsky said slowly, "Gorbachev came to London. He spent eight days speaking with Mrs. Thatcher on a wide range of topics."

"Of course," Lyubimov said. "The meetings went very well. Gorbachev was pleased with the conversation, and he and Mrs. Thatcher got along on a personal level."

"So you would like such meetings to continue to happen?" Gordievsky asked. "You're content with such meetings?"

"Who isn't?" Lyubimov's stomach felt queasy.

"As the chief KGB officer in London, I prepared the daily briefings for Gorbachev," Gordievsky said. "Through my contacts in MI6, I also prepared the daily briefings for the Prime Minister. They were substantially the same briefings."

The queasiness became a brick.

"I did this," Gordievsky continued, "so that the parties would find common ground. So that they could approach challenging issues from similar directions, rather than with one hundred eighty degrees of opposition. And it worked."

"You'll be a hero, when you reach the West."

"No," Gordievsky said. "I don't want to be a hero. I'll be an ordinary man, and disappear into some English village to live out my days. But perhaps, before I do, there will be more information that I can give the West to help bring peace."

"It's hard to imagine that you could do as much good for the world in the West as you did while within the KGB, briefing Gorbachev and Thatcher at the same time."

"True." Gordievsky was silent for a time. "But I've been betrayed. I don't know how, or by whom, but someone denounced me. I was brought back to Moscow. I've been under heavy surveillance. I've even been drugged and interrogated."

"K Directorate?" Lyubimov asked. K Directorate was the KGB's counterintelligence division.

Gordievsky nodded.

Lyubimov's blood ran cold. He scanned the other people on the train platform. Might the man reading the newspaper be spying on Oleg and Mikhail? Might the woman with the baby carriage be listening in on their conversation?

"You're leaving Leila," he said.

"The English have promised they'll bring her and the girls across. They'll trade for them, if necessary. Likely, I can help MI5 arrest a few Soviet agents who will be valuable as bargaining chips."

"Leila must be unaware of your activities, or you wouldn't leave her."

"I tried to tell her." Oleg's voice was heavy with grief. "She wouldn't listen. She's too good a Soviet citizen. Her family is a KGB family, and she can't even imagine why I would want to do what I've done."

"Perhaps she won't want to be traded to the West."

"Perhaps not." Gordievsky's voice brightened. "But since the escape plan included space for her, that means that there's room for you, instead."

• • •

Once they boarded the train, they lay on their separate bunks in silence. A couple of hours after the train left Moscow, Lyubimov climbed down from his bunk to stretch, and surreptitiously passed Gordievsky. Oleg was asleep, so still that, for a moment, Mikhail thought he might be dead. Even in sleep, Gordievsky's face had a waxy and unhealthy pallor. No wonder, if he was being surveilled and interrogated, and was now contemplating leaving his family behind with no guarantee of ever rejoining them.

But Gordievsky would be a hero in the West, whatever he said. Knighthoods would await him, meetings with heads of state. He would have private gratitude, if not public recognition.

Mikhail had already been standing beside Oleg's bunk for too long. Quickly stretching to be able to look both directions along the train car without attracting attention, he saw that no one was watching him.

He took Gordievsky's gun, checked that it was loaded, and then pocketed it himself.

He lay awake through the night, thinking. Had he rushed to join Gordievsky on this journey on mere impulse, a spur of the moment desire for adventure? Was he merely disappointed in his own career as a writer, and hoping to experience romance and thrills that might somehow sink into his work?

Or did he long for something deeper? He had enjoyed his time in Denmark, but he did not desire to return to the West. His experience and trustworthiness meant that he could enjoy perks like Glenfiddich whisky in Moscow without betraying his country.

But he couldn't get out of his mind the image of Oleg Gordievsky, meeting U.S. President Ronald Reagan. Oleg Gordievsky, being warmly welcomed by Margaret Thatcher. Oleg Gordievsky, receiving honors from the Queen of England. And Gordievsky had acted to bring peace—were the thawing relations between East and West not in the interest of the workers of the world? Wasn't the avoidance of nuclear war in everyone's interests?

Or perhaps it wasn't, if the poor remained enslaved to the wealthy. Perhaps true peace could only come by the defeat of western capitalism, a defeat that would be brought on by the mighty deeds of socialist heroes.

In the middle of the night, the train braked and Gordievsky fell from his upper bunk. Either because of exhaustion or because he had taken some narcotic, the fall that split his lip and splashed blood down the front of his coat didn't wake him. Lyubimov and another passenger lifted him and shoved him back into one of the lower bunks.

With only an hour to go before arriving in Leningrad, Mikhail finally fell asleep.

• • •

At the main railway station in Leningrad, they briskly walked toward the exit. Lyubimov gently pressed Gordievsky for an itinerary, and was ignored. With no taxi cabs in sight at 5:00 a.m., they paid a private car owner to drive them to the Finland Station.

In the car, crossing Leningrad, Gordievsky put his hands into his coat pockets. His face remained expressionless in a studied, controlled fashion. Beneath the blood, and with hair askew, it made him look comical.

He had noticed his missing pistol.

He wouldn't ask about it, though. If Lyubimov had taken the gun, then Gordievsky didn't want to give away that he'd noticed. And if Lyubimov didn't have the weapon, then Gordievsky didn't want Lyubimov to know that he'd been armed.

Lyubimov looked out the window at the city that was just beginning to yawn itself awake.

But in either case, Gordievsky's stress and alertness had just been pushed up a notch.

They piled out of the car at Finland Station, rumpled and malodorous, beneath the eyes of an enormous statue of Lenin. Lenin seemed to be watching Mikhail as the two men bought tickets for the 7:05 Zelenogorsk train, and even as the train pulled away, Lyubimov felt the hero's eyes boring a hole between his shoulder blades with the intensity of their stare.

Lenin had returned to Russia in 1917 at this place.

Lenin, the great hero.

And was this now how Mikhail Lyubimov was to leave it?

At Zelenogorsk, Gordievsky stood in line to buy bus tickets. Lyubimov feigned a dire and urgent need to urinate. Fearing that too long a separation would make Gordievsky suspicious, he asked at two stalls where he might find a telephone, and met only shrugs.

Finally, a woman with a face like a beet and a strong odor of tobacco and turpentine overheard him and offered to let him use her phone, for a price.

"My phone call is a matter of national security," Lyubimov told her.

"So is my hunger," she said.

He doled out a short stack of rubles and found himself standing in a short hallway with peeling wallpaper that had once been green, but had faded so much that it now looked like mud. It took him several tries through a KGB switchboard, but he finally found himself talking to someone who answered simply, "K Directorate."

And Lyubimov was suddenly uncertain how to explain himself. "I have information about a traitor," he finally said. "Gordievsky, Oleg. He's attempting to defect today."

"One moment."

Silence.

A new voice, a man's, flat and emotionless. "Budanov."

Lyubimov knew the name. "Colonel Budanov?" The man was a relentless bloodhound, famed for rooting out enemies of the Soviet.

"I was told you had information about Gordievsky."

"Yes. Oleg Gordievsky. The man is at this moment attempting to defect." The beet-faced woman slashed a finger at Lyubimov, warning him that he had taken too much time already. He glared at her, but she didn't retreat.

"And you are?"

"Lyubimov, Mikhail. I was posted with Gordievsky in Copenhagen." He felt he owed the K Directorate inquisitor more information. "Gordievsky believes I share his sentiments, and that we're defecting together."

"Where will the traitor attempt to cross the border?" Budanov asked.

"We're in the town of Zelenogorsk," Lyubimov said. "I believe he'll cross into Finland, but I can't be certain where. Perhaps Vyborg, that's where we're headed next. He says very little."

"So he doesn't fully trust you."

"He does not."

"I'll alert the border guards at Vyborg. However, Comrade Lyubimov, as you're the only man who knows where he now is, you may be the man in the best position to stop him. Are you armed?"

Lyubimov nodded, then said, "Yes."

"Don't hesitate to shoot Oleg Gordievsky, or even kill him."

Kill?

The woman tried to grab the phone from Lyubimov, and he pushed her away.

"I'll tell you something that few people know, Comrade Lyubimov. Consider this a state secret. While Comrade Gorbachev makes friends with the westerners Thatcher and Reagan, there are forces within the Kremlin who believe that he's making a mistake. He's caving to western hostility and lies, just when the West is about to collapse from industrial discontent."

"Yes, Colonel."

The woman grabbed for the phone again. This time, Mikhail pulled out Oleg Gordievsky's pistol and pressed the muzzle against her forehead. Erupting into a lava of curses Lyubimov could barely understand, she scuttled back into the depths of the house.

"Gordievsky is to be stopped at all costs," Colonel Budanov said. "An example must be made to all who would aid the West. But also, if there is any chance to create an international incident, it will be strategically advisable to exploit that opportunity. In particular, if American or British or other western diplomats can be captured in the act of attempting to rescue the traitor Gordievsky, then wiser heads within the Kremlin will be able to sway Comrade Gorbachev to a more correct way of thinking."

"Yes, Colonel."

"Or replace the General Secretary."

The line went dead.

Lyubimov rejoined Gordievsky in line as the bus doors opened, feeling the weight of the pistol in his jacket like an iron ball.

• • •

They rode the bus along a fine highway, wide and well-asphalted, a highway the Soviet road makers were proud to show to their neighbors, the Finns. The ribbon of asphalt wound its way through thick pine forest westward, toward Vyborg.

Lyubimov was exhausted. His heartbeat felt thready and inconsistent, his hands shook, and sweat trickled down his back. Gordievsky leaned against a window and appeared to sleep.

Lyubimov was resolved to arrest his friend, but how should he do it? In sleep, Gordievsky seemed almost childlike. Lyubimov could reveal his call to the K Directorate to Gordievsky and urge his friend to return to Moscow. That would be heroic. And surely, Gordievsky knew something about British intelligence that he could share with the KGB that would save him from execution.

Maybe even return him to favor.

Maybe make Oleg and Mikhail both heroes.

As the bus passed kilometer post 836, Gordievsky lurched abruptly to his feet. "I'm sick!" he called, staggering toward the front of the vehicle, from seat back to seat back. "I'm going to vomit, let me out!"

Lyubimov raced not to be left behind. When he thudded down the bus steps, the driver bellowed at his back, "We're not waiting for you and your friend!"

"Go!" Mikhail shouted, and waved the bus away.

Gordievsky writhed on the ground retching. Was he truly ill? Was this how his defection would end, in a spasm of vomiting on the side of the road, twenty-five kilometers from the Finnish border? But once the bus had disappeared into the trees, Oleg stood. He still had blood crusted at the corners of his nose, and he was thoroughly disheveled, but he grinned.

"Now all we do is wait," he said.

"If you're ready to tell me the plan, I'm listening."

Gordievsky considered this and nodded. "Two cars will come for us. They think they're coming for me and my family, so there will be room for you. They'll pick us up at a meeting spot three hundred meters up the road, and drive us across the border."

"It can't be that simple," Lyubimov said.

But he knew that it *could* be that simple, if the cars picking the defectors up had diplomatic plates. This was what Budanov had been talking about, the opportunity to create an international incident.

They walked up the road to the pick-up spot. It was a dirt turnout on the side of the highway, screened from the highway by a thick stand of trees, and Gordievsky settled himself against a rock in the woods to wait. Mosquitos buzzed and the forest stank of stagnant water and rot.

"I'm glad you're here," Gordievsky said. "Or I might be tempted to run into Vyborg and get a drink."

They sat in silence for hours. The mosquitos ate them alive, though they tugged their sleeves down their wrists to cover their hands and shrugged down into the collars of their jackets to protect their necks. Lyubimov could no longer think, and he reeled from image to image in his mind. Crossing the border. Death in a hail of machine gun bullets. A cocktail reception at the English embassy in Denmark. Gorbachev's death by firing squad. Gordievsky shaking hands with Margaret Thatcher. Lyubimov sitting with Ronald Reagan in armchairs at the American White House. The funeral procession of Mikhail Gorbachev. Nuclear warheads detonating in Washington, D.C. Denials from Margaret Thatcher, surrounded by a thicket of press microphones. Nuclear warheads detonating in Moscow. Budanov, sternly lecturing capitalist leaders on television. Nuclear warheads detonating where Lyubimov stood.

He was shaking when he heard the whine of car engines approaching from the east. Gordievsky whistled, and they both crouched in the brush to hide.

Two cars skidded into the turnout, breaking abruptly: a white Saab and a red Volvo. Lyubimov felt relief like an ice bath when he thought, for a moment, that these could not be Gordievsky's western contacts; a woman pulled a picnic basket from the trunk of one car and began quickly laying out a blanket, while two men emerged from the cars and stared at the highway they'd just left.

But then Gordievsky leaped to his feet and trundled from the brush, and Lyubimov's heart fell. The picnic apparatus was a ruse, it was cover.

And then he recognized one of the men: Ascot was his name. He was a British diplomat stationed in Moscow, and he was also some sort of minor English nobility. A count or a baron or something.

The English were using actual aristocracy to infiltrate the Soviet Union!

Lyubimov felt his nostrils dilate and his heart pound fast and hard. An international incident.

He pulled the pistol. "I'm sorry, my friend, but I can't let you go."

Gordievsky stopped and turned around. "You stole my gun."

The other man, not Ascot, was edging toward his car. Lyubimov gestured at him with the pistol. "Stand back." To Gordievsky, he said, "Would you have shot me with it?"

"Only if I had to." Gordievsky stepped slowly toward Lyubimov.

"But you don't have to. Now we can go back to Moscow. In fact, you can be a hero."

"I'm not going back to Moscow. They suspect I'm a spy for the West, and they're right."

"But you'll have tricked these capitalist spies into revealing themselves." Lyubimov pointed. "That man works at the embassy, and he's a baronet or something."

"Viscount," Ascot said.

Lyubimov shrugged. "Fat on the blood of the English workers, whatever your title is. Come, we turn them in, and we're both heroes of the KGB."

"Or we both leave," Gordievsky said, "and we're free men."

"You don't want to leave," Lyubimov said. "You called and told me to read Maugham. You told me what you were going to do, because you wanted me to stop you."

Gordievsky shook his head. "I don't know why I did that. Maybe it was a joke. I thought you would realize afterward, the KGB would realize afterward, that I had told you my plan. And then we could all have had a secret laugh together."

Lyubimov's hand drooped from fatigue, so he gripped his wrist with his left hand to steady it. "Instead, we go back to Moscow, and you and I have a laugh together at the fate of these capitalist spies."

A blue Zhiguli raced by on the highway, and Lyubimov's eyes flashed to look at it. At the speed it was going, it had to be chasing someone. Probably the Saab and the Volvo. Probably it had just missed them in the turnout, for the trees.

Gordievsky lunged forward, grabbing for the pistol.

Bang!

Meet D.J.Butler

Dave (D.J.) Butler writes adventure stories for all readers. He has been a lawyer, a consultant, and a corporate trainer. His interests include languages, guitar, hanging out with his wife and kids, astronomy, and history.

Sign up to get updates about Dave and his books at: http://davidjohnbutler.com/mailinglist/

The characters in this story are real - Mikhail Lyubimov was a colonel in the KGB, and is also a novelist.

Oleg Gordievsky is regarded as one of MI6's greatest triumphs, working as a double agent and playing a crucial role in avoiding nuclear Armageddon. He left the USSR in 1985 in Operation Pimlico.

Afterword

Well, they do say end with a bang. And with this shot, as history spirals off in a new direction, we draw the curtain on another set of Alternate Earths. In this collection we have seen flashes of inspiration change the fate of countries, we have seen movies made or not, and we've seen how the march of history affects not just great generals, but those who must endure history unremarked.

Tales from Alternate Earths is our biggest brand, we've returned to it three times now, but there are so many more worlds out there, so many more stories to tell. No doubt we will return this way again, in this world, or another.

Inklings Press continues to encourage new and upcoming writers as we publish our collections. And you can help. One of the best ways you can show encouragement to authors is to leave a review. Amazon and Goodreads are excellent places to do so. Reviews are priceless to authors, even if it's just a few words to say what the anthology meant to you. It doesn't need to be long - but each review can mean the world (one of them anyway) to an author.

To keep up with the further plans of Inklings Press, and the authors who have featured in our pages, you can check out the contact details below. We'd love to hear from you.

How to contact Inklings Press
Twitter: @InklingsPress
Facebook: Facebook.com/InklingsPress
Visit our website: www.inklingspress.com
Email: theinklingspress@gmail.com

Made in the USA
Coppell, TX
11 September 2021